Love
Letters

Love Letters

a novel by Eli Cantor

AN AUTHORS GUILD BACKINPRINT.COM EDITION

Love Letters:
a novel

All Rights Reserved © 1979, 2001 by Eli Cantor

AN AUTHORS GUILD BACKINPRINT.COM EDITION

Published by iUniverse.com, Inc.

For information address:
iUniverse.com, Inc.
5220 S 16th, Ste. 200
Lincoln, NE 68512
www.iuniverse.com

Originally published by Crown

ISBN: 0-595-18341-7

Printed in the United States of America

To my wife, "Pat"

Part One

Feb. 29

Dear Mr. Curtiss:

This is an unabashed fan letter, the first I have ever written. As I typed the date, it came to me that this is a leap year, but that does not lighten my embarrassment in addressing someone who is not acquainted with me and is undoubtedly too occupied to be afflicted with gratuitous correspondence.

Since I personally know some young people who have been badly burned by the "subculture religions" you describe in your impressive article, I found your views a breath of fresh air, especially coming from one with your credentials.

It occurs to me, indeed, that I should address you as Doctor, not Mister. But it would be untidy to ink out the salutation now. On the other hand, if I were to start fresh, I wouldn't. I mean, I have used up all of my daily quotient of valor in getting this page into the typewriter at all. Now that I am actually pecking away, I realize I have been hunting an excuse to roll the sheet out and crumple it into the wastebasket. I feel like someone knocking on a door uninvited. Still, I am writing to praise and not to ask for a cup of sugar, so I suppose that makes my intrusion acceptable even if it is presumptuous.

Your article is written in a human, understanding, yet firm tone that speaks to me very directly, and I suppose that is why I feel this letter is not altogether inappropriate. At the same time, I must confess a shyness that is unusual for me. I am not ordinarily a retiring woman. Yet here I sit, yes, blushing. I am sure that if I left my desk here at the window and went across the bedroom to my dressing table, I would see myself in the mirror as red as my carpet is blue. I can admit it because you are a stranger I shall never hear from (from whom I shall never hear?). I am 3,000 miles safe and secure from your reaction, whatever it be.

Now I am laughing at myself. Why in even the most proper world shouldn't I feel free to tell the author of this meaningful article that it is important to me? I do admire the balance and scope of your thinking, Dr. Curtiss, and I envy the precision and clarity of your expression, too obviously lacking in my own, as you see.

Please be sure I am aware of how engaged you must be, so that I expect no reply. Thank you again for your stimulating piece. It is needed so badly these days. I hope it is widely read and heeded. Unfortunately, the young people who would benefit most are the least likely to pay attention. Isn't that always the melancholy truth?

Very truly yours,
Margaret F. Webb

March 6

Dear Margaret F. Webb:

This is an unabashed thank you.

I regret to advise that your letter was the only fan mail stirred by my article. The rest has been more poison-pen type. Not a surprise to me, of course. The "religious leaders" who prey on the confused and gullible can mobilize torrents of zombie postcards. Legitimate religious groups, which are to be carefully distinguished, have held their peace. Revealingly, the hate mail identifies the fringe bunches in all their tawdriness, tars the choleric senders with their own soiled brushes.

Still, the dean of my college did feel called upon to remind me that discretion is the better part of valor for an assistant professor expecting promotion. Since you are a stranger, safely 3,000 miles away as you say, I can state my opinion of my dean as a soggy Milquetoast dipped too long in the coffee cups of his board of trustees. (You see that my critical sword is swung not only at outside groups.)

Your letter was most welcome. It promises a new friend, and that is always a pleasant prospect, even though we are a continent apart.

For myself, I am hopeful that the appeal of the far-out, synthetic cults and cultists will fade. As a sociologist I look upon them mainly as a form of and a sanctuary for youthful rebellion, which itself is largely a backlash against overpermissiveness in our society generally. Yet, even though I see the pendulum reversing, perhaps soon, it is painful and distressing to witness the damage being done to so many fine individuals and their families while it swings. I find the periodic scenario bleak indeed: Man invents the wheel of social order, then fractures its axles, then bewails the collapse, then reinvents the vehicle and, without having learned anything, repeats the sorry cycle. That is the subject of my next article, and I will be happy to send you a doleful copy.

I am glad you wrote of your shyness in sending a letter into space to an unknown person. It made you real to me. You have the advantage of me—at least you know I am an academic, and my field. All I know of you is your generosity of spirit in writing, and your stationery.

I admire your writing paper. It isn't gussied up with engraving or the flossy lettering I see in the chic ads. I sometimes wonder about the women who go that route. It might make a study for one of my graduate students, at that. What image of themselves do they think they are sending through the mail? Elegance? I am being too cynical even for me, but doesn't that seem like borrowing a personality instead of being one? Your stationery is refreshingly neutral. Your words don't need a stage setting.

What else can I deduce about you? I propose that you are not a woman who uses bright nail colors, you wear your hair simply, you dress casually, you don't show much jewelry but what you have is in excellent taste.

Also: Your typewriter needs a new ribbon, so you may be a writer, or on the other hand you may not have used the machine for a long time. Ribbons go stale in the air, you know; I learned that only recently. Also, your "o" punches holes. It put me in mind, variously, of a youngster with missing teeth, and/or confetti as if your punched-out circles are floating around somewhere, somebody's holiday. I feel cheerful writing to you; it is a welcome change from the somber temper the state of the world ordinarily imposes on me.

Unfortunately, I get no other clues about you, not as to your age, not even whether you are Miss or Mrs. Or is it Ms. altogether?

This turns out to be most pleasant for me. I haven't been in so genial a mood for a long while. Will you write and tell me my score so far?

Your letter, coming out of the blue as it did, was the kind of happy surprise I had forgotten could still happen. You will think me an unreconstructed sentimentalist, but it took me back to the felicity and expectations of Christmas Eves waiting for the presents that sometimes did materialize.

Please tell me about yourself. I very much look forward to hearing from you again if you would like to write.

Sincerely,
Brian Curtiss

March 13

Dear Dr. Curtiss:

I never did expect you to write back to me, much less so kind and friendly a letter. My first impulse was to answer with the "biography" you so warmly invite. But something else happened as I was considering how to describe myself. I asked, What will Dr. Curtiss know about me if I dutifully fill in the blanks, as for a job application, my height, color of hair and eyes, complexion, marital status, weight, club affiliations, hobbies, my age?

Given a most unusual chance to define who I am for a total stranger, I find myself challenged and suspended in an interesting way. Would the passport information above tell you a whole lot more than, say, my social security number?

Well, yes, of course, and I am not wholly serious. Yet, in a way, I am suddenly made conscious of how, always, when I meet somebody for the first time, one of my early-on questions (with what I am sure is a fatuous smile) is, "And what do you do?"

As if that would sum up everything one would like to know about an individual. It's the easy way to classify people, but there is so much it doesn't tell that is central to knowing someone—whether the person has a sense of humor (I think I do), does he like or dislike pets (I don't, particularly), does he enjoy walking (I do, greatly), does he favor chamber music or jazz (both for me), etcetera.

So I find myself hanging back a bit about myself, not because I hesitate to fill in the blank lines (mighty unglamorously it would be, I might state) but because for once it is possible for me to communicate with someone out of the ordinary way!

I must confess that something has quickened in me. It is intriguing to be writing to a man to whom I might be anything. *Tabula rasa.* (Was that Francis Bacon?) Just as, to me, it makes no difference if you are five feet short or seven feet tall, what difference if I am plain or beautiful, ancient or young, poor or rich?—though I would of course prefer the second choice in each category.

Don't you agree that this is, the only word for it, fun? Genial, as you nicely put it. I feel that way, too, and that I am making a friend. Let me say again I will understand if you are too pressed to answer, or if the diversion palls.

Reading this over, it occurs to me how many implications there are in the various ways one can ask "What do you do?" There is "What do you *do*?" and "What do *you* do?" and "What *do* you do?" and "*What* do you do?" I find myself wondering what *I* am doing!

Actually, my memory of "the emphasis game" we played in school was sparked by a sentence in your letter about typewriter ribbons going stale, where you say "I learned that only recently." Playing the game, we would go on with "Only I learned that recently" and "I only learned that recently" and "I learned only that recently," and your "I learned that only recently" and "I learned that recently only." Shifty word, that "only," isn't it?

Cordially,
Margaret Webb

March 21

Dear Margaret Webb:

As you say, *this* is fun, and most welcome to me at this time, for reasons with which I need not burden you.

I very much enjoyed your letter. Far from ending what you call diversion, it whets my interest. Like yourself, I have never done this kind of thing before. Frankly, I would have thought it somewhat juvenile, but to my surprise it is extremely pleasant, more like a door slowly opening into a room which, though only glimpsed so far, is clearly promising and inviting.

It is not so odd, come to think of it. What are strangers after all but potential friends whom chance has kept apart? Haven't you sometimes seen someone passing by whom you knew at once you would admire to know or, yes, even love? You did not venture because of society's confining conventions. I suggest that, at least in many instances, the loss may be greater than the hazard, though of course one must always use judgment.

I regard a stranger simply as someone who has not happened to be invited to a party I happen to be attending. It's as chancy as that. Haven't you observed of life itself that, while we plan and calculate and premeditate, everything important happens fortuitously, straight back to the accident of which sperm embraces which egg? Just think how people meet their spouse, get a job, and so on.

I was amused at the thought that you might see me as five feet short or seven feet tall. I cannot help but try to imagine your appearance. The correspondence itself creates a kind of mist out of which images inevitably start to form. But I can't conjure you yet, and I enjoy your notion of in effect remaining incognito. It has a savor and I find myself beguiled. You sent along a new clue, *"tabula rasa."* So you have studied Latin or philosophy, a *rara avis* these days. However, you are not quite on track with your attribution. While Francis Bacon was much admired by John Locke, it was the latter who spoke of the mind being at birth like a clean page for life to write on. That was in his "Essay Concerning Human Understanding" (cited variously as of 1689 or 1690).

Let me hasten to state I am not the pedant I sound! The above is my way of turning a scholarly cartwheel before you.

Perhaps, at that, it is not irrelevant to us that John Locke held a deep faith in basic human goodness. I'd like to compare notes with you. We are in tune on many more things than my article.

Incidentally, I noted that you spelled *et cetera* as one word. While I'm cartwheeling, let me mention it is two words. I learned that the nasty way when I had to correct it throughout my doctoral thesis, where I had overused it in any case. Actually, I wrote "etc.," at first, only to be confronted by a scholiastic don who quoted Webster at me in a spittle of indignation, "The abbreviation is not favored in literary contexts." I was flattered to think of my deadly dissertation as literary, but it didn't ease the drudgery of retyping the pages.

Now I look forward to another letter from *you*.

In friendship?

Brian Curtiss
(Please skip the "Dr.")

March 28

Dear Dr. Curtiss:

I applaud your cartwheel and hope that pleases you. It reminds me of a time long ago when a boy did somersaults for me—somersaults I pretended not to see and did not acknowledge, for which I am greatly sorry now. Perhaps I will tell you about that some day.

It just came to me that we write to each other on Sundays mostly. It does make the day more special to me. I have found myself keeping your letters. I take them out on the terrace of my apartment to read again. The weather here is ordinarily miserable at this time of year, but today is almost like spring. New York can have crystal blue skies, you know, and today it is setting off the skyline like a Miro or Calder lithograph, and the jet planes are coming and going like kites with their tails of vapor pluming behind. It's a vault of spaciousness that I can feel crossing, stretching, connecting, and I reread your letters almost as if we were talking. They have added a sparkle to my days, and I confess that I look for the mail with an impatience I have not felt for a very long time. You come into my thoughts airily and unbidden every now and then, always with an individual quality I can't quite capture or hold. I keep wondering about this. Of all the characteristics that might describe what is happening, the one that comes closest is *buoyancy*.

I wanted to share this with you. "To share this ..." What an agreeable sound that has. I suppose in due course it will lead me to reveal myself, such as there is to tell, but for now let us stay as we are. I suppose I have never had any relationship so completely free of any kind of demands, yet so real in its own way. I don't have a word for it, and that brings its own refreshment. We are such creatures of label and routine.

It occurs to me that I never think of you without smiling. And thank you for it. Thank you, too, for correcting "et cetera." My lapse gives me pause. Not because I do know better, but because it suggests that age is greasing the skids of my mind. That is a free clue!

Please never feel any pressure about answering or not answering. That is not where this (unlikely) relationship between us—whatever it is—is coming from.

Sincerely,
Margaret Webb

April 18

Dear Margaret:

Yes, Sundays seem to have turned out to be our days. For me, it is the only free time I can manage.

Today is Easter. Sometime I'll share more of my thinking about theologies, organized and unorganized, and listen to yours. Today it's enough for me to be praying by myself out here in back of my new home, lying in this hammock, in my own church columned by magnificent redwoods that are carrying my thoughts straight up and directly to heaven, a cerulean-blue sky, the heaven of Baal, Jahweh, Ra, Zeus, Jesus, Mohammed, Buddha, Quetzalcoatl, and the Navajo's Great Spirit, among Others.

My wife and I were fortunate to locate this house. One reason you haven't heard from me for a time is that we have been in the midst of packing, moving, and unpacking. It takes forever, a chore I wish on no one, especially with two small children. But I have thought of you and wished you could see the beauty that fortune has favored us with here.

Our apartment in San Francisco was inadequate even when my wife, Kay, and I were first married five years ago. As of today we have my daughter, Joanie, a proud and exquisite blond of four, and my son, Paul, a dynamo of two. Larger quarters were a necessity as you can imagine. (Are you a parent? Have you children? If so, how close in age are they to mine?)

My wife set about looking for a house a full year ago. We wanted Marin County. If you're not familiar with this area, it's north of the Golden Gate Bridge; compare your Westchester County and New

York City. But we found prices out of sight for our budget, and we had given up hope. Then a friend of Kay's was divorced (so what else is new?) and we grabbed the house. Ill wind and all that. It is only twice what we can afford.

What an experience house-shopping has been! I know that Easterners all have a notion that California, especially in this section, is a paradise climate. Let me tell you a few *facts,* as befits a card-carrying social scientist. Just next door, Sausalito has a tropical belt where, believe it or not, *bananas* grow. Extremes are the norm everywhere. One agent showed Kay a place in Marin where we could get a dynamite bargain because the husband needed three-alarm cash for Mafia loan sharks. As Kay was being shown the grounds, she came upon the wife and some children sitting in a shady spot. The woman couldn't contain herself. Desperate to assist a sale, she burst out to Kay, "Even when it's 102–103 degrees, it's always cool down here!"

Equable climate indeed.

We wanted a view if humanly possible, though houses out here are mostly crowded lawn-to-garage except for the very wealthy places. Our "wide open spaces" are another Easterners' illusion. Finally we were escorted to a height overlooking the Pacific. Magnificent! I was sold. Brand new homes along the ridge, modern (a bit istic for my taste but not disagreeable), but when we got out of the car I had literally to tackle Kay to keep her from being swept away. A veritable gale blows up there 24 hours a day. The wind was more breathtaking than the panorama. I realized why the houses had high fences, the more ironical because they blocked most of the splendid view.

Nor is the section we finally found without its penalty. Friends warned us that "redwoods grow on rain." I think I own (along with the bank, and a friend who took a second mortgage) the wettest acre in the U.S., though people up around Portland claim that distinction.

But it is worth it, and you can put the emphasis on any word in *that* sentence.

There is no way I can describe to you the dignity and the majesty of these trees. They tower 200–300 feet in the air, literally. Think of a 20–30-story building! These are pillars holding up the sky over my house, over my hammock.

One of my trees, Margaret, is ten feet wide! North to Oregon I have seen redwoods so huge the road cuts through the base. I am delighted Joan and Paul will grow up here. It will be hard to be petty surrounded by this grandeur (though people manage). The inspiration is real and profound, but one retreats into the house with some relief. Man needs his cave. These outdoor giants impose an obligation, a commandment, to be the best you have it in you to be, and that is a hard responsibility to confront without an indoor martini now and then. What do you prefer to drink? White wine is my guess. (Footnote: Some research indicates red wine may be better for you, and contrary to widespread belief white wine does not have fewer calories.)

I know where the peace comes from in the presence of these redwood trees. They are complete in their purpose and being. Nothing is missing. They are fulfilled, from root to crown, a celebration of what man can be if he ever gets his act together.

Brian Curtiss

P.S. As I mentioned my pleasure that my children will grow up here, another dollop of research came to mind. It discloses that people who live in the East have longer hospital stays than inhabitants of the West, regardless of age or sex. I can't even begin to start to formulate a hypothesis as to why this should be so, but it confirms Horace Greeley's advice, doesn't it?—especially with hospital rates what they are these days.

P.P.S. Though I had to be out of our game these past weeks, I did miss letters from you. I hope we don't correspond like ping-pong players waiting for the ball to come over the net. I should have dropped you a card at least, and am sorry I didn't. I'll depend on your kind promises to understand. It was truly family pressure time here to the exclusion of everything else.

April 21

Dear Dr. Curtiss:

Interesting that you wrote of pettiness. That was my vein when weeks went by without a letter from you. I had decided that if you did write again, I would not reply for at least the span of your silence. I had thought myself past such small-mindedness. I reminded myself that I had specifically foresworn pressure of any kind. Yet I missed your letters too much for common sense.

This is an admission which startles and disturbs me. Considerably.

The first flush of our unconventional acquaintanceship was pleasant indeed, but the more I reflect on it the surer I grow that we have nowhere to go with this lollygagging correspondence.

It is not that I now know you to be married and a father. I did not have the details but had no reason to believe you did not have your own close relationships, similar to mine. Why not leave it at that? Our casual "diversion" has been all that it promised, and I am ready to say that my husband and I will be delighted to meet you and your wife if we ever come to your area. As I trust you would get in touch with us if you ever come East—though none of my skyscrapers can match your redwoods, I agree. Actually, since my husband, Arthur, lectures widely, there may well be some occasion when we are near San Francisco. It would be a pleasure, as I say, to meet you and your family.

All the best to you, then.

Sincerely yours,
(Mrs.) Margaret Webb

April 24

Whoa:

I am not about to analyze you across a 3,000-mile couch, but it's obvious you are put out with me because I did not write for a time, *and* you are not ready to let more reality into our exchange.

I do understand that. There is a new element to be reckoned with when you know I have a wife and children, and when I know that you, too, are married. But I want to deal with actuality, not fantasy. I still believe we can and should have a friendship, and I want it because I like and admire the intelligent, sensitive, and seeking woman I hear between the lines of your letters. There is no reason in anyone's world why we should cut each other off, none at all that makes sense.

Like you, I am aware that what has developed between us has no easy name. It is fragile, to be handled with care. It is also a gift I do not want to return.

I can't insist, of course, but I genuinely hope you will reconsider.

Sincerely,
Brian Curtiss

May 24

Dear Margaret Webb:

Now it is a full month with no word from you. I hear your decision about us in your silence. I did not realize how anxiously I would scan the mailbox each day, how hard I would find it to accept that you do not wish to continue.

It takes little self-examination on my part to perceive that your first letter out of nowhere struck some nerve in me, a chord I did not know was waiting to be touched. That must be true or I would not now have this sense of loss. I did not expect it, I am not prepared for it, but it is there. It is a raw, a disconsolate, emotion. I find myself frowning through the day.

Our writing to each other need not have any goal or purpose beyond itself. I can understand your questioning what it can add up to, but that seems to me a false trail. Why do things always "have to add up" or "be heading someplace"? To me that is one of the unnecessary and unhappy aspects of our Judeo-Christian-Protestant ethic. People beat themselves over the head with goals, goals, goals. I suggest there are times when goals are relevant and times when they are not.

I have simply been enjoying our "lollygagging" (happy word!). Isn't that goal enough?

Perhaps I should not be conjecturing any of this. Perhaps you haven't written for some innocuous reason—you've been on vacation —or you have a career that takes you on travels. Or are you married to a millionaire who fancies world cruises? The incognito game has its disadvantages!

Or you may be ill, and that thought is disquieting.

If you have not been writing because you have consideredly chosen not to, I must accept it. Obviously we are in no grand opera tragedy and both our lives will go on their way. With regret on my part, though, I want you to know that plainly. Because I do have this ever-stronger inner conviction that we ought to keep knowing each other, you and I. Please do not be frightened away. By me, or yourself. There is nothing to be frightened of between us.

Let me add that my wife knows that I have been corresponding with a new friend in New York. She has her own relationships with others, and we respect each other's privacy. There is no problem on that account, in case that is in your mind.

Brian

June 7

Dear Dr. Curtiss:

I appreciate your writing and regret that my silence has given you concern. I did not answer because, frankly, I wasn't sure how. Your invitation to friendship is flattering and very attractive. On the other hand, as you have observed, you know almost nothing about me. My husband is not a millionaire, though we do go on an occasional cruise; I have not been on vacation; I do not have a career at present. Finally, and thankfully, I am not ill.

There isn't any question of wrong or right in my mind, but I do now question a correspondence that has no map or contour but the distance between New York and San Francisco. I cannot agree with you about free-floating relationships that have no direction. I am not a risk-taker, much as I sometimes pretend to myself that I am bold. Perhaps I was indeed too bold, even rash, in writing my first letter. The prospect of the friendship you offer now should be welcome to me, but I must answer by stating that I am not at all unsatisfied with my life and my friends exactly as they are.

I don't mean that to sound brusque. I suppose I owe it to you to spell out my own sense that I would not feel this way if our correspondence had not begun to make waves never intended or anticipated by me. The fact is that we did not meet at any party, and that we are strangers. I am regretful if this sounds prim or starchy. The plain and simple truth is that I have no room or desire for anything new or different in my life.

To you, this may seem ungrateful, stingy, and mulish. I plead guilty, without apology, and I would prefer to say no more. If I have reasons I have not stated, they are quite my own and in no way reflect on you. I tell you once more that I have enjoyed our exchange, but it is time to end it. Please do not write to me again.

Very truly yours,
Mrs. Margaret Webb

June 8

Dear Brian Curtiss:

They say a woman has the privilege of changing her mind. At the risk of offending Women's Lib, I will offer that excuse for my return to the typewriter. The fact is that I have spent hours wondering why I sent yesterday's odious note to you. All I know now is that I feel like talking to you again. Maybe it's the day, a ravishing June season here. If you were in the city, I would have phoned you this morning for a walk in the park. We live near the lake. Central Park is one of the most beautiful places I know, and I have been over much of the world. I would almost match it against anything you have in California, but that sounds challenging, and that is the opposite of my mood right now.

It's too bad that news stories play up the rotten stuff in our city. Over the many years I have enjoyed the park, I've seen one mugging. It was terrible and terrifying, to be sure. A half-dozen girls no more than 12 or 13 ripped a purse from an old woman and threw her to the ground when she resisted. Pure barbarism. I later learned that the old woman was a distinguished doctor whose broken hip prevented her from practicing again, so the loss was greater than money. Yet having said that, I must add that by and large our park seems as safe as or safer than many cities. Last year my husband was lecturing in Detroit. We had been told about a top restaurant a block from the hotel and were advised to take a cab! You can find trouble anywhere, poor New York is too much blamed.

This morning I sat near the lake thinking of your description of your wonderful trees. Did you know that this park was planted as a veritable arboretum? Except for rush hours, the roads are closed for the use of bicyclists and joggers. When the Philharmonic gives free concerts in the summer, it is a truly awesome sight to see over 150,000 people on the great lawn. It is hard to be happy in the midst of a crime-ridden world of muggers, pushers, arsonists, looters, and the rest, but we ought not lose sight of the great good things around us as well. Don't you agree?

In both autumn and spring the colors here are beyond description. Right now I am looking at a smoky, fuzzy yellow-green light that seems to be hovering over the trees, the light of the tiny leaves just unfolding, a kind of color-breath in the air.

There was a black puppy on the path, only weeks old, exploring life prancingly. His eyes were bright as he chased a beer can, and he panted with a spilling-over vitality that shook his little body as if it were all tail. To the puppy that tin can was nothing less than utter enchantment. If only we didn't lose our innocence.

But how keep it in a world where there are rats, too? That is the story I am trying to get out, I suppose. Unhappily and awfully, right beside my bench a slimy creature came out of a nearby copse. Slowly! It took its own good time crossing the open path, lacking even the grace to scurry furtively. I swear that rodent was sneering at all of us. Did you ever see a sauntering rat. It is horrifying. Perhaps it is a sign and symbol of our times.

The puppy went crazy on his leash. I looked up at the exquisite trees, the magnificent skyline, and down at the rat, so hideous and revolting. I heard children laughing in the playground across the road, and the screeching blare of one of the terrible radios turned up full volume to shatter the ears and the peace. Nothing is stable or secure any longer in this overloaded world.

I think that is why I have come back to the typewriter and a letter to you. I did not intend this. But when I returned home, instead of going into the kitchen for the tea I wanted, I found myself walking directly past our living room into the bedroom and to my desk. I needed to tell you the mixed-up things I have not told very well so far, and my hands were taking the cover off the typewriter. It was a consolation to have you to talk to, to think of you as "friend," and it was settling to me. I am able to close my eyes now without seeing the rat.

So here I am, fingers poised over the keys, wondering to myself, as I must, why I did quit writing to you, and why I demanded that you stop.

Oh, Brian Curtiss, I know the answer, and know it only too well.

There is one basic, unrelenting fact that must be filled in if we are indeed to continue. I am over 47 years old, dear young man. It doesn't matter that I don't feel old. What matters is that you, with your oldest child only a four-year-old tot, must be in your early thirties at most. It takes little arithmetic to calculate that there are close to 20 years between us and that I could quite be your mother! Under the circumstances I think you can see why I might feel we had proceeded with our letters about as far as was sensible.

My mood has changed now. The truth is that I don't understand "age." I don't know what "47-plus years" is supposed to feel like. On most days I feel better and more alive than when I was what people call "young."

I projected my confusion on to you, unfairly. As I think about it now more coolly, I can see no sensible reason why we should not be the friends you say we have become. So be it.

Yet, yet, yet! In honest truth I truly do not know or fully understand why a man in your position should want this correspondence. I am what can only be described as your garden-variety hausfrau, with the expected range of middle-class interests, a little fancier than some, others a little less fancy, I suppose—my family, my friends, some face-saving volunteer work at a hospital, occasional museums, some theatre, some concerts, some ballets (hardly as much as everyone talks of living in New York to enjoy the benefits of).

Let that clumsy parenthesis stand. It reflects the lumpy chagrin and guilt I often feel for not taking in more of "the cultural advantages."

In any case, Dr. Curtiss, I have nothing special to contribute, certainly not to a scholar and teacher like you. Nothing much out of the ordinary happens in my life. Or shall I say that the problems —like my son, Gary, who is not two years old but 22!—are too common and ordinary to be more than a passing footnote for a sociologist.

I suppose that, too, is a commentary on our society. Here I am, a woman about whom most people would enviously say, "She has everything." And my main feeling is one of being cheated. Rat on the path. When you *get* all you have been taught to want—security, a good marriage in a good home—you sometimes find it seems not enough, particularly when the so-called fruits of your life, like a child, turn out to be sour.

That's a blasphemy to draw the lightning, but today I am impelled to truth. It is also a caution that our "game" may prove not so cheerful all the way if we do, indeed, pursue it further. In any case, I am not yet ready to go on about either my husband, Arthur, or my son, Gary.

Do you write quickly? My letters sometimes spurt, like this one. More often they dawdle self-consciously. I stop to read and reread, concerned with the impression I am making on you. Everyone wants to be liked and admired, at least not disliked. Isn't that a universal (sociological?) truth?

I am not sure why I have allowed this letter the liberties it has taken with me. I scarcely intended to write as I have. Perhaps it is because I do feel, with you, that friends are people with whom you don't have to weigh every word.

> Without further weighing,
> Margaret

June 13

Dear Margaret:

Delighted to hear from you! I had about given up. Now that we have your reservations behind us, I hope we have turned on to a main road without more detours. I was pleased that you would have called me to walk in your park. I wish I could phone you the same way right now and invite you for a drink here. There is a quiet tavern in a grove of redwoods just up the road. We will some day have that drink, your city or mine, and I know it will be as pleasant as I imagine.

Speaking of pleasure, I just looked outside at Joan and Paul. They are playing in the sandbox I built for them. They are beautiful children, if I must brag on them myself. California does seem to bless youngsters with blond hair, blue eyes, apple cheeks, and golden bodies. I will send you their pictures one day, if you like. They grow so fast that what you see today is changed tomorrow, as you have experienced with your own son, I am sure. Tell me more about him when you are ready.

It's my day to baby-sit again. Kay is off once more to visit friends who have discovered a new guru. Gurus come and go around here like gypsies. Some are genuine, many are opportunists. I don't know

18   ·

anything about this fellow, but in any case the mysticism-cum-intuition way is not for me. I am a rationalist, at least for the most part. That's unpopular with most of my students. This crop believes the path to truth is through the debris of the well-blown mind.

I am an ancient fogey to my classes, which is ironic since I am not old enough for you! I wish you wouldn't make such a point of whatever our age difference happens to be. I just turned 30 last month, to be exact, and it hasn't the slightest thing to do with our talking to each other as we do.

Gaps! People dig canyons between them where there need not be any. One time a New York friend had a drink with me out here, and he ordered a Manhattan "made with bourbon." The bartender promptly retorted, "What in hell do you think we make Manhattans with?" My friend, surprised, explained that in the East the drink is fixed with rye unless bourbon is specified. Somewhere in mid-America, Margaret Webb, there must be a town where, on one side of the street, the bars make Manhattans with rye, and on the other, bourbon. The Whisky Divide!

That's how trivial, even comical, the "age gap" between us is in my view, and I trust you will make less of it as we go along. However, the age gap between four and two, and brother and sister, is shriekingly real outside at the moment. Joanie has turned the garden hose on Paul, and to escape getting wet he has, with infinite logic, jumped into the rubber pool and ducked his head under the water! I'd better get out there before he drowns . . .

Later, kids dried off and peace restored, I've come back to finish this letter. One thing has been on my mind a little. You refer to me as an "expert" and a "scholar." I suppose I should be both and, indeed, will try not to fail you if you should need my help in either capacity, but I like to keep my work in perspective. Have you heard this story? Dr. A is a man who counts how many apples will fall in a day on X's farm. Dr. B challenges him. Dr. C makes a living predicting whether Dr. A or Dr. B will prove correct. Dr. D arrives to predict whether Dr. C will be right.

Dr. C is an "expert."

Dr. D is a "consultant."

And the fellow who tells the story is a "sociologist"!

Margaret, I am thinking that it's more than time to exchange photographs since we can't foreseeably arrange a personal meeting.

I hope you agree. It's getting to be strange writing to some ghostlike image that hovers invisibly over your pages, and I suspect you feel the same way looking in this direction. I will if you will.

And, Margaret Webb, please stop addressing me as Dr. Curtiss. Even my students call me

Brian

June 16

Dear Brian:

I suppose I can if your students can. Still, to be candid, addressing you as "Brian" is going to take some getting used to.

An interesting sidelight occurs to me. When you wrote "Margaret" for the first time, I did not mind at all. I found it quite easy and comfortable. Why should it be a smooth transition for you and a bumpy one for me? Possibly a provocative question for Women's Lib?

But I have more important news. Last night my husband announced we have been invited to Montreal for the Olympics! The people own a large department store in Canada for which Arthur—have I told you he is an attorney?—has done legal work here. He tells me they have a grand old-fashioned mansion in a section called Westmount, and we are being given first choice of tickets for the Olympic events we want to attend. That is no problem for either of us. Just as we see eye to eye on so many things, Arthur and I are both great fans of the gymnasts, especially those Russian and Romanian darlings. (I always spelled Romania "Rumania," but Arthur has just bought some wine carrying "Romania" on the label, and Webster's says "Rumanians" use "Romanian" officially! No wonder they are known as a quicksilver people.)

I haven't looked forward to anything with such anticipation since —well, to be honest—since your letters began to come. (That is the truth, Brian, and I want to confess it to make up for the times I have been uncertain and hangdog about us.)

I *am* considering sending you a photograph. The difficulty is to find one that I think portrays me the way you might conceivably imagine me to be. I find this like thinking of the square root of minus one. The concept of "irrational numbers" has always intrigued me. If a *number* can be irrational, then maybe mysticism and all that isn't just hocus-pocus. But who am I to be lecturing you!

When you have seen my photo in all its nearly-48-year-old non-glory, you'll be dead sorry you asked for it. Young man, the difference in our ages, yours and mine, remains far more critical than your Whisky Divide and far from trivial. But I enjoy your sense of humor.

Still, I will take the chance of sending you a picture of me, if you will wait until we return from Montreal. We should have some up-to-date shots, and at least the backgrounds will be of interest. We will be back home the last week in July. I have never been to anything at all like an Olympics, and my husband and I are as excited as two kids . . .

Your friend,
Margaret

P.S. I must tell you, concerning humanity and its outlook, all is not lost! Today in the park I watched three children chasing a butterfly. They were some eight or nine years old. Despite their delightful, open faces, I was utterly terrified that they would tear the lovely yellow wings and torture the insect. To my joy, instead, when one boy finally caught the butterfly in his fingers, a little girl said—after they had all laughed and fussed over its beauty—"Now let her go, *and let her have her future.*" Those were the child's exact words. And they did let it go! And I wiped tears. Not everything is wrong with this old limping world.

June 20

Dear Margaret:

I hope this catches you before you have left for Montreal because I have Big News! A group at Princeton is planning a seminar in my field for October. If it comes off, I will be traveling East to participate. I could easily stop off for a day or so in New York and buy you that drink I have promised!

If Princeton works out, I hope your own plans will make it possible for us to meet at last.

Meantime if you hurry with a photograph, Kay and I will be able to watch for you when the TV cameras pan the crowds. I did considerable athletics in high school, until my leg was injured in an accident. The gymnastics are my favorites too. I find the feats incredible, both men and women. Please save up your impressions for me.

I have been thinking about you constantly, it seems, probably because there is now the possibility that we will actually come together face-to-face instead of letter-to-letter. I, too, am trying to get more of a handle on "us," and a story told by Alan Watts in his autobiography comes to mind. You might like to take it to heart, about us, as I have. The story is about Sir Walford Davies, then master of the King's Musick in England. Here is the passage in the book:

> Sir Walford was instructing an untrained choral group in hymn-singing. He started them out with some familiar hymn which they bellowed forth with gusto to impress the Archbishop of Canterbury ". . . who was, obviously, in attendance . . ." and the musical effect was terrible. But there was also present a small professional choir, and Sir Walford asked them to go through several verses of a completely unfamiliar hymn so that everyone could memorize the tune. "Now," he said, "we're all going to sing this new hymn. But one thing is absolutely important: you must not *try* to sing it. Just think of the tune and let it sing itself."

I wrote to you before that what is happening between you and me has no easy name or model. We ought not *try* for one. *"Let it sing itself!"* I am well content to do that.

In your last letter you confess your anticipation of my mail. Let me confess the same for your letters—and now (roll of drums) October may bring us together in the flesh! Be sure I will let you know the details of the Princeton affair immediately if it jells.

With fingers crossed!
Brian

June 27

Dear Brian:

My husband can't get away from his office before July 19, so I have a little more time than I thought before Montreal.

Your tidings about Princeton make me terribly uncertain once more. Of course I would very much like meeting you, Brian Curtiss, but frankly, I have mixed feelings at the prospect. I am trying to be as honest as I can with myself and with you. It simply is not easy for me. It is one thing to exchange letters. We are sheltered nicely behind our typewriters (did you notice I have had the "o" fixed?) and our postage stamps, but I must admit I *have* considered it a "diversion" and nothing more. It never remotely occurred to me that we might ever conceivably stand face-to-face, and I find that enormously difficult to imagine or contemplate. I expect I would be fearfully self-conscious, a frozen stick, and tongue-tied while you, seeing me in the all-too-human aging flesh, would wonder how you had ever let yourself in for such a disenchanting blind date.

I do not put myself down, Brian. I am a reasonably attractive woman as matrons go. I don't even discover any really worrisome wrinkles in my face. But my mirror does remind me, bluntly, that I was already more than 17 when you were just born!

As my 22-year-old son would say, Wow!

I cannot blink that stubborn circumstance, nor can you.

I will defer my decision about a meeting between us and let this simmer on the back burner while I am in Canada. I will let you know when I return. Perhaps we should not meet even via photographs. Anyway, you said Princeton was indefinite, so we need not make an issue of it now.

Since you have churned all this up, I have been taking a fresh look at myself, and I have been jolted. The mirror reminds me of something Richard Wright said, or maybe it was James Baldwin (shades of Bacon and Locke!) when he was an expatriate in Paris. One reason he liked living there, he observed, was that, sitting with his white friends in some cafe, the only time he remembered he was black was when he happened to glimpse his skin as he lifted his glass. You have got me staring at my hand, and I see the inevitable signs that no skin cream can erase despite the utopian promises of the cosmetics ads. We live in no utopia in any aspect of our lives.

Brian, my fingers have come off the typewriter, as if some force lifted them. What a curious feeling! The machine is telling me to stop, look, and listen. Very well. I have paused. What do I see and hear?

I see and hear what I do not wish the machine would be telling me so plainly now that I have resumed typing. The keys are declaring that I am fussing about my age in this letter as an unconscious or even conscious way of creating an excuse to avoid meeting you.

Not because of my age! That is transparent even to me. We would be meeting as acquaintances only, so what possible bearing could our ages have to do with it? No, my real reason is fear, or rather I should say a fearful and sharp sense of impropriety on my part. Despite everything, you *are* a stranger. I may address you as Brian and sign myself Margaret, but between us it is really Dr. Curtiss and Mrs. Webb, as it should of course be.

Now I have a feeling of really acid irritation. I don't like myself when I yield to pressure, in this case my own stiff-necked reference to "impropriety." What an arbitrary and priggish word that is! I am leaving this impertinent typewriter for a minute to let that sink in.

I have been out on the terrace for a long time. Our view is north, over the whole expanse of Central Park. Just below, there are white swans on the lake, but the setting sun is turning them to orange birds out of my old fairy tale books. You may be amused to know that we have what I can only call an upside-down sunset here. You see, tall buildings on the west side block the sun as it sinks lower, but the rays beam across town where they are caught to reflect blazingly in the windows of the Fifth Avenue houses. The windows literally catch fire, and I am watching a breathtaking battery of brilliant, dazzling flares as far uptown as my eyes can see. Tonight there are black clouds behind the buildings to the east, so the flares look like the gleaming eyes of wild animals in some dark jungle. Tigers, tigers burning bright . . . We may be in for a storm, but right now the air is summer, the park is a magic carpet relieving the stone city, the crowded streets. Sometimes the park looks to me like an Eastern prayer rug, with intricate designs made up of the lawns, ledges, lakes, gardens, playgrounds, ball fields. Do you know we still have a working carousel?

I come back into my bedroom with a sense of perspective, a sense of all the lives bustling outside, all the people in the streets, in the office buildings, in the luxury apartments, in the slums to the north. Bridges are visible, too. I can see the bridges making their vital statements of comings and goings, leading to roads east to Long Island. And west across the country. Reminding me again that you are not pieces of mail but a man. ("Bridge" has always seemed to me a wonderful word, from the time I was a little girl. There were so many rivers, even little streams, I could never get across.)

What Princeton has roiled up in me is not new, Brian. Lately, lying in bed with my husband sleeping beside me, I think of you across the country. It is almost as if I am in a spaceship so high I can take in the whole curve of the earth and the distance shrinks between you and me. When I feel so near, I am chilled with a pounding sense that something is out of kilter, that the connection of our letters has created stronger links than either of us anticipated. It is just because you have become so real to me that this relationship seems out of place in my life.

So! Having got that off my chest, let me tell you what I decided quite clearly on the terrace. (As Henry Moore said, or was it Noguchi? "One returns from a journey with new perspective.") I do not need to defer my decision about Princeton until after Montreal. I do not need to defer it beyond the next keystrokes, which say that I do want to meet you.

I am hardly impressed with my weather-vaning, you may be sure, but I think you will understand and even sympathize with my confusion. Nothing like this has ever confronted me before, and I am out of the habit of handling new things. I suppose that happens when one's life has followed a fairly steady and uneventful course. I have not handled my son's problems well either.

But we are not talking about problems, we are looking forward to a holiday together! If your trip becomes definite, write me your timetable so I can arrange my schedule to spend as much time with you as possible. As I've indicated to you, my husband travels a great deal and I am usually with him. It would be a pity, a crying shame, if you did come to New York and I was not here.

That was exceedingly difficult to get out, but I am glad I am able to say it, plainly and without reservations.

Your friend,
Margaret

P.S. Reading this over, I discover something else I want to share with you, Brian.

As you realize, when I began the letter I truly did not know how I felt about meeting you. The answer came in the course of the writing!

I started with an inner problem and just in laying it out for myself, came to the conclusion.

It is as if my typewriter keys do have a mind of their own. No— it is more as if I have had a good talk with Brian Curtiss, a talk with a close friend that helped me make up my mind.

Now I am rooting for Princeton to work out!

Part Two

July 4

Margaret!

Your rooting did it—Princeton is on! I will let you know the exact October dates and will count on your being free. By all means let us not be like Longfellow's Evangeline. Remember how the star-crossed lovers kept passing each other in opposite directions for a lifetime as they sought each other? Not that we are lovers or star-crossed, but it would be a travesty if I got to New York and you were elsewhere or unavailable.

Fourth of July today, almost a full six months we have been corresponding, and there's the pop-bang of firecrackers all around to celebrate our occasion!

It continues to be a good feeling just knowing you are there, reading my letters, telling me a little more about yourself each time, on the lines and between them.

About myself the most important thing to tell right now is my rage. I have just finally quieted down a little after a night-long fury so great that I was prepared to commit murder. Literally.

I am not exaggerating. I did not suspect that I was capable of such primitive violence. I urgently need to tell you what has happened, so viciously, here.

The road past our house runs west to Point Reyes and ocean

beaches that attract hordes of people on holiday weekends. Most are folks out for a family good time. But the Fourth has brought a rock and roll concert nearby and an invasion of miserable types. Among other things, these animals drop their garbage and beer cans all over the place—on their way to rally against polluting the environment!

I remember what you called the girls who mugged the elderly doctor in your park. "Barbarians." Too mild! What would you name the "people" who last night *took a hatchet to two redwoods at the edge of my property?* They didn't try to cut them down, they could never manage that. Instead, this parcel of savages slashed the trees in a full circle that cut through the cambium layer where growth takes place. They knew exactly what they were doing. It was squalid premeditated murder.

The chopping noise woke me up. It was about two in the morning. I thought someone was rapping on my door. Kay had gone to San Francisco. It might be her, or someone in trouble on the road.

I hopped into some jeans and ran outside. Nobody near the house. I followed the noise. I thought an animal might be hunting garbage, or a van broken down. Instead, I heard laughing, young voices obviously drunk or high on drugs, that raucous hysterical pitch you never mistake when people are out of control. But I never expected what I saw.

The mutilation was just ending as I approached the gang. They were hopping around crazily, braying like hyenas at their diabolical handiwork. Four young men (one openly masturbating), two girls, all bombed out of their skulls. In the moonlight I could see only too clearly what they had done. The slashed trees looked as if they were bleeding. My outrage tore my throat, I never knew I was capable of such a sound, more an animal roar than a human voice. It stopped them cold. They glared at me. One of them yelled—dared to yell— "Mind your own fucking business!"

Margaret, if I had a gun, I would have killed them all, happily, thankfully, without thinking twice.

I grabbed rocks and threw as hard as I could, wanting to squash those vicious heads. They ran like the filthy cowards they are. Ran laughing and sneering at me as I missed and missed and missed. I cursed myself for the way my rage was making my arm shake so that I couldn't aim straight. I chased after them but my leg doesn't let me run fast any more and they got to their car. I tripped and fell at the side of the road trying to pick up more stones.

And those evil bastards steered straight for me!

If I hadn't rolled away like a dervish, they'd have run me over, as purposefully as they had hacked the trees.

It was an incredible nightmare. I told myself it had to be a movie shot for a terror script someone was faking. How could such a thing be real? How would anyone, drunk or drugged or insane, have the thought of destroying redwoods like these? Some of these stands go back before Jesus Christ. A handful of fucking vandals cleaves the life out of them, for an evening's kicks!

"Fucking" is the word *they* left behind. Just to be sure everyone got the idea, this group of American kids celebrated the Fourth of July by carving their message into the bark: "Fuck you, one and all."

Eloquent inscription. At least they used the comma.

When I stood up, with my jeans ripped and my legs bleeding, I heaved another rock after their disappearing car. Aimless and pitiful gesture, aimless fast-burning fury and frustration—the way most of society today responds to the crimes the troglodytes commit against us.

What will these beasts claw apart next in their feral hunger to fill the emptiness of their hollow lives? They have already destroyed themselves. They are joyless, without souls. Their world has given them nothing to fear, nothing to follow. They have no God, no Hell, no Parents, no Law, so nothing is proscribed, nothing forbidden to them. It is the slippage of conscience in our society generally, an age of dehumanization. They are beyond reach. Without outer or inner authority to restrain them, we have no control, and our jails cannot contain them all in any case. They live by one rule only: instant gratification, taken as a supreme right, *their* right without regard to anyone else's. And when their meaningless lusts are surfeited, what else is left to them but destruction? It is their last possibility of asserting their lives, the only thing that affirms their existence, that leaves a mark to show they were on earth at all. Otherwise they are zombies.

How mighty they must feel if they can doom so sublime a creation as a redwood tree. What they did was not just malicious. Inwardly, they must *hate* these trees, because they cannot stand any reminder of nobility in any form. Their only hope of living with their stench is to believe that everything in the world stinks as noisomely.

It might not be so foreboding if, when the drugs wear off, these zombies felt remorse. But remorse is a human quality, and they are mindless creatures. The years of self-indulgence have pithed their brains. And mindlessness is a passion of its own, as a tornado or tidal wave may be said to possess passion.

Not even sex gives life to these walking corpses. That disgusting masturbation I witnessed was as mindless as the rest. Not even the girls paid attention.

And this species of brute does not have even a political cause to rationalize their foulness.

I think society does not take such vandalism seriously enough. This is not just an escalation of goldfish-eating. As a sociologist, I see these despoilers lacking in any personal commitment to meaningfulness in human life. If there is no commitment at the core—which has been the Family in the past—there can be no sense of commitment to one's self, or to a friend, an employer, a city, a society, a civilization. We are backing into a psychological anarchy. I take grave note of the (respectable!) theories that there is no such thing as insanity! To me, this is only another version of "anything goes," the very poison I am describing. It is mutiny against society itself. The price, I deeply believe, is not just a decline but a possible shattering of our world. A devilish apocalypse may be more imminent than is supposed.

I am writing more dismally than I had intended. I am shaken in every way by this profanation. If Kay were here I would be spilling this out to her rather than burdening you. I hate morbidity, but I am sick for my children. What world awaits them? Today a redwood tree, tomorrow the deluge?

I see a generation of destruction lurking, infected with the most ancient dark passions and corrupt purposes. The omens are everywhere, though largely neglected. Only note the spread of terrorism beyond international law or agreement. Neo-Nazis all around, including our U.S. A resurgence of anti-Semitism, Ku-Klux racism and the brutality they celebrate. To say nothing of the common vandals, bolder on all our paths every day like your rat in the park. Don't people see the broken street lights, the smashed park benches? The rats are chittering their warnings all too plainly, and our ears are plugged with the wax of self-delusion. "It's only kids . . ." No, we had better watch, listen, and take heed!

I have never felt as I did last night. I did not know I owned such hatred. I never fathomed that *I* could kill or maim another person, and certainly not with a bursting pleasure. That is the worst about barbarians. They make barbarians of us all!

Now I wonder about sending this letter. Why trouble you? The answer comes at once, and gratifyingly. I am sending this because Margaret Webb is my friend, and friends are for sharing the tough times as well as the good. This has been one of the meanest hours of my life. I needed to write. It says you are genuine to me; we are beyond pastime. Being able to talk to you this morning has eased the pain of last night a little.

Write if you have time before you leave.

Brian

July 7

Brian dear:

Your sad, terrible, and distressing letter just came, and I don't want to wait to answer. I am glad you wrote, glad there was some small comfort for you in sharing that nightmare with me.

I don't know what to say except to agree that you are too fearfully right about the venomous lunatics in our midst. In a minor way, I have experienced something of a vandalism experience here. Not as miserable as yours, but symptomatic and unsettling in its implications too.

Arthur and I live in a co-op, a grand landmark-type building with the kind of construction and appointments never to be seen again. We needed to automate our elevators. (For one thing, operators now run about $15,000 per man per shift. I am on the board of directors so I have the firsthand figures. Also, the building mortgage was due for refinancing, and banks want converted elevators. They don't want the expense of manned operations if they have to take over, or the cost of automating.) We tenants all agreed, though, that the automated elevators should not be the shoddy plastic cabs seen so often these days in even fine buildings. A committee, of which I was a member, spent hours selecting a fine walnut paneling, and we were delighted with the final result. Everyone agreed the expense was worth it.

I suppose you are ahead of me by this time. It wasn't a week before our handsome panels were defaced with the most awful gouging and graffiti. "Fuck" was the mildest of it. (My finger has to be forced to type the letters of that ugly word.) The marks were dug in so viciously deep that they cannot be repaired.

Who was the "perpetrator"? We have doormen 24 hours a day so it is unlikely that it was an outsider, unless a visitor. Possibly it was a disgruntled employee, or a teenager everyone knows is erratic. It could even have been one of us shareholders, with no more reason than your scurvy redwood vandals had. It could have been my own son, if it comes to that!

What *does* one do in such a world?

Our board tried hidden cameras, talked of television monitors, etc. I want them to try a reward, but so far they haven't.

Meantime, the elevator has become a disaster area of grotesque fun and games. More than one frolicsome hand now makes its thumb-nosing contribution. Also, there are small children in the building, and I suppose they find it irresistible to mark the walls once the breach has occurred. Now there are tic-tac-toe squares amidst the abounding obscenities. It is, I tell you, a trial to go up and down.

And this in a very upper-class setting, not a slum building with welfare families! Do you recall the shameful situation in St. Louis, where the terribly expensive government-subsidized Pruitt-Igoe buildings had to be razed because the tenants vandalized their own homes, using their elevators for toilets, throwing garbage out of windows, ripping out plumbing for the few dollars fences paid? No animal would do that to its cave.

I am sure you have heard of Cleopatra's Needle, the obelisk that stands near the Metropolitan Museum. It was a gift from Egypt in 1880. Its hieroglyphics were inscribed more than 3,700 years ago, over 1,700 years older than even your redwoods! It is an amazing single block of stone weighing 200 tons, rising 69 feet. Not as high as your trees, but perhaps more impressive in its own way, carrying the inscriptions, invocations, and praise of kings and gods of Egypt.

Lofty is the word. Man's reach for nobleness.

Today, the base is a scrawl of graffiti. Recently, some modern hero by name of "Lugo, 198, Bronx!" inscribed his love to "Boba, the Quean" [sic] to challenge Cleopatra and the ages. Pharaoh "Lugo"!

One thing that always strikes me about the graffiti is its swirling calligraphy, always arch in the worst possible taste. It is the flashy-flash of pimps who think their vulgarity impresses the world instead of filling us with contempt and disgust.

But what strikes me most as I stand before the historic obelisk is how *pathetic* the "Lugos" and "Bobas" are. How pitiful their pink and purple fugitive scrawl appears beneath the beauty of the carved images above.

But I agree with you about the danger of trivializing Lugo and Boba. Maybe it's mostly illiterate high jinks, but their spray cans may be chiseling as deeply into the stone as the original carvers did, and deeper.

Perhaps, as you observe, we are witnessing not just a sneering grunt out of ghettos but what may indeed be the handwriting on our society's wall. Maybe we should be grateful that we are dealing with spray cans and not yet with guns.

Are the hordes of Attila the Hun waiting and gathering beyond the gates? What does one do in such a time? The question keeps coming back. For myself, I am capable of murder, too, Brian! If I ever learn who vandalized my elevator, I swear I will gladly knock his (or her?) head against the defaced walls. Yes, they make barbarians of all of us, as you so accurately and terribly say.

I understand both your rage and your frustration, you see. We can only live as decently as *we* know how, I suppose. When I contemplate the daily headlines of crime, and worse, everywhere in the world, I find myself shrinking into my own apartment, my private life, with its own ups and downs, but with its own compensations. It makes me all the happier to know that you and I may see each other in the not far future now. Yes, I want your friendship, as I more and more want good and happy things in the rest of my life, and less and less of the ugly, unhappy, driven world. Knowing you makes it a little easier for me to ride my poor elevator without flinching or clenching my fists each time. What is the old saying? *Carpe diem!*

As my friends call me,
Peggy

P.S. When I typed that foul word "f—k" above, my mind turned to a little book my husband brought home last week, written by a young typographer who is a client of his. It is called *The Magic Type* and tells of an inspired designer who creates an alphabet so beautiful it cannot be made into ugly words. Of itself, it changes the letters of h-a-t-e into l-o-v-e, w-a-r into p-e-a-c-e, and so on. It is a charming literary conceit, isn't it?—and so much more! I would send you a copy but it is privately printed and we have only the one, which I obviously cherish.

July 11

Dear Peggy:

It is a privilege and a pleasure to call you "Peggy" as your friends do!

Your elevator and your obelisk depress me too. Unfortunately, we could match horror stories endlessly.

When I was younger (no laughter from you, please) my reaction was to do battle. The irony is that I did not take the barbarians to be the enemy. If anything I was on their side. In going through my necessary radical stage, I was taken in by the 1960s shibboleth that everything wrong with individuals and criminals is society's fault, not theirs.

Well, I continue to believe that young people should be the gadflies and goads, or society would stagnate. But the whole 200-plus years of this nation is proof of accomplishments uniquely achieved under a free political system. The world has not seen its like, and it should not lightly be dismantled. Today there is too much whining in place of ambition and effort. Most past immigrants had nothing but their personal determination in the battle against underprivilege, oppression, poverty, prejudice, scapegoatism. Instead of expecting free lunch and welfare handouts, their only demand was for opportunity.

To the extent that our society still fails to provide sufficient and equal opportunity, I fault it emphatically. But that is no justification for anarchy or laziness, for terrorism or the politicalization of crime. It is a sociological fact that within two generations of immigration, Americans of Russian, Polish, and Italian origin had the highest incomes of any racial or ethnic groups in the country. And they did it largely by lifting themselves by their own bootstraps, more credit to all of them.

As to what we, as individuals, can do, I agree with you about "seizing the day." I find myself believing more deeply each day that happiness, like charity, begins at home. I think it may also end at home. I see my own task now as making my family as secure as humanly possible, economically and emotionally. Then let howl the wolves over whom I have no control.

I know full well the argument that all tyrants need to succeed is that free men should do nothing, but what point was there in my throwing rocks at the empty air that night? My old companions would scorn me as a turncoat now, but I have lost my radical beliefs and enthusiasm, nor am I sure John Locke was right enough about human nature, at least as it exists in our industrial and postindustrial civilization.

In any case, there has never been a period without such distemper and worse, has there? Every era has known its prowling outlaws, has needed sentinels and protective fires outside its caves. Before you and I lose ourselves too thoroughly in black gloom, let's remind ourselves of the overriding fact that today more people are living *better* and less nervously than ever in history. The world is not all horror by a long shot, and I am sorry that my account of the redwood vandalism slid both of us into one of the swamps. Let's leave the grundginess and pessimism behind. Go on to the Olympics where, to paraphrase Tolstoy, you will witness celebrations of the best, not the beast, in man. I know it will be a fine time for you and your husband, and I will be impatient to hear about your experience.

Fondly,
Brian

July 15

Dear Brian:

Less than a week before we're off! Even my husband is showing signs of impatience. Ordinarily, he remains the phlegmatic one, pipe-smoking cool, who looks at you as if he is reading a cue card behind your eyes. It's what I call The Lawyer's Look. It can be disconcerting if you're not used to it, but I am and I don't mind. Our marriage is so solid just because Arthur and I are opposites in enough ways to keep the electricity flowing (without blowing fuses). My husband, for example, would *never* have started a correspondence like yours and mine. (Still, I would have thought it outside the range of my own possibilities, yet here I am . . .)

I suppose one should never presume to predict what anyone else can or cannot do. I know that people who see Arthur casually come away with a very one-sided view of the kind of person he really is. More than most, Arthur can present a misleading image. If you get to meet him, I know the words that will come to your mind. Coldly professional. Precise. Uncompromising. Enigmatic. And, arrogant. All plausible to some extent, but clearly there is more or I would not be the happy wife I am.

This same man *is* a fabulous raconteur, a warm and willing friend, a generous supporter of charities, and, quite unbelievably, a jazz buff. We have every record from Bix to Dizzie and before and after. Arthur has dragged me to the most improbable joints in New Orleans, Kansas City, Chicago, as well as New York to hear the old-timers and the new. All the musicians know and love him. "Here come de judge!" they call out when they spot him. If he had his life to live over again, he would play drums—in the style of his idol Gene Krupa!

A musician in legal trouble knows Arthur's door is open. If he is down on his luck, Arthur's fee will be a phonograph record or a photo of one of the greats. We have a fabulous collection, you can guess. Arthur's trouble was that his family was too poor for instruments or lessons, but I know he flagellates himself about music. Sometimes, after some drinks, he pounds the table praising the black boys, worse off than he ever was, who found some way to realize their love while he did not. He is a man who forgives himself nothing.

I will tell you more about this complex, always fascinating husband of mine as we go along, Brian. Life with him is seldom dull. It has been particularly absorbing to me to watch his reaction to your California address on the mail I receive from you. I must admit that with your first letter I had an impulse to hide the envelope. But that would have been childish and unworthy. Arthur had the grace not to inquire who "Brian Curtiss, Ph.D." was. Had he asked, I would of course have told him immediately. But then something of the spirit of our "game" caught me. It was mischievous of me, but I kept silent though I could see the question in Arthur's face.

Once the moment went by, it became difficult to bring the subject up. I am not sure why, Brian, but all at once it was cardinal for me to have something totally my own, absolutely private. I found myself shrugging off Arthur's asking eyes when he went through the mail. I said your envelopes were magazine mailings from "some outfit selling self-help psychology."

It was quite horrid of me, but I do know why I did that. It occurs to me that I have never in my life been free of people looking over my shoulder! Simply never! I went from my father's house to my husband's not only constantly sheltered but constantly scrutinized and *answerable!* I never even kept a private diary—significantly enough called a Personal in our Boston society. There, that's it! It is a brand new thought in my head. It makes me both out of temper at the past and exhilarated about the present. At last I have a secret! This relationship with you—tenuous, distant, "fragile," as you have rightly called it—is the *only* thing in my life I have not shared with someone!

Isn't that a momentous thought to give one pause!

Maybe it is what creates the buoyancy I mentioned. I feel it now as what my father would have called *bracing*. Yes. I am quite set up about it, though part of me knows I am a chowderhead for creating this maze against Arthur where none is necessary.

I saw that my husband did not buy my deception about psychology publications . . . he is not the attorney he is for nothing. But he did not press me, and I was grateful. He went into the library, and I smelled his pipe going strong, and heard the record he always plays when he wants a change of mood: Peggy Lee asking what life's all about. It's passing strange that that should be "Arthur's song" since his own *last* reaction to adversity is to uncork a whiskey bottle and go on a bender. Yet, as I say, who does really know what goes on inside anyone else? Anyway, I love the song, too, and especially the way La Lee sings it. (I wanted to be a singer once. If there is reincarnation I will rejoin drummer Arthur as Peggy Lee!)

In any case, I now keep your letters out of Arthur's sight. The mail comes up to the apartment after he has left for the office, so it isn't hard. I feel quite silly doing this because everything between you and me is so obviously and attestedly and wholly innocent and irreproachable. Brian, you are evoking parts of *my* personality I did not know I possessed, including deceiver! Once I began hiding your letters from my husband—and there is no other word for it than hiding—I was trapped. To confess our correspondence would seem doubly suspicious after I had denied it. Now and then I do have an impulse to clear the air, but every time I reach for the packet in my dressing table, something in me balks and bridles. Dammit, I *am* entitled to one experience purely and strictly intimate—Personal. But I suppose at the same time I am writing this as a kind of caution for you always to be discreet, as if there were any reason to suggest such an outlandish notion!

It is disquieting to have a secret from my husband, but it is also diverting. It has started me thinking more about myself, with a quite sharp and abrupt awareness of how much more of my life I have devoted to others rather than myself—my parents, my husband, my son, et cetera (two words, though by the way Webster does say the single word is acceptable; however, you are correct that the first style is preferred).

As I think about myself in this new light, I perceive that my preoccupation with my age is a reflection of *others'* image of me. You are righter about me than they are. I have a respectable regard for the calendar as you know too well, but I do not feel *old.* If our correspondence has brought me nothing else, this awareness, stimulated by you, is dividend enough!

Do you know the joke about middle age? "I can do anything I ever did, I just don't feel like it so much." It's a perennial at our club. (We are members at a place in Westchester. Arthur plays splendid golf. I flounder at tennis. Sometimes on a Saturday night if Arthur has had a drink too many, he plays drums with the band for a number or two. He does it quite well for an amateur, and everyone applauds like mad, including the musicians, because he so obviously loves joining in.)

The more I think about Arthur, the less I believe a man like him can ever be put on paper. He is too many things all at once. Did I mention he is an accountant as well as an attorney? How can I make it credible that the drummer I have just described lives by, with, and through actuarial tables? Literally. Sometimes I find it a nuisance, even a morbid shadow brought into our lives unnecessarily. But I try to see the amusing side, and I suppose it is amusing and even beguiling in a way. To wit:

At 55 years of age, my husband, Arthur Webb, calculates that (if he keeps his weight to the 160–165 pounds recommended for a male of 5'10", medium-boned) he should live to 74.5 years of age. That leaves him 19.5 years to go, and counting down. For instance, at two suits annually, reducing to one after age 70, he projects the purchase of 39 more suits. That's grisly! So is 39 more pairs of shoes. Then there are his haircuts. At exactly 17 a year, he has 331.5 visits to the barber left. You know, Brian, *331.5 haircuts remaining in a man's life does put things in a very different frame.* Next week, Arthur will have only 330.5 more times to go. Quite stingingly, that does not seem so terribly much, does it? It amplifies the clock too insistently for me. It has its droll side, to be sure, but it leads me to count how many more visits *I* have to the hairdresser. I dearly wish Arthur would quit his counting, but his confounded score sheets are taped inside our medicine cabinet where I can't avoid them every morning when I reach for the toothpaste.

Toothpaste! My husband has a separate and outraged fixation about that. His indictment is that manufacturers design brushes longer than we need so that people will squeeze out more paste than necessary! Arthur complains that people like me are sheep. If he were in the business, he would double his sales at our expense simply by making longer brushes. He did bamboozle me into settling for a dab morning and night, but—and I believe this is more than coincidence, Brian—since I have been corresponding with you I have been smearing toothpaste to my heart's content to the very last bristle on the longest brush I can find!

Arthur sometimes pretends all this is a humorous affectation, but I believe he is dead serious when he worries whether he is ordering too many business cards engraved. Arthur's idea of heaven would be to make everything come out exactly even—to use up his last toothpaste and hand out his last card just as Gabriel blew his horn.

If I have to have my nose rubbed in mortality, I would far rather consider how many *shaves* Arthur still has to go. At one a day (though he shaves twice when he has an evening speech) they now come to 7,117. *That* is a respectable number, and I wrote it on his chart this morning.

Our son, Gary, makes jokes about this hang-up of his father's. Yesterday he taped a poem to the wall of our bathroom. It is lugubrious, though it did give me a laugh. (Arthur hasn't yet told me how it struck him.) Gary wrote:

> *At a rate of one roll per month*
> *Of toilet tissue, neat,*
> *Time may be measured out upon this seat.*
> *But isn't it rum to hear the muffled drum*
> *Each time one cleans one's bum?*
> *Oh, ask not for whom the paper turns,*
> *It rolls for thee!*

That's Gary! Irreverent, disrespectful, absurd, and outrageously clever, don't you think? I hope John Donne forgives him. I do. After all, what is Gary to think when he sees 15 bottles of Arthur's pre-shave cached away "against inflation"? At one bottle per four months, that is a five-year supply. I am as irritated as Arthur at the way the prices go up on this stuff, but how much money will we really save?

There's the contradiction again. Arthur will put aside a tea bag to use twice "because it still has plenty of strength." But he will travel first class at any expense on even the shortest flight. And take a hotel suite for overnight though he will scarcely set foot in the extra room. And then he will raise the dust about a charge for toast for breakfast —and steal every piece of soap he can get his hands on!

Soap! Oh, my sacred aunt, I haven't had to buy a bar of soap since Arthur became a peregrinating lecturer on tax law. I have with my own incredulous eyes witnessed my impeccable, upright, honorable officer-of-the-court husband skulk in a hotel corridor until the maid is inside some room so he can snatch extra soap off her cart. At first Arthur claimed he was merely taking souvenirs. Now this exemplary stalwart of the law claims it is not stealing or pilfering because at today's rates hotels should furnish as much soap as anyone might want.

If any of this sounds as if I am putting Arthur down, be sure I mean nothing like it. On the contrary, I find his peculiarities endearing in their way. They make him human-size, though I must admit that sometimes he goes too far. I remember that on our honeymoon (*shall never* forget this!) he taught me that if a person needs both to clean eyeglasses *and* blow nose at the same time, the glasses should be attended to first, since two pieces of Kleenex will otherwise be required.

I don't quite know how I got off on this. I am again doing Arthur a considerable injustice. I should tell you less about his charts and more about how handsome a man he is, how well he is carrying his years, keeping trim and fit with squash at the Harvard Club (his partners are Cambridge men). I should tell you more of his public service, mostly behind the scenes, on important city committees. You have gathered that he is a leading tax attorney of national reputation —which, incidentally, doesn't make for peace with our son. Gary shoots from the hip, sometimes on purpose I think, about men like Arthur helping rich people "screw the government and adding to the poor people's load." Arthur stays calm for a while, answering logically. He points out that what Gary calls "fat loopholes" are mostly the government's use of the tax structure for positive social purposes. Arthur supplies persuasive examples: The country wants more decent housing for lower and middle-income groups. Private industry can't meet the need without charging higher rents than the people can pay. So the government enacts tax abatement as an incentive. That is not a "loophole" in the pejorative sense that Gary uses the term. But Gary doesn't want his heated prejudices cooled by facts. He yells "Dullshit," and then they go at it. Finally, Arthur loses patience, and I don't blame him. Gary has no interest except making Arthur wrong, so there is no way a dialogue can be sustained. My brother Ted never dared talk to my father as Gary talks back to Arthur. Ted today is a distinguished physician in Boston. I am not sure what Gary will turn out to be. Which one had the better father?

I have let this letter run on too long. Still, I won't be writing to you from Montreal, so count this as two or three. I felt sociable talking to you and didn't want to stop. Maybe it's a way of saying I have been feeling alone lately, though I don't know why I should, and in any case this letter has been about my family. . . . I am at the bottom of a page and should quit. If I use another sheet, I may have to add a second stamp. There is something of my husband in me, at that!

I feel as if we've had a walk in the park.

And I like it.
Margaret

July 16

Dear Brian:

After I mailed the missive yesterday, I came back and wandered around my apartment. I was restless. I looked at the furniture, our paintings, the Eskimo pieces we collect, seeing everything through new eyes—yours. What will *you* see when you come here in the fall?

The pendulum of which you once spoke swings in small arcs as well as large. I have noticed that with rare exceptions when children leave home they decorate in a style opposite the parents'. If mother and father had dark furniture, the new household will be light woods. If Victorian, modern, and vice versa, versa vice. My husband and I started with light pieces, though conservative enough in design. Arthur left it pretty much up to me, "the woman's province."

When we moved to this apartment after our finances improved, I found I preferred darker things, though not the heavy, looming furniture of the Boston house.

Mother is still up there, though Father died last year. Arthur points out that Father passed away at precisely 70.8 years of age to the hour, the actuarial expectation. My father was not a man to step off the straight and narrow in any regard. Mother lives with my brother. I mentioned Ted in my last letter. Father wanted him to be a lawyer too, but he couldn't complain too testily when Ted was admitted to *Harvard* Med School. Ted and my sister-in-law, Nadeen, a lovely woman who was his nurse, have the big house on Beacon Hill so there is plenty of room for my mother, even though there are four children.

I can close my eyes and see the old house. Smell it would be more accurate. My mother kept everything smelling of polish, including us (we?) children. I had to shine at school, at voice lessons, at elocution performances, at dancing classes. Dear Lord, how cliché-clumsy I was at Miss Dryer's, and petrified of both her and the boys. I had heard it whispered that if a boy so much as touched the tip of your breast, even inadvertently and in utter innocence, you would become pregnant. I kept my stern distance no matter how crankily Miss Dryer yelled. Mercy, *there* was a Gap-and-Divide, Brian!

It was impossible to win total approval. If I brought home four A's and one B+, I got a proper scolding. Even years later, when I was already married, my mother spent the first ten minutes of any visit criticizing my clothes, my hair, the arrangement of my furniture, or whatever else her eagle eyes lit on. As for my father, he was reduced to speechlessness when he first came to our New York flat. Our Picasso (small but genuine) was bad enough, but he literally sputtered at a New Guinea sculpture in our living room. It is frankly male, a very masculine figure, a compelling carving of its genre. Father bellowed, grabbed a towel from the bathroom and rushed to *diaper* the chief.

Looking back, not even my husband knows how miserable my parents made my life. Brian, you are the only person I have ever permitted myself to admit this to. I haven't been able to get it out even to Ted, whom I dearly love. That starts tears now, and I quite hate self-pity. I do not know what is the matter with me today. I didn't know this treacherous typewriter was going to take off this way. I suspect I have bottled up more than I have realized. For too long.

Let me go on, then, since I have started and you are patiently listening, dear friend.

Now I am looking at my typewriter and seeing not the keys but my father's face. I never saw the man smile, not one time. As a graduate of both Harvard College and The Law School, he never let anyone forget that the Harvard Club of Boston was the hub of the hub of the hub of the Universe, nothing less. And, it comes to me now, Father fancied himself the Hub of the Club. He was a Brahmin manqué, the absolutely most damnable, exasperating thing to be. A real Brahmin is so secure that he has no trouble unbending. My father had always to be ramrod. He was always playing to the Manor born, forgive the pun. He pretended our family had arrived with the Mayflower, although we all knew that his "patrician" father had founded our wealth on a horse-and-wagon coal and kerosene route.

Mother followed Father's pretense of an aristocratic heritage. She was as obsequious and submissive to Father as she was domineering and relentless with my brother, my sister, and me. Our lives as children were as brittle as the then-fashionable glass plants carefully set (as traps, I used to believe) on the spindly tables in our drawing room, and God help any child who ran about in that china shop. I think of your golden children free in their playground under your redwoods!

It isn't easy to face, or even to frame the thought, but I need to say to someone finally, though the date is late, that my father was a pompous ass! And more's the pity. Because he had genuine gifts and was deservedly respected throughout the state. But a mask worn long enough usurps the flesh.

The man was poisoned by his need for acceptance. He held all the prejudices that costumed his pose. He abhorred the Irish ("*We* go back to England!"), he even put down the Kennedy family as "up-starts." Need I say what he thought of "kikes"? Blacks—"niggers" to him—were unmentionable; they were simply off the human scale entirely, not the same species. Horrible!

Propriety above all! If we had a family crest, that would be emblazoned on it, you may be sure. Plus Father's motto: "Even when you are ahead, work and struggle as if you are coming from behind, for you *are* always behind the best that's in you!" In my youth I accepted that as true, moral, and logical, never recognizing it as a wicked and bombastic prescription for everlasting frustration and unending guilt.

Does the West Coast have our custom of the "mortgage button"? When you enter a New England home—more specifically on Martha's Vineyard and Nantucket, but throughout the area generally—you glance at the newel post supporting the bottom of the bannister. If it has a button atop, usually carved of ivory, you have the owner's sign that the mortgage on the house has been paid off! Few people know this quaint Yankee convention—how to boast with your mouth shut.

You may be certain that we Fairfields had the most beautifully carved ivory button on Beacon Hill. It was the largest possible diameter consistent with good taste, and it sat, in daily polished glory, broadcasting its self-satisfied message to every visitor. Few who entered our house did not know it, but Arthur had to ask. Trust him to notice. And Father proudly to show and tell.

Our freshly washed steps on Beacon, like the others up and down the Hill, rose between iron railings to the sedate front door with the lovely (and lovingly remembered) fantail above. I recall how that heavy door always seemed to need lubricating. When I was a little girl I believed it was somehow human, and actually harrumphed like a proper butler when it opened to a caller.

Ours was one of the grander facades, a Charles Bulfinch house, with Ionic columns and pilasters proclaiming dignity and wealth. And propriety, remember.

The household was pickled in vinegar rules. No exceptions unless you were ill. I rose on the split second, dressed and ate by the clock's minute hand, was out to school so precisely that Greenwich could check the time by me. I sat for tea with a ruler-straight back, my hands clasped knuckle white in my lap, head up till my neck felt broken, chin in till I couldn't draw breath, only to hear mother scold me for slumping.

Genteel. Diapers on sculpture! Now that I think of it, every trip we took to the art museums was carefully routed to avoid the Greek and Roman statues! I grew up hardly realizing I had a body. One attended it as discreetly and quickly as possible behind locked doors. Sometimes I think my father would approve of the custom of one pygmy tribe in which, I read somewhere, meals are eaten with backs turned, it being considered indecent to be seen in the act of dining. (Though it wouldn't have been indecent that the dish might be an enemy's flesh!)

People were never to be naked, except to bathe. At night, I put on a tent nightgown before I slid off my petticoats and "unmentionables." I still do, come to think of it! And my husband, come to think of it, has never remarked on it one way or another.

The conversations in that house were edifying, when I could manage to hear them. Somehow everything interesting took place after

I had been sent upstairs to my room. I did overhear quarrels between my father and Ted. I remember one when Ted must have been about 17 (I about 14, and Clarissa, whose separate tale I will write another time, 23 or 24). Ted wanted permission to go to some affair that didn't suit my father. Ted was losing his case of course, and blurted in desperation, "You only live once, you know!"

But my father had a clincher for that clincher. Oh, how the walls shook with it: "That is always the excuse for cheap pleasures! *Happiness* is the exercise of *maturity* in the overcoming of *temptation!*" At Radcliffe some years later I recognized the Spartan and Kantian philosophy, but with Ted it seemed only tyrannical.

Ted had the manliness to persist. "I'm going," he said doggedly. "I've made up my mind!"

Father floored him with, "That's easy when you have little to make up." (As I recall, I later came upon that sophomorism in, of all unlikely places, Aristotle!)

Later I heard my mother venture, "Aren't you being *too* strict, William?" And good old father had another chisel-ready sermonette: "It is necessary for children to have someone to whom they must always show their best side. It helps them remember it exists!" Father was not a man to match wits with.

My childhood catechism: "Abjure desire" (I hadn't the foggiest as to what desire meant). "Lust is a scourge." (That sounded like some kind of floor mop to me.) "The path to redemption is self-denial." (Later, after Tennessee Williams, I tried to make a joke: Had there ever been a Streetcar Named Redemption? Ted didn't think that was funny but I still, perversely, do!)

There is something about my trusting you that is allowing me to write this way. Things I have been reluctant to talk about with anyone else, even Arthur, come stepping right along. I get into a strange and mysterious rapport with this typewriter. I don't have any touch system so I have to keep staring at the keys as I type, and I swear they mesmerize me. At moments like this the machine seems to take over. I feel as if I am a ventriloquist's dummy, except that I know only too well that the voice I am sending out to you is my own, my most private own.

Well, you have in your way invited me to let my hair down. Now that you see its length and its tangles, you are probably regretting our turn toward greater familiarity, but I have taken you at your word. And I thank you for the opportunity. It *is* very good to have Brian Curtiss for my friend.

Best,

Peggy

July 14

Dear Peggy:

I have a feeling that this letter will cross one of yours in the mail. We have been quite faithful correspondents, haven't we? I suppose new friends always have more to say to each other than people who have rummaged in each other's closets for years.

This is a brief note to assure you that Kay and I are not going to be deprived of any of the joys of parenthood, including chicken pox. Both Joanie and Paul are down with it, and Kay and I are up with it most of the night.

Does Gary remember (or care about) the nights you were up with him?

I don't mean to sound cranky. I'm just exhausted and wanted to say hello to someone who's been through all this before. Somebody's yelling from upstairs, I don't know whether it's Joanie or Paul, or Kay.

So long. Itchingly?

Brian

July 17

Dear Brian:

I got your news about the chicken pox just after I sent my letter telling something about my own childhood. You wouldn't have received it before you wrote "itchingly." That may not be a joke! I remember when Gary had that illness. My doctor-brother Ted was quite concerned about me because no one recalled my having been through it when I was a child. (It amazed me that neither my mother nor father would have that in their memory. So much for people who are sticklers for form!) On the chance that you may not be aware of it, chicken pox can be a very nasty disease for an adult who hasn't had it before. It's worth checking out, and being as careful as you can.

After all, if you get sick, who will I have to share my confidences with? I have been reading over my effusions and have my own bad case of ambivalence, including embarrassment at letting my typewriter take over without restraint. You will not be able to credit it if I tell you I am often taken to task for "keeping everything to myself." I have never found that surprising. I find it difficult to talk to our men friends about myself. I am seldom with other men except with Arthur at a social gathering or a business function, and there is always something less private everyone would rather discuss anyway (unless one is in psychoanalysis, which I am not).

As to women friends, I have very few with whom it would seem suitable or easy to talk about myself intimately. So, strangely enough, as we have observed, the very distance between you and me makes it possible for me to feel the closeness that I have been expressing. That's the positive side. We are really having the conversations we would enjoy if we were across a table, as we may be in the fall.

Meantime, my last letter must leave you with the impression that my childhood was second in misery only to David Copperfield's. That's not really fair to anybody. I was surrounded by people who didn't understand as much as they might have, but they weren't ogres. My childhood was not all grim, far from it. In the first place, there was genuine comfort in knowing where the boundaries were settled and marked. As I reflect on it now, I can see that being assigned a role is not wholly pernicious. It is confining, but it imposes order and provides assurance against temptations and crosscurrents before one is old enough to deal with them.

I see now that an assigned role can be viewed as cultivation of one's roots, quite in the same sense that gardens and fields are cultivated, with the weeds of haphazard desires pulled out, allowing the useful plants to grow and flourish.

True, sometimes it's difficult to know whether one is part of a cabbage patch or a flower garden, but the principle is the same.

My father constantly quoted a definition of law by Harvard's John Maguire, "Those wise restraints which make men free." The professor was talking about the rules of society, but I can see the application to the self as well, of course. Don't you?

We did have good times together, all of us. There were outings, and sometimes sailing on the Charles, and trips to the Cape, and down to Gloucester (I still don't know why New Englanders say "down" when they speak of going *north*. Wouldn't one more naturally say "up"?) I got lost outside of Gloucester, to the great consternation of the family and the police. There is a large area on Cape Ann known as Dogtown Commons—I am not making this up. The Dogtown Commons is filled with huge boulders for what seems to be miles and miles. The Pilgrims used to hide from Indian attack behind these giant formations. I remember pretending I was a Pilgrim and my family were Indians coming to burn me at the stake. I wasn't found until near dark and was spanked so hard I might have preferred Indians at that.

For me the absolutely best time was the long summer visits I had for several years with my mother's parents, starting when I was about seven. How they could be so different from her I do not know, unless her personality altered after she married Father.

My grandfather (on Mother's side) owned a drugstore in Medford, one of the small towns north of Boston, then quite rural. There will never be anything so heavenly in life as those hot lazy afternoons when I would perch on a high wrought-iron stool at the cool marble soda fountain. The propeller blades rotated slowly over my head, fanning the exotic mixture of medicinal and soda-fountain odors of the store as I ate (licked, sculpted, devoured, surrounded) the special "Grampa Frappay," as we named it. It was lavishly concocted of love and every flavor of ice cream that could fit on the enormous banana-shaped dish. The generous scoops were ladled over with chocolate syrup, whipped cream, chopped nuts, all topped with maraschino cherries and flanked by the split banana. What bliss, with never a thought of any such thing as calories—a word happily not even in our vocabulary then. My grandmother fussed some, though. She was sure my stomach was being ruined for life. My grandfather would vow, promise, and pledge it was "The Last Frappay," but we managed to sneak in at least one a day when Grandmother wasn't looking, or was pretending not to see.

A smile and soft word from anybody in the world undid me at the time, and my grandfather added a sweet, spreading generosity. I was not the only child who didn't pay at that magic fountain. The dear man created odd jobs for the poor kids of the neighborhood—like sweeping the spotless floor—so he could pay them with sodas and sundaes, feeding not just their stomachs but their pride. I will never forget his kindnesses or the way he chuckled when he decided that my tower of ice cream could fly the banner of still another cherry. And the way we would both cry out with laughing consternation when it slid off. "Muckle!" he would shout, "that one's alive!"

As my mind wanders back, my typewriter keys are changing that red cherry into another round object—a white marble. Bear with me, Brian, I want to tell you about my White Marble. It is another thing I have never mentioned to anyone before, not even my husband.

It was a Medford summer when I was nine, I think. My room overlooked the backyard where, best of all to a city girl, there was a little brook. It trickled over pretty stones between my grandparents' property and the house next door. That was a neat yellow frame place with white trim. It intrigued me because I was told "Jews" lived there. People "like us" had nothing to do with "people like them."

There was a boy of about my age who played every day on his side of the brook as I played on mine. Do you remember when you wrote of doing cartwheels for me? Every day when I came outside, that boy would pretend he did not see me and would throw himself into a seizure of acrobatics. Although I made believe I wasn't looking, I admired him mightily. Indeed, as I recall, he did successions of somersaults such as I may not see at Montreal. I never applauded, I never nodded, I kneeled to sail my boat of twigs and leaves as if there was no one else present.

His name was David. I heard his mother call him many times. He had a shock of curly black hair over a pale, thin face. I remember his eyes most. They were dark and piercing. They seemed to burn with questions when he glanced in my direction. On my part, I kept trying to see whether he had horns under his hair. I thought that was why my heart jumped in my chest when my eyes met his.

Oh, Brian, do you know that to this day I find it hard to admit what I inwardly knew was true then? I loved him. I was in love with that sweet boy, David, with all my soul from the first moment I saw him. I wanted more than anything in the world to cheer his somersaults. I wanted more than anything in the world to cross the brook and play at his side.

No one guessed, of course, including me. One morning David was standing at the brook, obviously waiting for me. He did not launch into his acrobatic display. Instead, seeming even paler than always, he said something to me. It was so soft I could hardly hear, and my knees shook. "I have something for you." His voice was trembling with his own fear, and I was petrified.

With that, he threw something across the brook. With a reflex, my hands flew out and caught it. It was a red box, small, about an inch square. It was flimsy and scuffed. There had been some printing on it, perhaps the name of a perfume or some such, that he had tried to scrape off. He said, "Look inside," and hopped back until he stood by the cellar door of his house. He watched me from the distance with wide eyes. I looked around to make sure no one was witnessing, and I opened the red box. Inside there nestled a white marble, a perfect, smooth white globe, beautiful as a miniature moon. A piece of paper was folded inside. It said, "I love you."

My heart leaped with joy. I thought it must burst my body. I had never felt anything so magical, so wonderful in my life. I called out, "Don't you dare, you dirty Jew!" I flung the box back.

Without a word, he bent for it and, with an angry look, threw it across to me again. He disappeared down the cellar steps. My grandmother called from the kitchen window, something like, "What's going on out there, Margaret?"

I cupped the box to my chest and raced up to my room. I kept whispering to the box, "I love you, too." I loved him, and hated him for making himself the scapegoat of my confusion. Does that make any kind of sense? What a mess people are, young and old.

Oh, David, how I wish I had applauded your beautiful performance, all for me. I was the unworthy one. How I wish I had crossed the brook and kissed your cheek. How I wish I had thanked you for your heartbreaking marble, and told you I loved it and was in love with you. Please forgive me, David, wherever you are.

But you are Brian, not David. I must discipline this typewriter by stopping right here!

Peggy

P.S. If I ever got a chance to talk with Gary long enough to ask him about his childhood memories the one thing I know surely is that he would neither recall, nor care about, the nights—like all mothers so many, many nights—I walked the floor with him when he had measles, mumps, whooping cough. But, relaxed as I am beginning to be about writing to you about almost everything else, I still feel an inner restraint about Gary. I am astonished enough at how far I have come with you. Let it be . . .

July 18

Dear Brian:

Writing to you as I have the past few days seems to have opened the floodgates of memories I have held to myself these too many years. I've told myself I am saying too much to you, then remind myself again that it has been you urging me to be more open. I accept the invitation again, without waiting for another letter from you . . .

Right now my mind is rummaging back to when I was 22 and my father brought Arthur to dinner. They had been conferring on some case. Although Arthur was, unaccountably to my father, out of Columbia, he was acceptable as an undeniable legal talent.

I was just out of Radcliffe and about to start on my Master's in English. (That made me feel even more put out when you corrected my "etcetera," and I should say it was not without some slight asperity that I mentioned in a recent letter that Webster does also accept the one-word version.)

I intended to be a high school teacher of English, but I fell in love instead. Arthur is still a man women turn to look at. He is not very tall but is soldierly in bearing (he was a colonel in the war). He has stayed lean and tanned. With the years, his moustache has turned salt and pepper, and his craggy face softens into a quick smile that reached me from the first.

Married and moved to New York. Away from my parents at last, I could breathe for the first time. We had only three rooms, but to me they were more than a mansion. I registered for graduate school at Columbia and promptly became pregnant. It turned out to be a miscarriage (and Gary did not come along until later), but it delayed my career plans for the time being.

To my surprise, I also discovered that I enjoyed the housework that maids had always done for us in Boston. To this day there is a considerable satisfaction for me in housecleaning. I know it is supposed to be the lowest form of drudgery, but my enjoyment may not be as odd as it sounds. I can understand, for example, why someone would like to get up in the morning to be a house painter. There is a clearly defined, finite space to cover, a specific and well-marked job to do. Your work has immediate, visible, satisfying results. This square foot that was dirty before is clean after. As I work along, I know when I am a quarter done, a half done, all done. That is extremely gratifying, whether it's washing dishes or vacuuming rugs or ironing clothes. I have domestic help here, of course, but what I am saying is that I don't at all agree with people who think such work is deadly.

Indeed, I admire men like my husband precisely because they can tackle jobs the results of which will not be visible for weeks, months, even years, and perhaps never! That takes a special kind of maturity and hardiness. Maybe it is why Arthur insists on polishing his bicycle himself. At first I urged him to take it around to the bike shop, thinking it was more of his tea-bag nonsense. But then I realized that for him steel-wooling each spoke of a wheel is like my cleaning each tile of my kitchen floor (when the maid is off). Have any sociologists studied this aspect?

Of course, the party line in our social circle is that housework is no way to spend a life, and that a woman like me should be "doing something with herself." So, until Gary was born I spent the first years of my marriage teaching and taking occasional courses toward a Ph.D. By the time I earned all my doctoral credits, Arthur was on the lecture circuit, traveling almost every month for consultations and conventions, and to Washington regularly.

I didn't like staying home, especially later, after Gary started in private school. Writing a thesis would have meant considerable separations from my husband. My teaching and my accumulated credits had proven me to my friends and well-wishers and ill-wishers. It wasn't too difficult to decide I would rather be with Arthur. I enjoyed exploring new cities, meeting new people with him. It wasn't as if I was giving up a brilliant career. I would be lying if I said I didn't enjoy sitting with governors, senators, judges, the President himself on two occasions. I was exceeding proud of Arthur and proud to be introduced as his wife when the spotlight picked me out on the dais. Reflected glory, but why not? In my own way I have been a decided help to Arthur (do you realize how many times I have had to laugh at the same jokes?). I have had no misgivings or apologies about being an "ABD" (All But the Dissertation) instead of a Ph.D., and I have none now. I am with my husband because I want to be, and I am doing exactly what I want to do with my life, with my consciousness fully raised so far as I am concerned, thank you to the would-be Raisers.

Sidelight for Sociology: Why at most business conventions are the wives' programs designed by antediluvians who think all women are capable of is tatting or working a handbag kit or watching a cosmetics demonstration? There are hundreds of relevant subjects, as proved in the table of contents of any contemporary women's magazine. Wives would appreciate serious speakers and forums as much as the men appreciate their business and professional programs. Here is The Distaff Stereotype in a particularly insidious, wasteful, and distasteful manifestation.

I think of my mother again, the other side of this coin. At 72, she has about 13 years to live by Arthur's charts. We don't get to visit more than twice a year, which means seeing her only 26 more times in her life! That is a jolting and sobering thought.

One good thing about my husband's charts. They make me more tolerant and patient. In the past, I would flare back at my mother when she nagged at me (about my hair, etc., as I've mentioned to you). Now I hold my peace. She never heard me before, and she certainly won't hear me now, so why fuss? Do I expect to change her at this time of her life? I am fortunate and grateful that my brother and his wife are ready, able, and willing to care for her. She has her own little apartment in the Boston house and a nurse-companion so it's not too bothersome to them, but of course it's my tradition to feel guilty.

I interrupted to go to the kitchen to make myself a cup of tea. I suppose it was the association, thinking of my mother. She drank tea endlessly. When I was a girl I used to wonder why she never seemed to have to go to the bathroom. She poured cup after cup inside, and she just sat and smiled or scolded or wrote at her desk but never once a step to the john! (Do Sociologists know why it's called "john"? I know that the man who invented water-closet plumbing was named Crapper, but was his first name John?) I imagined grown-ups had special containers within.

Children's imaginations. I have mentioned my sister, older than me by some years, named Clarissa. She was a hauntingly beautiful girl and young woman, the beauty of the family. She escaped my parents in an unusual, though tragic, way. Before she died five years ago, a spinster at 50, she had long withdrawn into a world totally of her imagining. I say tragic, but who knows? In many ways, Clarissa may have been the happiest of us all, the most enviable . . .

She was a feisty and high-spirited girl always. While in high school she went with one of our aunts to visit friends who had moved to Santa Fe. She fell in love with the city. In the summer before she was to enter Radcliffe, she asked my father for permission to return to Santa Fe. My father's answer, bellowed for all of us to take to heart, "No daughter of mine will trollop alone about the country!" Clarissa apparently had a stubborness inherited from him. If she could not go to Santa Fe in fact, she would go in her mind. She was always resourceful.

At first we thought nothing of it when her room began to be stacked with Western books, magazines, maps, Indian lore. We considered it a bit quirky when she indulged her interest to the exclusion of everything else the family was doing—refusing to come to concerts with us, and the like—but why shouldn't she do what she preferred?

Until we found her subscribing to Santa Fe newspapers and immersing herself in the place as if she truly lived there. At first I chided her, but it was soon apparent that it was more than an idiosyncrasy. Clarissa would dress in a disordered Western style and come to the top of the staircase to announce she was off on a shopping trip to such-and-such a store on Canyon Road for a sale on jodhpurs (that "hp" instead of "ph" remains a constant trap for me). She would turn back to her room and later call me in to show me what she had bought. What she had were pictures of boots and things clipped from the newspaper and pasted in a scrapbook. To her they became actual. In the same way, she would recount to me imagined trips to Indian pueblos of the area. I was fascinated by the names—Tesque, Pojoaque, Namé, Picuris, Cochiti, Taos. She made them come alive. I think she came to know as much about the area as the local experts.

She would refuse most food from our kitchen, saying she had just dined at "the best Mexican restaurant anywhere, El Paragua." (I must tell you that Arthur and I traveled out that way a few years ago and there was indeed such a place, some miles north of Santa Fe, with unbelievably delicious dishes.)

On Sundays, Clarissa's room would become for her the Chapel of Loretto, the Santa Fe church with the famous spiral stairway that seems to have no support but faith. She followed the Santa Fe opera faithfully, buying and playing records of the works as they were done during their season. In her deranged mind she attended the theatre performances, concerts, rodeos. She would chat with me about people mentioned in the Santa Fe news as if they were old and dear friends of hers. At first I was frightened and upset, but then it became a kind of game to me, and the doctors my father brought in did not discourage it.

It was amazing how Clarissa literally memorized the social columns, lamented over the obituaries, dressed up and danced in her room at the weddings. I later learned that she even sent presents. Once she took me into her confidence and, brokenhearted, I saw the "gifts" she was preparing. They were quite pathetic—a pressed stale flower, a gray chocolate, a dingy ribbon off an old Christmas package; and a pitiable note she proudly showed me to attest the reality of her dreamworld, signed, with the loops and swirls of madness, "Your Close Friend, Clarissa Webb."

How many startled residents of Santa Fe must have wondered through the years what eccentric was playing such an odd joke. But it was all terribly real to Clarissa. She had sent for a Santa Fe telephone book, had all the addresses. If my father hadn't taken the phone out of her room, she would have spent hours speaking to strangers.

When Clarissa was about 30, she became engaged, in her mind's world. Very proudly she boasted to me that she was not going to become one of our street's shrunken spinster ladies. She held out a newspaper photo of a handsome cowboy who had won a rodeo. With a razor blade she had cut apart each word of the caption, lifted her own name from her high school yearbook, and painstakingly pasted up an actual announcement of an engagement, with her own photograph montaged alongside the man! If the difference in typefaces hadn't woefully revealed her madness, you could have sworn the item was legitimate. Clarissa herself was flying with joy. The clipping became irrefutable proof. I was to be her bridesmaid and she would invite Ted too, but neither Mother nor Father, because "Wayne would shoot them on sight" for their cruelties to her.

A week later I found Clarissa prostrate on the floor, weeping inconsolably. Beside her was a newspaper from Santa Fe opened at a report of "her cowboy" being killed in a motorcycle accident on the road to Albuquerque. Her fantasy was pathetic but her tears were no less real. Clarissa wore black for the rest of her life, and would hardly speak, even to me.

I don't know, Brian. If my sister's brain created her joys and sorrows, were they less actual to her than ours are to us? Maybe we are all just phosphorescent, in the same way that all children ask at some time how we know we are not dreaming our lives. And not just children, some distinguished philosophers have taken this doubt very seriously, as you of course know. I remember what you wrote about rationalism being more to your taste than mysticism. Well, yes, I suppose we must live "as if" the world is as real as it seems to our senses to be. (I forget the name of the philosopher whose credo that was, but then, the purpose of a liberal education is to leave you with ideas and notions, not necessarily names. Yet I have this irritation about not remembering so many things I once knew so well!)

When visitors to the house asked for Clarissa, she would come to the top of our staircase and shout with great indignation, "They all know I have moved to Santa Fe!" Standing above us in her Western outfit, she would scold, "Everyone knows I am not here any longer!"

As indeed she was not.

Looking back, Brian, I think my sister *enjoyed* her madness. It was harmless enough, God knows. If it hurt my parents, I can only cheer dear Clarissa the more. I have my own vein of hatefulness and asperity, as you see.

As I reflect on Clarissa, it comes to me that she freed herself from Beacon Hill as I never did, though she fought the rope so hard that when it broke she went hurtling too far.

Dear Brian, if I go on, much as I want to, you will wish I had remained incognito. I have enjoyed these visits with you the past few days. Apparently I have needed very much to talk to someone, and you are the best someone I know. How pleased I am that I can let my hair down with you! You asked for friendship, and this is one of its burdens.

Peggy

July 20

Peggy, dear Peggy:

I did indeed ask for your friendship, and it is a treasure to me, not a burden. You must never again say that. Learning about you and your family is fascinating and ever more rewarding. The truth is that our letters bring us closer to one another than people who see each other every day. With those around us we tend to talk about the mundane stuff—What channel do you want now? Pass the salt, please. Is the laundry back? The assignment for tomorrow will be. In writing to each other, you and I get down to what we are thinking and feeling. It is a bonus, although it doesn't make up for the frustration I feel at not being with you, especially when you are what you call "unsettled." I am glad your typewriter keys do take over. Often, our thoughts are what we find we have expressed, as our lives are what we find we have done.

Tonight I am more angry than usual at the tyranny of distance. Our "farness" is palpable to me right now. It is a physical barrier I could scrape my knuckles against. It occurs to me that distance is a force, a power, as strong as a hurricane, as effective as a gunshot. I'm thinking of a news report I read last winter about a Chicago boy who was playing on an ice floe that broke loose from shore. His screams for help were heard (oddly enough) by a woman on the fifteenth floor of a building across Lakeshore Drive. She called the police, who fastened belts together and reached for the boy, now submerged in the water. They *almost* got to him, short by less than an inch. The boy drowned. Less than one inch became the measure of a life. Distance is a power. I resent it, and October seems forever away.

I am looking forward to meeting your husband, too. He sounds like a most attractive and many-faceted person, and I must say I find his actuarial view of life persuasive. Too many of us exist as if we had all the time in the world to get around to living. A decent regard for death's daily stalking is a healthy perspective.

I was moved by your accounts of your growing up, especially your wonderful Medford grandfather, and your deeply affecting story of the boy David, his somersaults and his marble. At the risk of awful sentimentality I would like to think that somewhere he knows today that you did secretly applaud him and, as you say, loved him. I don't for a moment minimize the emotions children have. I believe they are strong and true because they come out of great need and at the same time innocence. I hope David does know you cherish his white marble. I hoped to find my own as a gift for you among my children's welter of toys, but none of their marbles is white. Nor could I find a pure white one in the stores. White is not exciting enough for today's jaded youngsters, I suppose.

I thank you, too, for taking me into your confidence about your sister. Obviously your Clarissa was dear to you. I must confess to being troubled, though, by your concept that happiness may be found in illusions. That is exactly what we both fret about in the case of the drug users and the junk religions.

I may be hypersensitive about this at the moment because Kay has taken off "to explore a new space" with her friends in San Francisco. She will be gone for weeks, and I am left with the children. Fortunately, I have no classes this summer, and I can do most of my research at home. I enjoy Joanie and Paul, but at their age they have no way of comprehending my need for time and quiet, and I can't afford summer camp or sitters. I'll manage somehow, as we all do when we must.

I had planned to enclose a photo of myself with this letter, but I can't find a presentable one in the whole batch of family albums I turned up. I doubt you want my baby pictures (naked on a bear rug!), nor the proud soberface in cap and gown, and I certainly won't show you the petrified father scared he will drop his infant any second. And so on. All the recent shots suddenly seem too blurred or too overexposed or just plain blah. Looking at them through your eyes there isn't one I want you to see. I understand the way you felt. Somehow the man who is writing these letters is not in any of those pictures. I'm not sure where the devil he actually exists. That will take some thinking. Maybe it's my way of saying that, in honesty, I am as fearful as you about letting you see what an ordinary fellow has been at this end of our correspondence all along.

Hold on! The kids are fighting outside. They are over the pox, with no lingering results, thank goodness, and they are all charged up with new energy. . . .

Well! Between that last sentence and this have passed several hectic hours. The danger is over now so I can return to the letter, but I am still shaking.

What happened was that just as I went outside to separate the kids in the fight they started, Paul threw a handful of sand directly into Joanie's eyes. I was petrified he had blinded her. Irrationally, I cursed Kay. I had to race Joan to the hospital. Waiting for the medical report, my heart stopped. For Joanie to be blind! Thank the Lord, the doctor found no serious damage. Sometimes I wonder how children grow up at all. When I was a kid, a girl neighbor and I decided to spy on each other through a keyhole, on opposite sides of a closed door. As I placed my eye in position, my friend decided to stick a pencil through. Luckily, her mother appeared in time! God protects drunks and little children. But who protects sober fathers?

Have a splendid time at the Olympics.

Brian

P.S. The philosopher you want is the German, H. Vaihinger. In 1911 he published *Die Philosophie des "Als Ob,"* "The Philosophy of 'As If.' " He was among the pragmatists who in effect said that all the esoteric concerns of philosophy don't really matter that much —whether the falling tree in the forest makes a sound if there is no one to hear, whether the world has an objective reality or exists only in or through the mind, and so forth. We must live *as if* the world is real, as if life is meaningful, as if humans have purpose, as if there is right and wrong. This, apparently, is how you feel. And I don't disagree. It is too easy to get lost in the cat's cradle speculations. I prefer William James: What is true is what works. That is not amoral. It does not imply, for instance, that the end justifies the means. What it says is that we must trust our senses and our feelings and our consciences and live by common sense and consensus. I can buy that without any problem.

My head knows what physics teaches—that substance is really space, and surfaces are formed by a myriad of electrons dancing in random equations. But my *hand* knows better. This desk is solid! (Remember Bishop Berkeley, the kicking of the rock, and the "Ouch!" that declared the stone to have objective reality?)

But this is no time to plunge into the whirlpools that philosophers have been flailing in for thousands of years. What matters is that our relationship works, yours and mine. That is true.

P.P.S. Crapper's first name was Thomas. But there was a *John* Harington who was said to have invented an indoor privy earlier, so your thought about the use of "john" may have some basis.

July 30

Brian!

I found your letter when we returned from Montreal and was distressed to hear about Joan's accident. Since you did not write after that, I assume she is fully recovered. What can one do with a two-year-old? As you say, it's a wonder any of us grow up.

Thank you for bearing with my pre-Olympic outpourings of telling the too-dull story of my life. You are kind to receive them so well. I can only repay by inviting you again to tell me more about yourself.

As for the Olympics, everything was perfectly marvelous, simply super. With incredible great good fortune, Arthur and I had seats right in front of Comenici when she was sweeping her tens on the bar. She was a bird in space, a calligraphy of the body beyond even dance or sculpture. I have not thought of it this way before but Gymnastics, though it owns no Muse, is as much an Art as any!

The least of the athletes were beauty incarnate to me. I learned what it means to be "lost" in admiration. This letter is full of superlatives, I see, but I do want to communicate to you my sense of wonder if I can, and this is one occasion when no superlatives can be hyperbolic. So here I go with all stops out—and a flying feeling it is for me, almost as if I were vaulting myself.

First let me say that until now I never perceived the meaning of Athletics with a capital "A". *Every* human value is involved! Heroes are restored to the world, which so desperately needs them. I saw man and woman and woman and man use themselves beyond capacity, beyond endurance, beyond exhaustion—but not beyond spirit.

I heard the gasp for life-air as if it were coming from my own bursting lungs. I saw the stretch of bone that wracked my own body. I knew their racing heartbeats shuddering in my chest.

Are there no limits to human potential? Today the unbeatable four-minute mile is slow. I've read of a man who celebrated his 60th birthday by running an ultramarathon of 36 miles across the Firth of Forth in Scotland!

I used to think ballet was the ultimate. For me, this is more. These magnificent superhumans are proof one can go beyond the ultimate. Even my father would have had to admit, finally, the presence of total excellence.

Captivating to me, too, is that the sheer beauty exists not only in the events where one expects grace, like diving and gymnastics. I now understand the *artistic* form of *every* meet, from track to shot put. Arthur calls it "the final mathematics of the human body." Yes. I understand that as I could not have done before (and also realize there is more sensitivity in Arthur than I have sometimes credited him with).

No metaphors can express the glory that flooded every contest we attended. Arthur's warm companionship added to the enjoyment immeasurably. We were both overwhelmed not only by the height of the achievements but by the underpulse of brotherhood we saw on the fields and off. If you watched the parade of the nations' flags on TV, you must have caught something of the spirit. It put me in mind of how athletes in ancient Greece were given safe conduct passes to move through enemy lines if games were going on in times of local wars.

Yet, even as I write of that universal spirit, I must tell you of one Soviet judge who kept marking down non-Russians in the men's gymnastics. I don't know if this is part of the official record, but Arthur and I saw him very clearly, arguing endlessly and crudely with other judges. Finally, Olympic officials had to threaten to expel him—at least it seemed that way from the stands. It would have been good riddance. But he seemed the exception to the rule.

You, particularly, would have appreciated the discipline and control visible in every motion in every event. Every nuance of skill and strength is calculated to the nth degree. The young rebels you and I have written about need to witness how a pole vaulter cannot argue with the bar. He clears it or he doesn't clear it. Arthur echoed my point, mentioning music. About that, at least, my parents were correct. One reason they insisted on lessons—singing in my case, as I think I've noted in passing—was to teach us children that a C is a C is a C, not C sharp or C flat, and that there are such things in life as plain right and plain wrong. In a world where there is so much fudging—and applause for it!—that lesson of music is needed more than ever.

Lest you get any unwarranted notions about my musical talent, let me interrupt myself to add that I am no more a singer than I was ever a gymnast. I am only saying that my musical experience, limited as it was, did help me grasp and more deeply admire the virtuoso performances of the athletes.

Speaking of myself as a singer, I recall that my only distinction came at a children's church concert where I was a soloist, though why I was selected I can't imagine. How proud my parents were! How eager I was to appear in the white vesture with the blue angel collar. How bursting, at all of eleven years old, to display how faithfully I had practiced and rehearsed. How I yearned and longed above all for the grand impression I would make on my mother and father before all their friends and our relatives when my entrance came. How gloriously I would burst out over the chorus in the climax, "Oh, Savior . . ."

I reached the passage creditably and sucked in the breath I needed to issue forth the bravura notes that would bring down the house. My eyes burned at the conductor, riveted on his baton for my entrance. My lips parted, my jaws strained open, my mouth as wide as I could possibly get it, my chest expanded and ready—only to have a moth fly into my throat. Astonished, I gulped, choked, and swallowed with a terrible clucking squeal. Poor moth to have been immolated in such a feeble flame. Poor Mother and Father, mortified by me yet another time. Poor me, shamed once more before congregation and the world.

Sand in one's eyes, moths in one's mouth, pencils through keyholes, white marbles thrown back across a brook, how indeed do we survive?

Now that Montreal is over, Princeton is ahead. I am filled with new anticipation. Thank you for enclosing the program announcement of your panel. What a prestigious company! You might even pass muster with my father!

Now the prospect of seeing you, in just two months, is startlingly real. Somehow, with the Olympics intervening in my book, our meeting seemed very far off, quite nebulous. Now Brian Curtiss will suddenly be no game, no pretend, no incognito. I am not playing my own version of Santa Fe! It is a new exuberance. And a new chill.

In Montreal, since I had more time with my husband than we manage at home (especially when we had to walk for hours to the equestrian events because cars were backed up for miles on the only access road, the one example of poor management we encountered), I thought again of talking to Arthur about this correspondence you and I have been enjoying. (Did you notice the long parenthesis my typewriter shoved in there as a way of delaying the point of my sentence? Obviously I feel stupid and guilty about having started on the wrong foot with Arthur about your letters, and now it is horridly difficult to get over to the right foot!)

Anyway, to sum it up without dangling interferences, I never did get around to discussing Brian Curtiss.

I am thinking that now, with this Princeton announcement in my foolish hand, I can put things straight, and even invite Arthur to meet you. I am certain you would enjoy each other.

I have not forgotten my promise to send you a photo when I got back from Montreal, but you must give me a chance to catch my breath. I want that picture of you, too, and of the children. You tell

Paul that if he ever dares to throw sand at anyone, Grandma Margaret will fly out on her vacuum cleaner and paddle the tar out of him. (Gary says that if he has children he won't bring them up the way we did—*au contraire,* he will raise them "with the back of his hand." I quote him exactly.)

It is good to be back in New York. No matter how stimulating it is to travel, getting home is always special. Arthur and I do enjoy this lovely apartment. We wouldn't trade it for all the magnificence of our friend's mansion. Home is home, is nest, I suppose, as no place else can be. Good to be writing again, but I am a little tired.

Au revoir,

Peggy

P.S. I do want to add my thanks and my awed admiration without delay. I could never in a million moons have recalled Vaihinger. He was not, after all, one of the luminaries in the philosophy firmament. I am impressed again by the depth and range of your knowledge. Sometimes I fantasize how it would be to take one of your classes. In a way I am your student, and enjoying it mightily.

I did try to look up the *"As If"* when it first came to mind, but found I had lent my *History of Philosophy* to someone long ago, probably in a burst of enthusiasm over some discussion we were having. Of course the borrower swore solemn oaths of speedy return, and of course I have never seen the book since and never will. I am sure people do mean to return books, but somehow they don't get around to it.

Upon which I must blush and admit I am not holier than thou. Sometimes when I dust our bookshelves, I find volumes I have borrowed from friends. I have even taken them down to return, but next time I find them on my shelf again.

Since you know so much about so many things, Brian, why is that?

Aug. 8

Peggy dear:

I thoroughly enjoyed everything you wrote about the Olympics. You are more than an excellent reporter; I got more of the spirit of the games from your letter than from anything I read or saw on television, and I don't say that because I am prejudiced in your favor, which I am. I had not thought of Athletics in the way you put things. It is a fresh and enlightened point of view, much to take in and ponder. Do you know, I have looked through the sociological literature, and while there are many studies on the role of athletics in society, including mystical and even occult aspects, few consider sports as an *art* in the sense that you put forward. I think your insight is valid and important, and I am going to discuss this further here. It may lead to some interesting examination and redefinitions.

I did keep scanning the crowds on television, though it was witless since you have refused me your photograph on one pretext or another. I suppose I can't complain too crankily because I have done the same. But this week a friend on campus took some shots of me that seem promising, so I may have a picture for you shortly.

You and I have our two-way connection along so many life wires. I'm glad you sing, though sorry about the moth. I keep wondering why such devastating things happen so gratuitously, and usually to the innocent and well-meaning. In my experience it's the conscienceless bastards who sail along merrily. Every house they buy goes up in value, every stock they touch soars, every poker hand fills in, every door prize is theirs. (When *I* have four kings you may be sure someone else holds four aces!)

I agree entirely with your observations about the importance of early musical training. Music is salubrious as well as inspirational. My mother played the piano a little, and I practiced a little. If you like, send me some of your (easy) songs to practice, and maybe we'll have a session in New York (with Arthur on drums!). It would be an added pleasure indeed to make music together, but I am a terrible sight reader because I can never anticipate what's coming and I run out of fingers.

It might have been different—as so many things might have been different—if my mother had lived. She was a cultivated woman for a farmer. We lived up in Montana. It wasn't much of a place, just some Hereford cows (beautiful brown-red with white faces), some pigs, and chickens. My father quit real farming after the 1930s drought out there and went to work for the railroad. A hired hand did the work while he was off on his job. Still, it was a great place to grow up poor. For you folks, Custer's Last Stand is a paragraph in an encyclopedia, but Little Big Horn River isn't too far from where I was born.

Your writing of your fascination with Indian names strikes another common note between us. Montana has many tribes, of course —including Shoshone, Blackfoot, Sioux, Crow, Cheyenne, Kootenai, Kalispel, Assiniboine, Arapaho, Flatheads, Gros Ventres, Chippewa, and Cree—all with their own fierce pride and clan loyalties. I think that is where I got my first sense of how important tribal dynamics are in the world.

I saw it, too, in the ethnic impulsions of the general population mix. I grew up amidst a veritable UN. New York is supposed to be a melting pot, but we had neighbors—albeit at considerable distances —who were Scandinavian, German, Russian, Finnish, Yugoslavian, Italian, Norwegian, as well as Canadian and Mexican in origin. My mother made it a point to take me to their celebrations whenever she possibly could, so I had a quite elaborate view of the world outside even though I was a country boy.

Do you know that Montana is called the Treasure or Bonanza State? Not just because there was some gold but largely because it ranks third in the world in the production of *sapphires,* just behind Thailand and Australia!

And would you believe that a farmer neighbor of ours had a camel? It seems that years before the Federal Government experimented with camels in the region as military beasts of burden. It wasn't a success, but apparently a few lusty descendants survived. At least there was one around for me to ride as a kid. I was as enthralled as if it were the Pyramids in the background instead of the Absaroka Mountain range.

(Footnote: I just came upon reports of archaeologists who have found remains of camels going back perhaps ten thousand years, here in the U.S. It raises thoughts of an ancient land bridge again. Maybe it's symbolic. Did man once have one world physically, only to lose it?)

Remembering my camel ride reminds me of another improbable combination. I'll wager you know as little about it as I did about your mortgage buttons. Where do you think one of the Montana centers for cut sapphires is? A place called Yogo Gulch! The name often comes to my mind when I am reading books about Yoga, though of course there is no connection. It's a smile, though.

All around our house there was the rose-colored bitterroot my mother favored. There were many Sage Hens. The weather was often much milder than Easterners believe. Chinook winds coming off the mountains in the winter and early spring would warm up quickly. They'd melt the snow while other sections were in deep freeze. I still remember my father teaching me that the winds lowered in temperature by precisely one degree for each 183 feet they descended. That reckoned to a drop of a full 30 degrees by the time the winds got down the 5,500 feet to our level.

My world was rich with a landscape of every imaginable color. To this day I don't know why writers always settle for "green" as ubiquitous. Nature is every shade of sienna and umber and yellow and orange and pink and rose and blue and gray and purple and black, and more. Our fields of bluejoint hay, and bunch and grama grass, were lipped by rolling hills with soaring mountains in the distance. They always drew my eye to the reaching sky, sky, sky. There was so much sky it seemed not to be separate at all, just an upcurve of the distant earth, as if the mountains rose on the horizon fading into a faint gray-purple-blue to become air and dissolve into the sky color and curve back endlessly to make a seamless vault of heaven-and-earth. It was soul-inspiring, of great peace.

The Utah and Northern Railroad, for which my father worked then, had a single-track branch that skirted our land. The tracks passed onto a wooden trestle I couldn't keep off. It bridged a hell-deep canyon where our pastures fell off the map, like the early maps of the flat earth. You don't see that kind of trestle any longer except in old Western movies. (I liked what you wrote about bridges some time ago, wanted to tell you then, and got sidetracked on to something else.) How I loved walking those tar-and-oil stained railroad ties. I was about the same age as you were in Medford, when you were (not) playing with that boy David. I'd hurry as fast as I could, daring myself, and quaking in my boots at the abyss dropping below. It was filled with trolls and giants out of my fairy tales, all reaching ominously for me. I knew I wasn't supposed to look down; my father had taught me that. But that's all you need to be told, isn't it? The waiting pit was a magnet drawing my eyes out of my head. And I was always in terror of a train, though I well knew only one freight a day came through, and that one long before I was even out of bed.

The summer I was 12 my mother was killed. I am grateful I had that many years with her. I remember how different she was from our neighbors. Though she had their strong, muscular frame of country stock (the kind you'd cast in a pioneer movie), her face was delicate. She had sensitive tastes, inherited from some ancestor who must have been a craftsman or artist in the old country (her line was Flemish, my father's English, like yours, but no Brahmin of any kind). Mother played the piano with a gentle touch and, as she would laugh to me, "With enough wrong notes left over for Beethoven to write another piece."

She greatly admired Beethoven, his simpler pieces, like "Für Elise." I think it's unfashionable among modern pedagogues to play things like that and "Humoresque," but if so, I would take hard issue. Such pieces are the grass and flowers and bees and birds through which one first meets nature. Time for the storms and Rocky Mountains of sonatas and symphonies later, when one is grown enough to take them in. (I am only now coming to the profundities of chamber music.)

My mother told me how Mozart wrote sonatas when he was eight and nine years old. It was easier for me to believe as a child than it is now. The other night I heard his violin and piano pieces written in 1765—already Sonatas No. *11 through 16!* Amazing experience, but it only confirmed what I have always believed about those geniuses like Haydn, Bach, Mozart. They didn't so much create as plug into the music of heaven and write down what they heard. At least in the case of Mozart, it seems to have been as effortless as it was prodigious. To think that he died at 35. I simply do not understand God, unless He was jealous. Genius is not a strong enough word for a contribution like Mozart's. Who is your favorite composer?

The summer I was 12, my cousin Carl came up from San Francisco to spend his vacation with us. Carl is about my age, the son of my mother's brother, my "Uncle Joe" whom I have mentioned. Uncle Joe reminds me of your grandfather and the "frappays" he made for you. But it is Carl I want to write about now—need to write about now, since I have started with my mother's death.

Carl, about my age, was already a wild kid. His idea of fun on the farm was to roll a heavy log onto the railroad track to see if the locomotive could break it. I managed to get it off. Or he would start up the ladder to the top of our silo with a baby pig in his arm, intending to see if he could hit a pile of hay on the ground with it. I had to wrestle him to stop that. Just last year he thought nothing of stealing $500 from Uncle Joe, who works day and night, in all weather, at a ramshackle stand on Fisherman's Wharf selling crab legs to eke out a living. Carl whined that he had to pay a gambling debt or be hurt. I couldn't stop that. Carl was a miserable, rotten, mean-spirited kid as a boy, and I'm afraid he has not improved with age.

That summer we had a bad-tempered bull on the farm. My mother begged my father to get rid of it, but the animal earned considerable breeding fees around the county. My father named the bull "Gentle," as if that might transform the evil temper. I tell you, when that damned critter looked you in the eye, you wanted to skedaddle the hell to high country fast. Carl and I were sternly warned to stay away from the enclosure where Gentle was securely locked in. But one day when my mother was in her vegetable garden nearby, the bull somehow escaped. He charged her like the morning locomotive. We never knew how that devil got out, though to this day I remember seeing Carl around his pasture that morning. He swore up and down he was nowhere near it, and I still cannot believe even Carl would be so viciously reckless, but in my bones I feel he was responsible.

My family broke up after that. My father would not stay "where I have to walk in her blood." It was a graphic way of stating his sorrow, but a devil of a sentiment for a boy to have to remember.

My father sold everything, including the piano, and we moved away down to San Francisco to be near Hildie and Joe, who were our only family in the West. A couple of years later, my father got a job with the Chicago, Milwaukee, Saint Paul & Pacific line, and moved to Illinois, where his own people owned a considerable dairy farm south of Chicago. He took my sister, Frances, along with him. I haven't told you about Frances, but we two grew up very close. Frances is ten years younger than I, and in some ways was my baby as she toddled around the farm. To me she was as pretty and as much fun as all the other young animals. I suppose she might have been a calf or colt so far as I cared. I loved her, and cuddled her, and fed her when my mother was busy with chores. At the time my father decided to shift to Illinois, Frances wasn't even in school yet, so it was easy for her to move along. I, on the other hand, was a grown-up 14 and a freshman in high school, with new friends. The last thing I wanted was to pull up stakes again. So it was settled that Frances would go and I would stay with my aunt and uncle. They wanted me, and I loved being with them.

Carl and I developed a sort of truce. I suspected even then that he was sobered by a secret guilt over my mother's "accident." But I couldn't prove anything, and I put it out of my mind.

I couldn't prove, either, Carl's intent in the next disaster he caused. At 16, he was already a heavy drinker. I was tempted to tell my uncle, but the "teenage code" (understandable but so hurtful to so many in so many cases) kept my lips sealed. We then lived in an apartment of a typical San Francisco frame house, just off the well-known California Avenue where the famous cable cars run. Webster Street has its own steep inclines. One day Carl spotted a motorbike parked near our building. I saw his log-on-the-track expression. "That bike's gonna roll and kill somebody," he said. With that, he hopped on the machine and released the brake. Like a fool, I jumped to stop him. I was afraid he would wreck the bike, get arrested, bring more trouble to Uncle Joe. Carl headed right for me, playing the chicken game. I leaped for my life but couldn't get out of the way. He broke my leg, a nasty multifracture. The bike skidded away, dented a car, nearly smashed a baby in a carriage, and wound up a wreck. Carl got up laughing, without a scratch. The four-aces man.

Uncle Joe had to borrow heavily. I was in the hospital for months with a leg that wouldn't knit properly. As you can imagine, I have no great love or admiration for Cousin Carl, much as I love and esteem Hildie and Joe.

We do seem to exchange stories of malevolence, but then there are so many of them in this world. I'd rather stick to thoughts of Princeton, New York, October, and you!

Fondly,
Brian

Aug. 10

Peggy:

Okay, Finally. Herewith. Enclosed please find a picture of the man you have been writing to. Let it speak for itself.

The end?
Brian

P.S. You will want to know that Kay is home. My work goes more easily. The children are well. No sand throwing, no mumps, measles, or poison ivy lately.

Aug. 13

Brian!

What a great, earthshaking surprise in my mail this morning! And what a revelation of the fact that you are not to be trusted! All that flimflam you have been feeding me about self-doubt and disappointing me! Why, you turn out to be one of the most handsome men I have ever laid eyes on!

Seriously, it is fascinating to see how different you are from everything I now realize I have been imagining. I thought of you as dark-haired, you are blond; I expected dark eyes, they are gray. You are bronze, not scholarly pale; you look like an Olympic swimmer, or a lifeguard out of a glamorous travel brochure. (At the hotels we visit, I always wonder where the "beautiful people" of those four-color photos have gone to.)

Oh, Brian Curtiss, how can I exchange a picture of dowdy me with a pinup man like you?

I am searching again for a photograph of myself, but it's clearer to me now than ever that I won't find anything I can risk mailing.

Badly out of sorts,
Peggy

P.S. I stare and stare at your photograph and wonder how Kay can be insane enough to be seeking bluebirds outside of the backyard that holds a husband like you!

Aug. 14

Brian:

Looking still for a picture to send, I find your friendship paying off in unexpected ways. You have required me to get into corners of drawers and closets I haven't touched in years! I have found a score of things I thought lost or stolen, old shoes, broken umbrellas, unstrung tennis rackets, and ten years worth of out-of-date calendars (sent every year by Arthur's insurance agent, while I rush around to banks and such trying to get a calendar for my desk).

The family photographs are scattered all over the place, and it is simply shameful.

This is a strange phenomenon. Friends tell me the same thing. Most everything in our homes is tidy and shipshape, except for photos. Aside from a family album or two, snapshots get tossed into a messy catch-all drawer after the first oohs and ahs. (I'll wager that *you*, steeped in research techniques, are well organized.)

Schools should teach filing as a required course from kindergarten, especially these days when everyone has to tangle with so many records for taxes, credit cards, insurance, and the rest.

Has just daily living ever involved so much paper work in any other age? (A doctoral thesis in your field?)

I always promise myself faithfully that *this* time I will not let more than one day go by without marking the photo envelopes and filing the negatives in case we want enlargements or more prints. But I simply never do get around to it. Then it's hell on wheels, as it is now, to remember where I put what. This morning I came upon a promising envelope, only to find the first baby pictures of Gary along with a batch of snaps of Arthur and me in Hawaii two years ago. Don't ask me the filing logic that combined the two subjects.

The photographs make my mind wander to when they were taken. I am staring at the pictures of Gary when he was four, your Joanie's age, and still a miracle to me. A miracle with a mind of his own even then. Here is a birthday picture to remind me of that very well. Gary was making a mess in a corner of the room, and I called to him to stop and come across to me. He balked. "Why won't you come?" I asked him. "Because you'll give me a reason," he said.

Enjoy them, Brian, while you can. They do sprout so unholy fast. Here is Gary as Macho-Football High School Hero. Here is another of the girl he took to his senior prom. Oh, that prom! It includes a famous family story that may amuse you. Knowing what I've told about some of Arthur's inconsistencies, it won't surprise you that my husband saw no point in purchasing a tuxedo for Gary when one could be rented. I couldn't argue the point since Gary would have precious little use for any suit unless it was denim. So off to a rental shop went Gary, with me in tow to instruct the tailor sternly that the necessary alterations must be perfect.

The poor man was seasonally harassed as you may imagine, but he promised faithfully that Gary's suit would get special attention.

When Gary dressed that night, the ceiling fell in. The confounded tuxedo hung like a potato sack. It was plain to me there had been a last minute mix-up in the packing and delivery. By now the store was closed. What to do! I was as incensed as Gary. The store simply had no right to be careless about a transaction they knew to be so important. A budding life could be shattered; no one could appear at a prom in such a ridiculous outfit.

Well, said I to myself, if they could be so irresponsible, so could I! I grabbed scissors, needle, and thread. I slashed wildly at pants and jacket. I ripped seams willy-nilly. The suit was ruined for anyone else, but I did not care. It fit Gary well enough for the night. Indeed, I have seldom been prouder of my courage, skill, handiwork, and motherhood.

So I sent Gary off to his date in a blaze of righteous glory; only to find when Arthur and I went for our coats an hour later that there was another tuxedo hanging in the hall closet, where no tuxedo should be.

You have guessed it, of course. In the day's excitement, Gary completely forgot that he had hung the rented suit in the wrong closet. When it was time to dress, he had grabbed his *father's* suit.

So, with Arthur cheering me on loyally, I had devastated his own superexpensive tux (in which, to make matters worse, he had to give a speech the following night), while Gary's rental hung innocently waiting, all promises kept.

That episode did nothing to improve Arthur's relations with his son, and it took some time before my husband would speak to me again, although quite clearly it was no fault of mine, was it?

As I get this close to writing about Gary to you, I come to the realization that I am still not ready for that. I don't mean to be mysterious, and surely you have inferred by now that we have problems with our son. Yes, they grow fast, and they grow arrogant, rude, sullen, unruly, perverse, evasive, and other unpleasantnesses. I swear I don't know where all the animosity and hostility come from, and I hope you are spared it. Let me get off this. The tuxedo story is at least amusing. The rest can and should await another time.

I am pleased to hear that Kay is back with you. More and more

I realize that wives and husbands should *cherish* each other. In the end "mothers" and "fathers" find themselves *not parents* but *people*. In the end they have only each other to depend on and take comfort in. From that point of view children are a snare and delusion. I am not being bitter, only honest. You are not old enough to appreciate the verity of what I say, but believe me it is too true. I witness it in every family I know, without exception, without exception. The most a parent can hope for from a grown child is tolerance, not love.

But I do want to get off this!

I am looking at photographs again, and become aware of an interesting fact. My husband and I have very few photographs together. The reason is easy, of course—on our travels I am snapping him or he is snapping me. Occasionally, an amiable stranger offers to take us both, but then Arthur's expression always shows his anxiety that the camera will be stolen. (Has never happened yet.)

Why don't you send a picture of Kay? I would like to know what your wife looks like too.

What a pile of stuff I have been turning up. Good Lord, we still have cartons of books and records we never unpacked when we moved here. Cartons of my graduate notes and books—*forgotten!* How guilty all this makes me feel. I wish you hadn't started me on it! (See how easily I blame you for what is my fault. That's "Webb's Law": If people have any chance at all to blame someone else for what they have done, they will do so. Reminds me of a story Arthur uses in his speeches. An inventor boasts to another that he has designed a computer that is like a human. The other asks if the machine can think. The inventor says it can't, but if it makes a mistake, it blames another computer! Arthur makes sure he has at least one laugh per page in his speeches, which comes to at least one per 2½–3 minutes. Since his subject is usually taxes, I think he needs more frequent jokes. And better ones?)

Surrounded by my new-found possessions, I am struck with the notion that people like me need at least two lifetimes—one to take the photographs and another to enjoy them. We must have 3,000 slides of our trips, slides we never look at, slides that probably don't even fit the new projector Arthur bought last year. (Why can't those chowderheads standardize their machines?) And all this to say nothing of the miles of records and books that line the shelves in every room of our apartment.

Did I say we need two lifetimes? Make it three! I did an "Arthur Webb calculation" this afternoon and counted over 1,000 phonograph records. Figuring 45 minutes per side, if one devoted a full 40-hour week to nothing but listening, it would take 42.5 weeks, almost a full year, to play them all! And that's to say nothing of time for FM concerts, for television, or the books and magazines that have piled up, with more coming all the time.

All this by way of delaying my choice of a photo to send. I am considering three at this moment—the finalists in the Mrs. Margaret Fairfield Webb Cross-Country Beauty Contest. The bathing-suit picture, though an obligatory part of a pageant, is out! I have not realized how much weight I have been putting on. A fresh round of dieting starts as of tonight, again!

The second shot here isn't too bad, but it's dishonest. The white outfit looks like a tennis player's, and I'm hopeless on the court. Let it be runner-up.

This third one here now is probably the woman I am. It was taken by Arthur when we were in Yellowstone last year. Arthur had Old Faithful timed to the split second, so your attention will be diverted by the geyser, and in any case my face is sufficiently in shadow.

So I now move the first two pictures aside, and with the third in the spotlight, front and center stage, and the orchestra playing the familiar pageant song, I place your photo beside mine.

A mistake! Ah, Brian, dear Brian, the distance is not just miles between this strong young man and the, oh, nice and modish enough lady whose idea of action is waiting for a geyser display. That won't stop me from sending you the photo, but not with the thought that it will bring us closer. On the contrary, my reason is to make our relationship more realistic. Now please take a hard *unblinking* look at your friend Mrs. Webb, without sentimentality or self-deception. There is no sleeping princess here waiting for Prince Charming to kiss her awake. Far from it.

Brian, I could not bear to be in front of you and see your eyes drop in disappointment. That would unravel me entirely. I think, now that you have the incontrovertible evidence, we should both reconsider the wisdom of a visit.

Uncertainly,
Maggie Webb

Aug. 16

Maggie!

First you give yourself away by signing "Maggie" for the first time. That is the opposite of good-bye!

Second, since I know your honesty, I cannot understand your self-deception. Your photograph shows you to be an absolutely eye-catching, obviously exciting woman. In any company, young or younger.

As for your age, which obviously shows, let me say I am solidly in the camp of those men who know that women do not develop genuine beauty without some years. Beauty needs tempering as well as temperament. Kay, for instance, has the latter in full measure, but lacks the former quite completely. She is pretty, and physically a head-swiveler, but not yet beautiful.

You are, actually, much as I imagined. You do wear your hair—brown like my mother's—straight back. Your eyes are straight as bullets, like hers. Your smile comes across without anything held back. Not many people smile that openly. I like your squarish jaw, too, it speaks your anger with the evil around us, but your generous forehead and your wide-set eyes tell of your tolerance as well. The strong bones of your face say you are tolerant of everything but intolerance, and to me that is the signal human credential.

Incidentally, you don't look in need of dieting.

I cherish your photograph. All morning long I have returned to my desk to open the drawer and look at you. Each time there has been a returning excitement. It is almost like touching you, taking that walk in your park. The prospect of seeing you in October becomes more and more real. I am delighted. Until now I suppose one would say our relationship was "budding." I feel that with our exchange of pictures it has flowered.

Why does your beauty touch me as deeply as it does? I have been thinking about this since I opened the envelope and felt that the woman in the picture had always been somewhere in my life. The scientist in me speculates. I suppose that not every man responds as I do, but I have a theory about "beauty." It proposes two possibilities.

One is that we are drawn to people not because we admire their brains or prowess or personalities, etc., but rather because they remind us—in looks and/or action—of someone we have loved and received love from in our earliest years. It may be a parent, a grand-parent, an aunt or uncle, or even, I suppose, a teacher, or a family friend.

Or, the second possibility suggests, we may be attracted to the exact opposite of some early figure, to conceal an emotional reso-nance we do not wish to remember or acknowledge on a conscious level, because it was too strong, positively or negatively.

Either way, the resemblances need not be overt. Indeed, to work their magic, I would assume they would have to be subtle, illusive, behind the scenes so to speak.

I am staring hard at your picture to test my thought. You do not resemble anyone I remember, yet there is some half-reminder that catches my heart. It is in your high cheekbones, in the way your eyes seem to turn up slightly at the corners, and especially in the small lift of your lips, as if you were about to call someone, call to someone softly and pleasantly. Are you of a tribe I would have sought out in olden times? Does this explain how "natural selection" leads mates to each other out of all the possible combinations? *There* is a Ph.D. subject! And note that it works negatively as well. Just as your picture spells Instant Attraction for me, I have felt Instant Dislike for utter strangers on occasion. There have been times when if I were an animal, I would have growled and bared my teeth, though these poor unaware people were just going about their ordinary business, doing me no harm.

The thesis should explore evidence that an individual's appearance may trigger an inner response of the basic genes. I think there has been some such work with animals. Perhaps there is a subconscious current in each generation that spins a mating web in the interest of species, tribe, clan. If so, we are not conscious of it and have no control over it.

Perhaps I have just provided a psycho-sociological extrapolation of what poets have said better less ponderously, "Love is blind."

There's the difference between teacher and artist, and now you see what a figure I cut for my students. Still, I won't apologize. All this is more polite than whistling at you, as I would want to do if I passed you on the street!

We actually have to make some plans for Maggie Webb and Brian Curtiss to meet! Since we will be on your home ground, why don't you suggest how we should manage the earthshaking event?

Brian

Aug. 18

Brian:

I can't pretend I don't enjoy your exaggerations about my virtues. Also, I think your theories are profound, and I hope we have a chance to talk more about them when we are together.

When we meet! My first thought was that I would invite you to my home for a family dinner.

But the more I consider it, the less I like it. It comes very clear to me that you and I are taking nothing away from Kay or Arthur, but what we have *is* just between the two of us. As I have indicated to you, that has been part of its special joy for me.

It has not been easy for me to make this decision, but in stone honesty I find I want to meet you *alone.*

I am amazed at myself. I feel smarmy. And I am enjoying this!

So, to start with, dear Brian, you will let me know exactly when you will arrive, and I will clear my time. It will be a great pleasure for me to show you my New York, and you can buy me that famous drink we have been waiting for so long.

I am glad you picked up my signing "Maggie." I have few friends closer than you are to me now. Yes, the budding is flowering, and I am glad of it. Suddenly October is forever away!

Fondly,
Maggie

Aug. 22

Dear Maggie

And I have no closer friend.

As usual, we are on the same wavelength. Your thought about meeting by ourselves is exactly what I hoped, but I hesitated to be the one to broach it.

Please choose a hotel for me. On the inexpensive side if possible. A place you find agreeable, and preferably with a dim, uncrowded bar, perhaps with soft piano music.

I enclose my timetable, will arrive at Kennedy in the evening. That is 45 days—1,080 hours away . . .

My thoughts are of you.
Brian

Aug. 25

Dear Brian:

I read your letter again and it penetrates that I am to rent a hotel room for you. Talk about improbable! I never dreamed that first letter would lead—but I've said that too often.

It's silly but there is also the, I suppose inevitable for me, embarrassment of an unworthy thought in the back of my head. Brian, am I expected to reserve a single or a double room? Does Brian Curtiss have it in mind somehow that I will be meeting him not just for a drink but for a tryst?

That is absolutely unfair to you. Nothing you have written has even hinted that impossible question. It's a measure of my insecurity and my jitters that such an utterly fantastic notion should occur to me.

Brian, have you ever found yourself picking up a book idly and happening on a passage that hits something right on the nose? I was reading a favorite of mine this morning, Louise Bogan, her *From the Journals of a Poet,* and came to two such stoppers:

The first reads, "The great kindling power of passionate love, which in age we either do not have or do not allow ourselves to feel ... with women the inhibition is particularly strong: there are so many ways in which they can make fools of themselves."

With your letter on my desk, those words burned my eyes with new meaning I could not deny. God knows, and you do, that I have never thought of our correspondence as anything but a growing and welcome friendship, and I assure you that there is no passionate love for you kindling any power in me.

I think what hit me was Bogan's last phrase, "there are so many ways in which they can make fools of themselves."

I am sure you know I have no such intention.

Bogan has another sentence, one that struck me in a different vein, "C. Parker saying at breakfast, 'But 66 is *young, young*' (She is 75.)."

It recalled a story my husband tells, supposed to be true, about Oliver Wendell Holmes and Louis Dembitz Brandeis when both were venerable Justices of the Supreme Court. They stopped at the top of those august steps one summer evening and watched the Pennsylvania Avenue secretaries parading below in their summer frocks, jiggling various parts of their anatomy as they went by. The 90-year-old Holmes is said to have sighed to octogenarian Brandeis, "Oh, to be 80 again!"

I give you one more chance, Brian Curtiss. You see by this letter that I am quite off balance at the prospect of our meeting. Before I embarrass both of us by reserving a hotel room here, consider whether we would not both be better off if you went directly to Princeton. I say go to New Jersey, bless you, be brilliant and wonderful as I know you are, but leave a poor aging lady in peace.

Or must I keep shivering for 42 more days, 1,008 hours?

Maggie

Aug. 29

Dear Maggie:

Shiver on! I am arriving in New York per the schedule, and you are joining me without further discussion.

Single room or double? It never occurred to me. Not that I am an Innocent. I suppose it didn't come into my head because I don't think it is something we can or should talk about. Whatever we feel is right for us is the way things will be or won't be . . .

That's a nifty story about Holmes and Brandeis. I have a night class for senior citizens coming up, and they'll enjoy it. One thing, though, I don't believe Holmes for a minute. I believe he said what he did only so Brandeis wouldn't suspect old Oliver was sneaking off for a rendezvous around the corner.

Last night Kay was out with her group, and I was pleasantly alone. I put your picture on the piano and played it. You were a waltz. God made three-quarter rhythm to remind men that all is not gloom-doom.

For our New York drink, my dear, pick a bar with music. We'll waltz.

Brian

Part Three

Sept. 3

Brian dear:

Enclosed is the hotel confirmation for your single room.

This hotel has no bar, and no music.

I am not in much of a mind for drinking or dancing anyway as it happens.

Things have changed drastically here since my last letter, and nervousness over meeting you is the least of my concerns at this point. As it happens, I am doubly glad that you are coming because I want very much to talk to you about Gary. Things have come to a head with my son. Sickeningly.

Gary was away all summer. We received one desultory postcard, saying he was backpacking in the Adirondacks, working at odd jobs, "having a wonderful time." He came home last week. He was surly, withdrawn, no civil words shall pass these (newly) bearded lips, certainly not to his mother and father.

Last night he told us what he was really into. He has joined a religious group, one he refuses to name. He has made many life decisions. He will not return to Columbia for his senior year, and he will certainly not go on to law school, that abomination of abominations. He has found the vocation for which he has been searching all his life. It is a religious revelation. But he would not name his Group or his "Teachers."

My husband asked Gary why, if he found his new people so inspiring, he would hide their identities. That was when my suspicions were fired up, remembering your article especially. He said, "Because you'd try to get me out!"

He is right, of course, but Arthur went too far too fast in my judgment. I have never seen him so out of control. He got Gary's back up with an unwise and intemperate ultimatum. "If you leave college don't ever come back to this house!"

I tried to get between them to say they were both being irresponsible, but they raged at each other right past me until finally Gary shouted something I did not grasp for a moment but now will never forget. "They are right!" he screamed at Arthur and me. "You are both the Devil!" With that, he rushed out, and left home.

Arthur is in a fast-burning rage. I am absolutely frustrated, demoralized, and miserable. I saw something like this coming. Gary's room was full of pamphlets and weird-sounding garbage from dozens of the groups you wrote about in your article, and obviously it was this concern of mine that led me to write to you in the first place. Now I need to talk to you, Brian, not only as a friend but as an expert in these matters. Let me give you some background on Gary, as honestly and truthfully as I can, so you can think about it before we meet.

You've picked up hints that not all has been well with my son. He has been in and out of trouble for years. Early on, as a freshman in high school, he was arrested for stealing hubcaps with some other boys. "A lark." There was a later arrest for breaking windows. "A Halloween prank." Then in school he was caught smoking marijuana. "A juvenile indiscretion."

I handled all of these incidents myself, without telling my husband, because I was afraid of what Arthur might do. I was especially afraid that, with his stringent sense of the law, he would let Gary go to jail. It was a prospect *I* could not face. In each case I managed to get Gary off, in my custody, without a record or publicity.

I feel now that I was terribly mistaken. If I had let Gary suffer the consequences of his actions, he might have learned his lesson. His dropping out of college now is, I see, part of the same pattern of irresponsibility, to himself and to us. But how could I accept it that *my* son was a *criminal?* For me it was sheer impossibility. So I pulled these and other chestnuts of Gary's out of the fire.

And it backfired, as I might have expected. Grotesquely. Instead of stirring gratitude in him, all I did was feed his adolescent cynicism. He turned it on me full nasty force last night. Before he left, he accused *me* of being a liar and a hypocrite to whom he owed no respect or apology, and his *proof* was the way I had shielded him from punishment when I knew he was wrong and guilty!

And if I had not helped him on those occasions, he would accuse me just as cruelly of not caring!

Oh, they have their own Catch-22, these young fiends!

How easy and reasonable it sounds when "the books" advise parents to warble, "Oh, dear child, your *act* was wrong and bad, but that doesn't mean I don't still love *you* ..."

That is simpering nonsense. I did not love Gary when I had to go to the police station or the principal's office. I was mad as hell at him, and I should have let him know it from the word Stop!

Maybe he would not then have guitared Arthur and me to death with a vile little ditty he composed for our benefit, "Mine eyes have seen the coming of the glory of the Clods!" He made it clear he was singing it about us and our friends, you may be sure.

One thing that horrifies me is how ordinary all this is! Obviously, Arthur had finally to be told, and we proceeded to give each other the standard parental strokes, "He's young, he'll grow out of it." "He's young, he doesn't really mean to be insolent." "He's young, there'd probably be something wrong with him if he wasn't kicking up his heels this way."

For a while we seemed to be right and wise in our forebearance. Gary got good marks, entered Columbia, settled down. But it was all surface. Gary was getting smarter, craftier. He decided there wasn't much percentage in rubbing his golden geese the wrong way. He became a big man on campus—until they found him stealing money from the college paper, all the more idiotic because he didn't need it.

I was heartsick, but again, according to my lights, went to his rescue. I had to get Arthur involved this time, but managed to persuade him to give Gary another chance. I was shameful, Brian! My conscience troubled me badly. It was as if I had acquiesced in the stealing. But at the same time, isn't it written that parents are supposed to stand by their children? If anything, *I* felt guilty. Somewhere, somehow, I must have done wrong or Gary would not have gone off the track.

I think Arthur conceded because he has always recalled an unhappy incident with Gary that occurred years and years ago, when Gary was only four or so, about the age of your Joanie. We happened to be visiting friends in Westchester who had a cottage with a lake about a mile away. After swimming one afternoon, Gary grabbed the keys to our car. I scolded that keys weren't toys, upon which he very deliberately dropped them into—of all places—the window well in the car door. Unrecoverable, of course.

Arthur whaled Gary mercilessly and made the boy run back to the house with him for extra keys. My heart broke as I saw Gary's little feet pounding away to keep up with Arthur's stride. Arthur ran the small boy the full mile and back, and Gary could hardly stand or breathe when it was over. I know that my husband has regretted that afternoon ever since. I think that is why he has never thrown the book at Gary as I believed he might.

Then, after his sophomore year in college, Gary announced he was taking a year off to backpack Europe. There was no way we could dissuade him. There were months of silence, until a telegram from the U.S. Embassy in Athens! Gary had been hurt on the island of Mykonos, in a particularly ugly way. The story as we finally learned it was that he was with a group that got stoned on LSD or its equivalent and hallucinated themselves into being war tanks that had to defeat an enemy. The enemy was the town bus, parked at the beach. Our doped-up heroes charged the bus with their heads, my dauntless son in the lead. Smashing his head, he fell unconscious and rolled into the water. If some of the "square" tourists hadn't pulled him out, he would have drowned then and there, to the cheers of his comrades.

The Greeks wanted Gary in jail, but Arthur managed to get him home. This time Gary was contrite. He returned to Columbia, a year behind his class, but at least on his way to law school again.

It helped that he fell in love. Her name is Lorna. Arthur and I couldn't have been more pleased and hopeful. Lorna is a lovely young woman, bright as can be, a glowing personality. She is beautiful in a special way; in the old days she would have been described as comely. She is everything I would have wanted in a daughter had

I been able to have another child. Gary had known her at college as a freshman, but she wasn't one of his crowd (thank goodness!). When he returned to school after the Mykonos misadventure, it was a little awkward that she was a junior while he was a sophomore, but it didn't stand in their way. Lorna will be starting law school herself this fall, and Arthur has not been joking about offering her a place in his firm when she graduates. If we know Lorna, she will make Law Review without much question. She is one of the bright spots in our life, and we have Gary to thank at least for that.

He himself continued to be erratic, unfortunately. Just before school ended this past June, he became evasive and distracted again. Even Lorna couldn't reach him. He refused to bathe, for one thing. I can tell you, Brian, that it is very difficult to feel kindly to someone who smells bad, even if he is your own son. That, in turn, made me feel so monstrously guilty that I went out of my way to be nice to him, per them damned books.

Gary with his cleverness worked out an especially provocative way of mocking Arthur and me. He left notes, ostensibly for his journal, all over the house where we could not miss them. I am sure you will recognize the charming sentiments. "I am being what They want me to be, and losing Myself in the dirty process." Or plain snide, "People like my mother and father are playing roulette with life and death and betting on a number that isn't on the wheel. No wonder they are The Losers of Life!" And one time, "Why is man, as Emerson said, 'a god playing the fool?' " I answer (wrote Gary), "Because man has turned from God!"

That didn't surprise me too much, given his roomful of assorted tracts. But that note rang a warning bell in my head somehow. I took it to be Gary's way of telling us he was becoming involved with a group like the Jesus Freaks, Hare Krishna, the People's Temple, the Moonies, or one of the others you wrote about.

It was very disquieting to me, because I personally distrust them all, but I decided to wait and see.

Well, I "saw" this morning. I went in to clean Gary's room, which he had left an unholy mess, and found a document plainly left for me to read. I pass on only some of the choicest sentiments of my dear son:

"Most people in this sorry world live downbeat. A few manage upbeat. People like my parents live *side*beat, which is the stupidest waste of all, for they have not even the emotions of insecurity, poverty, hunger, and misery." (Those, now, are the exalted states?) And . . .

"Parents believe they have authority over children on the basis of birth itself. But what is my 'mother' really to me? Oh, I am not ungrateful for her nurture, but the woman named Margaret Webb is not the author of my life as she takes herself to be! Nor is my father. *The two of them are only and nothing more than the conduits of Creation,* the *happenstance* bearers of Creation.

"I come not from their Bodies, which are empty shells, but from Non-Being, *through God.*

"This means my 'parents' have been my custodians, nothing more. The egg and sperm they claim as theirs belong not to them, but only to God. This is proved by the scientific fact that the egg and sperm contain the protoplasm that is immortal, i.e., Godly.

"So the power and authority of parents are only what they may reflect as *servants of God,* and not of their own being or merit or worth."

Now, Brian, please give close attention to the rest of what Gary's message contains, because I think that, with your broad knowledge of these groups, you may see a clue to the organization he has joined. Gary continued with:

"This is what is meant when my beloved Teacher states that *my parents are the creatures of the Devil.* Literally. For they presume to be masters when they are only servants.

"Thus I learn the clearest lesson of all. I will never find or achieve my own true self and selfness *until I free myself from the devilish hold of my parents.* They may be well-meaning sometimes, *but they are ALWAYS of the Devil!*

"This is what my Teacher teaches when he teaches me to '*Hate* your mother and father! *Rip apart* all your family ties for they are your chains and bondage!' "

On and on in that foul, hysterical vein, Brian. Is that crapulous litany familiar to you? Can you identify it? You can imagine how appalled and desolated I am that my son should be caught up in such vileness. It is not just perfidy and blasphemy, it is sick. (For the first time I have a sickening thought about Clarissa's madness, for she was indeed out of her mind, no matter how euphemistically I have described her situation. Is there a strain of mental illness in my family? I never considered it before. I know of no one else, but then, given my parents, they would never speak of such a skeleton in the closet.)

If I sound distraught it is because I have tried and tried to understand. I have tried to reassure myself that this is another passing phase, that Gary has been duped like thousands upon thousands of others and will come to his senses. But my heart is breaking. I read his notes and can't believe my eyes. Arthur and I creatures of the Devil? Is this the joy we believed a child would be to us? I am losing my son to some insane "Teacher," and it is more than I can cope with.

I need to stop writing for a while. Then I will either tear this up as too intimate a family matter, or I'll continue it later. Excuse me now.

Later.

Obviously I did not tear the letter up. I find there is nothing I cannot share with you, and that is the true measure of how improbably far we have come with each other without even meeting. Now I want and need your advice very specifically. I have talked this over with Arthur very seriously, and it is clear to us that Gary is beyond our reach. It did not seem the time or place to tell my husband about you and me, but I did suggest that I would try to find out about the people who do deprogramming and that sort of thing, if we can find Gary in the first place. Please give me your suggestions as to how we might proceed. I am hopeful, as I have indicated, that the jargon I have passed along will help you identify the group.

I have talked with Lorna and wept with her. Gary confided nothing in her. He has slammed her door behind him as he has slammed ours. That only dismays and unnerves me the more. What a tide and pull there must be for someone like Gary to cut all of us out of his life this way. Inevitably I keep asking why, why, why. You wrote some of the reasons. I recall agreeing strongly with your observation that society is paying the price of disenchantment among the middle-class young largely because they have had too much too soon too easily. But now I find even the good answers not enough, they don't really explain Gary for me. And isn't it also true that most of our young people are more like Lorna, preparing themselves sensibly for real and useful lives? Why should Gary be among the few who would rather respond to a message like "Hate and despise your mother and father!" What a profound irony it is that such irreligious blasphemies should be pronounced in the name of religion!

I have a great and terrible rage in me, Brian. If I ever learn who the soul-swindlers are in Gary's case, I promise I will try to hurt them as badly as I can.

What an irony, too, that I, who suffered at the hands of my parents as Gary never did, returned only respect and acceptance while my son, to whom I gave everything, spits in my face!

That is wrath, not self-pity, and no apology do I make for the bitterness of it!

How often I have heard, from the pulpit and from my father, that Satan is real. In my heart I always pooh-poohed it as theological bombast. But I swear I am coming to believe now that (I think it was Pope John who proclaimed it) in this age the Devil himself is literally walking among us.

Now he has my son! Please help us if you can.

Maggie

Sept. 7

Maggie dear:

Your letter was held up by the Labor Day holiday and I didn't receive it until minutes ago. I am dropping everything else to answer at once because I know your grief and distress. I am not sure how I can help "professionally," but if sharing Gary's problem with me is some comfort, please know that I am at your side.

First let me say that this is a time to try to keep things in perspective. Statistics show that many like Gary return home after a relatively short time. They do come to see through the frauds after some exposure. Others take longer. I suppose it depends on how much resentment (against parents, society, teachers, self-fear) they have to work out of their system. Self-doubt is part of it, too. It isn't just rebelliousness, it is often the individual's anxiety that he won't be able to hack it in the adult world. He retreats to a promise of sanctuary from the world's problems, of making a living, facing competition, and so on.

Most important for you right now, there is evidence that going after the runaways only solidifies their resistance, sometimes just when they may be ready to return by themselves. Then it becomes a tactic of integrity to them to reaffirm their loyalty to the group, and the group forms "a covered wagon circle" against the outsider.

Whatever his particular reasons, you have to accept that Gary is not simply running *to* something but away from something else. In most cases it is *not* the parents, though they are made the scapegoat, as you and Arthur have been. Our books are full of case histories of Garys who seek every kind of excuse not to grow up. These "Peter Pans" are, I find, the quickest to turn to cults that supply the *appearance* of mature activity, while treating the individual as a dependent infant. Some of the outfits wrap themselves in radical causes, some in flags of nationalism, others in religious robes. Who can bad-mouth patriotic or religious orders?

I have colleagues with much more experience in this area and will discuss Gary's situation with them thoroughly, be sure. I think I do recognize the mouthings you sent along, but I want to make sure before I get you and Arthur off and running. This is too important for mistakes of any kind.

Meantime, let me offer a few observations sociologically speaking. None will be new to you (as so little of sociology really is when translated into everyday language), but they may help you with the perspective I am recommending. Since I am near Gary's generation, as you have pointed out occasionally, I know one basic certainty in cases like this. Neither you nor your husband nor anyone else, including me, is going to understand Gary while we view him in terms of what I can only call a middle-class frame of reference.

To start with, we had better recognize that the word *accomplishment*—which is the middle-class lodestone—has only negative meaning for many young people currently. They see it as a false value, "soul-destroying." With cosmic humor they are blind to their own self-contradiction. On the one hand they applaud the struggle of the poor nations seeking just the living standards they deplore as materialistic at home! After all, what have fathers ever wanted for their families throughout history? Nourishing food, decent shelter and clothing, an education, some amenities, a few luxuries and laughs where possible after survival needs were taken care of, PLUS the fundamental *sine qua non* in our society, the opportunity to fulfill individual talents and aspirations.

All this our own country has provided with a bounty beyond what could have been imagined only a few generations ago. We consider necessities what our grandfathers could not even dream of as luxuries. Yet today this incredibly magnificent achievement generates its own irony. It is spit on by its own beneficiaries, who choose to see only the warts and not the wonders. I think of what André Malraux wrote in another context, "The absurd was a question, they have turned it into an answer."

Unhappily, our society furnishes all too many blemishes to support the injustice collectors who seek disenchantment in the first place.

Ah, but why do we have so many of such seekers these days? There is a critical question, and I ask it every year in my classrooms. One meaningful answer, to me, is that we must understand the source of a primal anger that fuels the engine of rebelliousness, in whatever form it happens to take with particular individuals.

One supportable hypothesis is that *all* young people are inflamed against parents from infancy. As Freud observed, parents are infant-tamers, the acculturators, the suppressors of all the natural, feral, libidinous desires of human blood. Infants must learn the tricks. They roll over obediently at the crack of the whip; they jump through flaming hoops for the smile and candy that reward "good" behavior, though many do snarl and show their fangs before the final surrender.

Or what looks like final surrender.

Inwardly the hatred and animosity flares and grows. The rages may be sublimated, denied, repressed, transformed, or expressed in the masks of neuroses, but they persist.

I see a universal theme: "I hate my mother and father, but it is absolutely taboo to admit this hatred even to myself in darkest secret, and surely I am forbidden ever to act on it. Yet I must express this fury somehow or burst. So watch out, society! I will find a surrogate to battle instead of my parents! *Any cause, feud, youth gang, cult, or utopia seeking recruits will find my rage ready to enlist!* Only give me some small pretense that the Cause is just, that God is with you, that the Territory is bounded, and you have me, body and soul!"

(A true case history reported by a public school teacher: A girl of about ten opened her lunch sandwich and screamed, "No cheese? I hate the *world!*")

This kind of thing, I deeply believe, is why Irish kill Irish, why

Moslem Lebanese battle Christian Lebanese, why different language groups in India will march for mutual slaughter, et cetera ad nauseam. To say nothing of our own black-white conflicts, or of the rampant terrorist gangs that serve "Glorious Causes" while they murder innocent people.

I am convinced that man would invent rifts if there were no flags to rally to, no economic, political, territorial, or social enmities to tap the cauldron of inner human hate. Blue-eyed people would discover that brown-eyed tribes must be swept off the face of the earth. Redheads would have to kill brunettes. Short people would wage war on tall, ad disgustibus . . .

In the outside world, a man can find the counterparts of all the hurts he suffered helplessly as an infant. Later we witness the undifferentiated hostility and revenge in the form of Nazis against Jews —all the sorry sagas of inhumanity back to Cain.

When a Gary, following this unconscious dynamic, turns from his family, it is a method of dealing with unacceptable feelings in a way that may appear acceptable. He is safer if he substitutes ritual for emotion and reason, safer still if he hands over his discontent to a messianic Leader. It is my observation that the young people who have rebelled hardest against parental authority (*or* who have seemed most docile!) are the first to abdicate their lives to absolute dictators.

It is a mockery that our country sanctions and encourages these self-proclaimed prophets with tax exemptions. But I suppose that is a price a free society has to pay. Your husband knows better than I the legal concept that it is better for ten guilty men to go free than for one innocent man to be punished, and so, too, better for ten charlatans to be unmolested than one genuine religious organization to be circumscribed. (And who, in the first place, is to determine the genuine? Which are true apostles, which are the cynical peddlers, the embezzlers of property and souls?)

Religious freedom is a glory of this country even though it is abused and costs personal pain and disaster. I hope we remain strong enough to afford the luxury; a weak society will not sustain it.

Like you, Maggie, I can unfortunately move from the general problem to its personal impact. The prime example in my family is Carl, the cousin I've told you a little about. His way of dealing with the world, parallel to Gary's, is not to try to raise himself up but to knock everyone else down. He tells my uncle he's a fool "to work your balls off when you could go on welfare."

(I must interrupt to tell you of a new slogan scrawled all over our campus lately: "Get the rich off our backs!" I find myself wondering who is riding whom these days. To me, the middle-class is the donkey carrying the load. What with taxes, subsidies, inflation, theft in high places, millions of public employees goofing off daily, and the whole welfare mess, it seems to me that never before in history have so many taken advantage of so few!)

Cousin Carl's approach is summed up in a challenge he poses: "What's so great about all them big-shot names? Presidents, writers, stars, they all take a s—t just like me, don't they?" And his clincher: "Albert Einstein went to the crapper no different from me, didn't he?"

Uncle Joe gave him the answer. "But Einstein came out with the theory of relativity, and all you contribute to the world is your stink!"

I'd rather remember the many happy things about Uncle Joe and lighten up this letter for both our sakes, Maggie. Your "Grampa Frappay" brought to mind a family anecdote of my own. One summer when I was about nine, Hildie and Joe took me to the beach one day. My mother, who was a stickler about food, directed Aunt Hildie that I was under no circumstances to be permitted the frankfurter I'd be sure to try to wheedle. Hildie kept her promise by taking all of Joe's money when we got into bathing suits. After swimming, Uncle Joe and I just happened to pass the hot-dog stand. I knew my uncle had no coins, so I swallowed my disappointment along with my saliva.

Next thing I knew, Joe was racing me around the beach house with two delicious-smelling hot dogs in his big hands. He twinkled and winked as we gobbled them. Only years later did I learn that Joe had given the vendor his gold ring as security. The ring was Joe's only possession of value. The vendor could have closed for the season and absconded happily. He didn't. There are decent people everywhere. Your Medford grandfather and my San Francisco Uncle Joe (and the hot-dog man!) would have hit it off.

Except, to complete the story, Hildie felt honor bound to tell my mother, and I was administered a "castor-oil sandwich." Did you ever have one? It's a dollop of chocolate syrup to start, then the castor oil, and more syrup on top. You gulped it fast and mightily, praying you wouldn't taste the castor oil between the chocolate, but I always did. Miserable, foul stuff! I suppose it wouldn't be punishment otherwise.

Maybe Gary (and Carl) should have had a couple of heavy shots while growing up.

The one thing about Gary about which I have no question is that the bridge home should not be burned. Try to get your husband to agree. Everything and everyone changes, including your son. If he has sought a cause, remember that, by definition, a cause involves loyalty to something outside one's selfish interests. That is not all bad or negative, even if it is misguided at this stage of Gary's life.

We could both wish Gary worked out his hang-ups with less pain, but this may turn out to be even a good thing in the long run. Don't dismiss that possibility.

I have a strong sense of who you are, Margaret Webb, and I doubt that *your* son will "rip all ties with parents," no matter what his new Leader enjoins. For one thing, as Ben Franklin said, "An image is a better teacher than a sermon." Gary has had your image and your husband's to steer by—images of decency, common sense, and affection. Let him disillusion himself about the other. If it doesn't happen within a reasonable time, then you may have a different type of problem, perhaps psychological. Don't jump to conclusions. For now, I counsel patience. We'll be together in less than a month and can talk this out further then. As you can imagine, I am counting minutes now!

Yours,

Brian

P.S. I see I have written a lot about perspective. "The earth and sea are full of robbers, and the great part of mankind is evilly disposed." That was a letter by a 14th-century businessman! (Name was Francesco Datini, of Prato, Italy.)

And there was Roger Bacon (no relation to your Francis) who wrote *in 1271* that "more sins reign in these days than in any past age . . . justice perisheth, all peace is broken." A woman, perhaps like yourself, bemoaned that "all good customs fail and virtues are held at discount."

Yet the world has somehow survived, and we know its blessings as well as its shadows.

Still, adding it all up, I suppose I am not too sanguine. I wrote a poem in freshman English that I wouldn't change today, and it may amuse you. It is titled "God Got The Shakes?" and goes like this:

> The world is full of falling things
> Fledgling birds out of trees
> Thee's out of me's
> Children dropping mom's best dishes
> Atom bombs like flying fishes
> Virtues are failing in all our lands.
> Maybe it's not such a good idea for Him, at His age,
>   to have the whole world in His hands.

Now you see why I became a sociologist instead of a poet! Anyway, a somewhat earlier poet put it better. Here is England's John Gower, writing in 1393:

> for now upon this tyde
> men se the world on every syde
> in sondry wyse so dyversed
> That it welnyh stant all reversed! (Exclamation point mine.)

Sept. 12

Dear Brian:

Your letter helped. I thank you. Just its objectivity reminded me that Gary's case isn't so unusual these days. While that's hardly a comfort, it does, I suppose, tend to alleviate the guilt I told you I have been feeling.

Your quotations put me in mind of *King Lear,* "In cities, mutinies; in countries, discord; in palaces, treason; and the bond cracked 'twixt son and father." Today's headlines!

And wasn't it Socrates who long before Shakespeare bemoaned the lack of respect shown by children to parents and predicted havoc for the society?

What you help me see more clearly is that I need to distance myself more from Gary, as all my life I needed to distance myself from my own parents. (I didn't rebel or join any lunatic group, or "go to Santa

Fe," but I did carry the *Baghavad Gita* around conspicuously, to let Beacon Hill see that I wasn't just a member of the common herd. I could never get very far in that book, but that wasn't the point in the first place.)

I see another important thing here, too. I need to distance myself from my husband. We have been arguing fiercely and endlessly about Gary. Arthur insists that when Gary walked out of this house he died for him. He wants no more talk of Gary in his house. *His* house, Arthur calls it. Not mine?

I am flooded with cutting memories. *Arthur* decided Gary should be a lawyer. He promised Gary a car for acceptance in law school. He never asked or considered what Gary might prefer. You wrote about some Leader now commanding Gary's life. Isn't that what my husband did with him? And with me???

It has been subtly done, of course, and not without my cooperation. If I am a puppet in part, I must take the blame for helping to string Arthur's wires through my loops. But I decidedly do not like or enjoy the picture of myself I am grasping now. Why do I find myself quaking-afraid to talk about Gary to his father? Let Arthur explode! I can hold my own!

Ah, but can I, or is this bravado, easy enough to write in a letter going cross-country to you? Perhaps I have known Arthur's inner volcano all these years and chose to buy safety by backing away from any confrontation that might ignite it.

If this is what Women's Lib has been saying, then I'm sorry I have been too starchy to listen. The corrosion for me, Brian, has never been the so-called drudgery in the home—I've written to you about my actual enjoyment of cleaning. No, what bugs me is being a second-class citizen in my own mind. I see that my pattern has been to defer to the first-class person just because he is the male! I tooled this into myself because confrontation with my husband would shake the whole framework of my life. Me and my aborted "ABD"!

I have never perceived any of this before! That is what frightens and disheartens me as much as anything. I am decidedly ready to have my own consciousness raised right now, even if I have to hoist myself by myself!

Gary is *not* dead for me, and I will not have my husband killing my son for me!

If I was overpermissive with Gary, so have I been with Arthur, dammit! I look back now on the thousand restaurants *he* has chosen, the ten thousand television programs *he* has selected, the hotels, the vacation times and places, always *his* preferences, on and on. Oh, it always seemed for good and proper reason. After all, he was the one exhausted by the breadwinning labors. But what I see is that it was not Arthur who effaced me. I effaced myself!

I myself elected to be the man's shadow. *Mea culpa!*

I chose to deny myself. *Mea culpa!*

I forfeited my brains, my feelings, my wishes. *Mea maxima culpa!*

Damn, damn, damn!

I am seeing my husband in a very different and unfriendly light since this crisis over Gary. I think you are absolutely right that we must not burn the bridge over which Gary may want to come home one day. I think Arthur is absolutely wrong to insist it must go. I will persist in what I consider right.

Brian, I cannot believe I am writing this way to a man I did not know until so short a time ago. I am grateful I am able to. I am grateful I will see you in only three weeks. I think you will be meeting a quite changed woman from the one my former letters have led you (and me!) to expect.

Maggie

P.S. I like your poem very much and am delighted you thought to send it. I promise not to bother you with effusions of my youth, but I did write one stanza after Clarissa died that I would like to share with you. I called it "Clarissa's Poem."

> She opened the door she never knew was locked,
> and freed to the sun a girl she never knew within.
> She stood then, wraith and real, a masked figure
> Dreaming in the unaccustomed light
> With lost eyes and empty seeking,
> Ears of grief, lamenting lamentation itself, crying out!
> How can I have lost what I never owned?
> Oh, that is the most lost of all!

Sept. 15

Dear Maggie:

Your poem moved me. I think, of course, you were writing as much about yourself as about Clarissa. I suspect depths in you that you hardly know. I am sensitive to them, have been from the beginning. I will not be meeting a changed woman, only one who has come through the door "freed to the sun."

We have a cleaning woman in once a week. She is a dear old lady, bright and cheerful always, although she could complain of rheumatism and neglectful children if she wanted to. This sunshiny morning (smog-free here for a change!), I greeted Tillie with, "It's a good day, isn't it?"

She came back to me with a loud laugh, saying, "Any day I'm alive is a good day!"

Wow!

I don't know whether the sentiment is hers or whether she picked it up somewhere, but it blew my mind. May it be of some cheer to you.

Tillie bestows another pearl of wisdom I am glad to pass along. It is a Test for Happiness. You are to repeat three times: "This too will pass."

If you are left feeling happy afterward, you are sad. If you are left feeling sad, you are happy!

Think that one over. I love it!

I have some news from this end. Remember the tree-killers? They came back for more of the sport and were caught by a forest patrol. They were arraigned yesterday.

They are shrewd cookies, of course. The first thing they did was issue a ringing pronouncement that they had cut the trees as a protest for American Indians! "This is how the white man has killed the Indian and his culture, which are older than the redwoods!"

They have dared to make that proclamation, killing trees the Indians have held holy!

There are no crimes any longer, there are only political protests!

I'll keep you posted on what the court does with these unspeakable slobs.

I've been giving a lot of thought to how decent people can live with the bugs crawling out of the woodwork everywhere. It suddenly occurred to me that I—and millions of others—are living right on top of the answer. We all know that the San Andreas fault runs smack through our area—there have been enough earthquakes to remind us if we tend to forget. Yet there is a fatalistic acceptance of the situation. People just don't think about it. They invest their fortunes and their lives, building as if nothing will ever happen, although the geologists are quite unanimous in their warnings of danger.

You put your finger on it, Maggie—you and old man Vaihinger. People must live *as if* nothing untoward will ever happen.

But a decent respect for the possibilities of earthquakes and barbarians is indicated all the same. Which brings me back to Gary. I would guess in his case his convictions and allegiance to his group are on the thin side—more exploratory than ready for dedication. Where conviction is shallow and uncertain, it is held the more fiercely against outside challenge. So, though I think I may now know the cult he has joined, my advice is the same. Wait.

There will be time enough for decision when I am in New York.

I am affected by your confidences about your husband, and I cheer the new responses and ideas that are coming from you. Perhaps when we talk you will get them in clearer focus. I feel as much your very close friend as you feel me to be. You have become a signal part of my life. Let me tell you that your inner strength and character keep coming across to me.

Only 465 hours!
Brian

Sept. 29

Dear Maggie:

No word from you in two weeks! What has happened? By the time this letter reaches you it will by only a couple of days before we are to meet. We ought to complete the arrangements.

There is a perversity about the countdown to my visit. It grows longer for me as the time grows shorter. I look at your picture until it blurs, and I wonder how it will be to hold your hand, to touch your fingers with mine, hear your voice, sit near you.

Please write as soon as you possibly can.

Brian

P.S. Would you like a laugh? In a formal paper on my desk, I came upon the following sociological definition of "love." It is from (I swear and attest) a "Conference on Love and Affection" and states, in all the academic sobriety of the scholarly enclave: "Love is the cognitive-affective state characterized by intrusive and obsessive phantasizing concerning reciprocity of amorant feelings of the object of the amorance."

Maggie, may I consider you the object of my amorance?

Sept. 29

Dear Brian:

I am sorry I have not been able to write. My world "welnyh stant all reversed," to quote our Mr. Gower. I have needed time to take in the changes here, and I didn't trust myself until I had my mind clear or, as the youngsters would say, got myself together.

I am not at home with Arthur at present. I am staying at Lorna's place, for a while anyway, and that will explain the new return address you undoubtedly noticed on the envelope. Lorna's studio apartment is small, but like the darling she is she has made a place for me.

It is hard for me to believe I am here. It is hard to accept that I have lived with Arthur Webb for over 25 years and scarcely known him.

How *does* one understand others, Brian? Listening and observing are, perceptibly, not enough. They only establish that someone is out there. Can one ever get inside? Openings have to match, like lock and key. But I think nobody fits that perfectly, no matter how much love there may be, no matter how much sharing. Maybe it is better not even to try to turn the lock, for that gives the illusion that the bolt has turned, the room entered, while all the time we are really standing out in the cold.

You are wondering what happened, and I am stalling because I find it so difficult to contemplate. From one point of view, very little has happened. From another, everything!

A little over a week ago I went to my desk to answer a letter from you (your date Sept. 15). Something was visibly wrong when I opened the drawer. My packet of your letters and your picture had been moved. My maid never touches this drawer. Gary has not been in the house. Only Arthur could have done it. Arthur alone.

Still, I told myself not to jump to conclusions. Maybe Arthur was looking for a pen or an emery board or something and handled the letters without thinking. In "the old days" I would have let it go at that, but the new me asked Arthur straight out that night.

Brian, in its way that hour was the stickiest and most distasteful of my life. Quarreling with Arthur over Gary was one thing. Opening up this very private matter was quite another.

I won't take you through the fight we had. It grew quite snappish. We were both inflamed by guilt—mine at having withheld knowledge of your friendship from my husband, and his, that he had indeed invaded my privacy.

When two people feel both guilty and in the right, the fur flies. We each said ugly things. I recognize that years of pressure were finally bursting out of me. I did not suspect that the same might be true for my husband—to the point where, after I had explained our correspondence, *he forbid me to meet you!*

That was too much! I could not believe my ears. I demanded whether he would go to court for an injunction to stop me. I said that if he had read your letters he knew perfectly well how totally innocent our friendship is, and he should be glad that I would have your counsel about Gary. His reply was that if I had been sneakily writing to a strange man behind his back, he did not know what else I would feel free to do behind his back when I met you in October! My husband dared to insult me with that, in a tone hoarse with revolting and totally unjustified implications (as you so well know)!

You can guess how I answered that man! I told him I would damn well write to whom I pleased and meet whom I pleased when I pleased, including you on October 5!

And I proceeded to storm out of the living room into the bedroom where he followed me to watch with unbelieving eyes as I did pack a suitcase. Then he gave me a smile that said he knew that I was putting on an act. And do you know something, Brian, he wasn't entirely wrong. If he had spoken one word of apology, I would not have continued. It felt too artificial to me, too much like Nora preparing to slam the door heard round the world. Not my style at all.

I felt a strong impulse to back down. This could not be me, actually going through the motions of walking out of the house. That was off the scale of possibilities for dutiful, compliant, tractable, sensible Margaret Fairfield Webb. My heart was thundering in my chest. It seemed to me Arthur must hear it, and understand, and help me not to be swept to rashness by the fury that made my hands tremble. I was harrowed with an inner conflict, appalled at myself, yet somehow tall with a head-raising courage that was challenging every obedience I had let life wring from me since the very beginning. Somewhere in me I knew that if I gave way to the fear and uncertainty, I would never respect myself again. Yet in the same moment I knew in my heart that one soft word from Arthur would turn everything around. One part of me prayed he would take me off the hook, muffle the challenge I did not truly want to stand up to. That part of me wanted desperately to have things as they were, peaceful, quiet, even bovine if you will.

But—and now I am glad of it, elated—instead of reaching out to me, Arthur barked like a marine sergeant, "And where the hell do you think you are going? What the hell do you think you are doing!"

My own thing! I wanted to scream at him, but there was a wedge of bitterness in my throat that made it impossible for me to do anything but grab the suitcase and make for the door. I am glad to say that I gave Arthur a considerable shove on my way. As I careened by him, I could see that Arthur was stunned, perhaps not so much at my actual leaving as at his having misread me so completely. My only regret was that I couldn't be on both sides of the bedroom door as I slammed it behind me. I would dearly have loved to see that smug, superior smile get wiped off as my husband realized I was not fooling, that his puppet strings were actually severed.

This has not been easy to write, as you can imagine. I feel messy, addled, disloyal to my marriage. After all, was it such a terrible thing for a husband to read a wife's mail?

Yes, dammit!

If I am unfair to Arthur, well, let us say he has been more than unfair to me. I did honestly, always, want him to know about you and me, it just never worked out appropriately. I was wrong, but it is no excuse for his rough-riding.

Now I am looking forward to seeing you even more than before.

Incidentally, in explaining my falling out with Arthur to Lorna, who has been a brick and a lifesaver, I told her about our correspondence and our upcoming meeting. She would like to meet you, too, while you are here, and I will arrange something for the three of us. I am sure you will admire Lorna as much as I do. She may be able to cast some light on Gary that will help us all.

Now I can't quite imagine myself taking the cab I will ride to Kennedy in a couple of days! I can't really believe I will be standing at a gate straining to recognize Brian Curtiss coming off the plane from San Francisco to shake hands with Margaret Webb! If you see a woman there with a rose in her mouth it will be me to keep my teeth from chattering with the suspense.

I can't believe it!

Maggie

P.S. You ought to know that I am fully intending to return to home and hearth, perhaps even before you arrive. I expect that Arthur is quite upset by my unprecedented conduct, so it is taking him a while to make the first, conciliatory move for which I am confidently waiting. Meantime I am feeling my oats, and I like the feeling. *See you soon,* Brian Curtiss!

Part Four

Boston!
Sunday, October 10th

Oh, my dear Brian:

What a letdown, what a diabolical disappointment, what a fizzled fiasco!

This is the first moment I have had to write to you since I was forced to leave New York for Boston instead of meeting you. It was fortunate that Lorna could pinch hit for me, at least to welcome you to New York instead of leaving you stranded altogether. I know she has explained the family emergency. You will want to know that though the stroke was massive my mother survived it. But it has been nip and tuck for days here, with considerable family upset all around.

I still can't credit what happened. I was on my phone calling a cab to meet you at Kennedy when the other phone rang, from Boston. So there I was, incredibly, getting on a shuttle at La Guardia while your plane was coming in just miles away. We probably passed in the air, at that! I couldn't help but recall your mention of Evangeline somewhere in our correspondence. I'm sure you didn't mean it to be prophetic, but it seems to have been in the end.

Obviously, I was worried about my mother, but furious with her at the same time. It was as if she had purposely reached down to foul things up, the way she always interfered if I wanted to see someone

106 ·

she didn't approve. And of course she would not approve of you since "everyone knows" that "a married woman does not meet a stranger."

My mother! She came out of her stroke singing loud, "I'm off to see the wizard!" before she went totally silent. Figure out that bizarre flash if you can. What personalities does *she* have cloistered in her secret places that none of us has ever suspected? This, too, has given me pause.

Despite my vexation at the way my mother spoiled our plans, I found that I cared about her and was genuinely concerned. I had wondered whether I would feel grief if she passed away. Seeing her helpless in that hospital bed, tears came. No matter how much gall there has been between us, I cried for my mother. Brian, I give up trying to follow the tangle of the torrents of our lives.

It is a tangle. A new tangle for you and me. I must tell you now that I am no longer sure there should ever be a meeting between us, or even more correspondence. Hear me out. It has taken me a prayerful time to reach this decision, and it is why it has taken me so long to sit down to write.

My husband came up to Boston with me, obviously. Just as obviously, the family never dreamed of providing separate rooms for us. With Mother critically ill the last thing I wanted was to make more waves, so Arthur and I wound up together in one of the guest rooms with one double bed. I must say that Arthur offered to take the floor, but that was silly, especially after we had used the plane ride to have a good talk, calmly at last.

Having thought it over, Arthur said he understood my being put out enough to go to Lorna's. He apologized for opening my mail. He recognized how irreproachable this correspondence has always been. More important, he said, without my prodding, that he should have respected my integrity, should have recognized my right to my own things, should always remember that I am a separate person and not his Siamese twin.

On my part, I conceded my senseless mistake in not telling him of your letters at once. Not that he should ever have shared them, but that I should have been open and not secret. I was misguided. In fairness, I had to ask myself indeed how I would feel if I regularly saw mail to Arthur from some woman in California about whom he never spoke. As is usually true, there has been considerable right, as well as wrong, on both sides of our family argument.

I find my fingers slowing on the keyboard, but I am forcing them to go on typing what must be written now. Brian, I find that I must face into some very disquieting considerations about us that have been brought to the surface by this episode. When I sat in that plane for Boston, watching other planes in the sky so angrily and wondering if you might be close by just across a cloud, I was absolutely miserable and I was shaken by the way I felt. For the first time I could not deny how very much I had come to look forward to being with you. I was—shocked is the only word—to find that my disappointment was far more than casual. It was deep and it was painful. Flying in that Boston plane *away* from you instead of riding out to greet you brought a shattering revelation. You have come to mean more to me than I had ever suspected, or want, or can accept in my life.

I did not want Arthur beside me. I wanted you. It cut to the bone.

Writing this now I feel naked and afraid. I see myself standing alone in the center of an endless, icy landscape. In a wide circle around me are all the people I have ever known in my life. They are sliding around me grotesquely, friends and strangers, every face I have ever seen on any street, in any store, on any train or bus or ship or plane. Everyone is waiting for me to speak, but I don't know what to say. The only one who is missing is you, Brian, because I have never seen you except artificially, your surrogate picture. During rationing in the war (World War II, before you were born!) there was a cartoon of a cannibal stuffing his mouth with pictures of people torn from magazines. A fellow cannibal asks, "How is that dehydrated stuff?"

What I am saying is that you are not *in* my life, Brian. Not in my life except in some dehydrated way. I don't know why I am saying this, I don't know what it means exactly, but it is true for me.

It *is* my way of saying I must now keep you out of my life. The circle has no place for you. It is an unblinkable fact that I don't know where to fit my nameless feelings about you into my life. I don't know what to do with you, Brian Curtiss.

I'm sorry this is all coming out sort of fancy and dramatic. The reason is that I still cannot say, plain and outright—I now know that I am in over my head with you.

Since nothing can come of it, except drowning, I need to stop. Period. Ring the curtain down. It has been a game, done.

Maybe Providence in the form of Boston knew what it was doing after all. It is probably far better that we did not meet.

In fairness, since I was the one who began this correspondence, I suppose you ought to have the chance to end it. You can write to me at home. I am not staying at Lorna's any longer and will be leaving Boston for New York tomorrow morning since Mother is doing quite well now.

I regret the turn this has taken, and will always think of you as a good friend, but I am sure you agree that my first loyalty is to my marriage, as yours is to yours. I am certain that you, like myself, have never doubted that for a moment. You must forgive a woman who has apparently had an interval of unsuitable vulnerability. Put it down to the weakness of years. Apparently the "liberation" philosophy is not for me. In any case, we ought both to heed the sage observation made in—of all places—a television show on Masai Africa my family watched last night: "The wise hunter wastes no time on the chase he knows he cannot win."

As a last word, let me say that Lorna tells me you are even nicer than I had led her to expect. She was much taken with you, and you no doubt with her. Her red hair is glorious, isn't it? I hope you two will exchange letters, and so I may have some news of you from time to time. Good-bye, then, Brian Curtiss. Believe me, it is best this way.

Margaret Webb

Oct. 17

Dear Evangeline:

I simply do not know how to answer your letter. I have a long list of persuasive reasons why you are wrong about ending our correspondence. On the other hand, I have to respect your judgment.

Needless to say, missing you in New York was a devilish disappointment to me, too. The fact that Lorna is a delightful young woman did not make up for my sense of being cheated. I had my own turbulence in me about meeting you, you know.

Maggie (Peggy? Margaret? Mrs. Webb?), we have talked so many times about being on the same wavelength. Let me tell you I share your sense of disjointed circumstances between us and your disquiet about our relationship. Our near-meeting aroused much the same reactions in me as you describe in yourself. There was not only my flaring resentment at "Boston" but an intense sense that my feelings were much stronger than they had a right to be.

I can't honestly say your African homily is wrong, can I?

There is another reason on my side why your advice may be wise, much as I dislike it. There are developments that may bring my work to a new pitch soon. This started at Princeton, where I had a chance to talk with people from UCLA who are interested in some of my thinking. Specifically, I am limited in my present post because this faculty tends to stack the disciplines like separate bales of hay in the fields of academe. My own inclination is to explore much more widely, everywhere that the field of sociology interfaces with everything else, from anthropology to zoology. I am now writing up a proposal for the UCLA people, and they indicate I may have a good shot at a post opening up in Los Angeles. It would be as associate rather than assistant professor, and that would be an ambition of mine come true sooner than I thought probable.

I do not relish the thought of pulling up stakes and going through another move with the family. I would miss my redwoods badly, I'm sure, but the future is even more important. It would probably be a healthy change of scene for Kay as well. If I get the UCLA appointment, I will be in a whole new ball game and, especially since I also want to continue with the book I started, there probably would not be much time for anything else in any event. So I am following my thoughts to their conclusion, a conclusion I am reluctant and unhappy to reach. But I must match your honesty and admit that perhaps an interruption (and I shall consider it temporary, not a termination) of our correspondence would not be out of order on my side as well as yours.

I don't want to say any more. If I continue, I will be getting into feelings I have no right to express.

I do have a right, though, to ask you please to keep me in your thoughts, Maggie, as I will keep you always in mine.

Say hello to Lorna for me.

Not happily,
Brian

Oct. 22

Dear Brian:

I am pleased to have your last letter. Your sensible views—no more than I expected of a man like you—make it easier for me too. You know you have all my good wishes for your family and your career. I certainly hope you gain the UCLA post, and when your book is published, as I am sure it will be most successfully, you must send me a suitably inscribed copy for the proudest place on my bookshelves.

All this has been an unexpected joy for me, but you are right and I am right about what is right right now . . .

Margaret

Nov. 6

Dear Brian:

Lorna tells me that in a letter to her you have mentioned that Paul and Joan have measles. I suppose you know that is another of the treacherous bugs relatively harmless in childhood but dangerous for grown-ups. If you didn't have measles as a child, you must be sure to see a doctor at once.

You are fortunate that both children came down at the same time. That was true of the chicken pox too, wasn't it? Usually siblings have these things in tandem, which doesn't make it any easier for the parents.

No need to answer and, as we have both agreed, better not to. I just thought I'd give you the benefit of some motherly advice . . .

Margaret Webb

Nov. 20

Dear Margaret:

The children are fine, and so are Kay and I. But I have another excuse I can use for writing to you again. I think you want to know about our redwood vandals. I would send you a news clip of their court appearance except that it was apparently kept out of the papers. The update is that all of our barbarian friends are released on probation!

In such a world, I am more than ever convinced, one retreats to tend one's own garden. Call it surrender, if you wish. As I've told you, there was a time when I thought the answer to all the wrong things was the clenched fist, the march of protest, the personal effort, the political campaign, the community mobilization, the "writing-to-Congress." All valid, but I have lost my enthusiasm because I have lost my belief that the problems are responsive to personal activism. In my own way I am a cop-out, a defeatist, I suppose, but when it comes down to how I run my own life, I must confess my feeling that What's Happening Out There Today seems just too big and beyond the reach of my angers and my philosophies. I'm beginning to think that the peasants of the world have always been right. It doesn't matter all that much who is on top. Through history the names change, the titles, and the colors of the pennons, but the forces at ferment move in their own unalterable patterns.

Let me admit I don't admire my position. I am uncomfortable with it, it even seems morally wrong. Perhaps one day I will remember how much difference a Martin Luther King can make and get back in the fight. I suppose I can never really stay out for long. I am haunted by words Pablo Casals once recorded, "To live is not enough. We have to take part in what is good . . . I am unhappy when people who have the duty of pronouncing thought—to act against injustice—they stay still in their houses."

Well, I am not exactly still. My rage has not turned silent. We also fight the good fight who cast light, who teach, who point ways, which is what I hope I do on campus. Today that may be more to the point than the activism that wins the applause of radicals and do-gooders, and is too often subverted in any case.

I hope that you, and the spirit of Pablo Casals, a kind man, will understand and accept that I seek my own house, at least for this time. If it is a form of defeat or surrender, let me confess I am disheartened at the magnitude of the evil and uncaringness I see in so many, many people all around me. I will light my little candle against the dark as best I can, but for now my major concerns remain my family and my career.

The trouble with tending my own garden is that a large place in it is empty. I miss you, Maggie. Badly. When I, too readily, agreed that we each had good reasons to step back from each other—at least for a time—I had no intimation that I would feel such a loss. I have a profound sense now that we are *not* right in cutting off our friendship. In this sorry world, I repeat, we ought not be so quick to forfeit the few decent and happy things that happen to us. To me, that seems almost an invitation to the barbarians. If we turn our own backs on our gifts, how can we complain that Attila wants to take the rest from us?

I am immersed in my projects and my family, yes. But a significant part of my experience has miscarried. That's an understated way of saying I miss you terribly and want you back. I want the letters from you that came to mean so much to me.

The more I ponder us, the more I think we are victims of an idiocy, a deficiency, not of our making. I am not talking morality or theology or even psychology. I am referring to linguistics. You may wonder what the devil I am driving at. Just this: *The English language does not have enough words . . .*

For example, as relating to you and me, a man and woman can be "friends" or they can be "in love." There are no meaningful nuances between, no sensitive spectrum of words such as the real world demands. ("Affection," "confidant," etc., are hollow and not to our point at all.) *And,* in our society, where there is no Word there is no Reality. Remember "nominalism" in your philosophy courses? To name a thing is to bring it into existence. In the same way, to deny a name is to banish being, to banish us. The first proposition is, of course, arguable. The second is not.

Why aren't we willing to "let it sing itself"? I want the singing to go on, Margaret, uncertain overtones and all. To me the silence is not only painful but false, and unnecessary. How can I persuade you? Perhaps it will help to make you smile about it. I see in one of my professional notices that the National Science Foundation made a grant for $84,000 (which I could handsomely use!) for a study of "passionate love" as against "companionate love." I was gratified to note that this grant was tagged with a senator's Golden Fleece Award for wasting tax moneys, but the phrase "companionate love" sticks in my mind. Would you feel comfortable corresponding with me under that license?

I realize I am running the risk of coming on too strong, but I feel contentious today. Anyway, not to take risks is the same as death; all life is risk. You closed me off because we don't tuck neatly into some social slot, and I went along because I did not know how much you had come to mean to me until I no longer had you in my life. I cannot put it more sincerely than that.

Margaret, God said, "Let there be Light," not "Let there be A Word"! Please think hard and conscientiously about this. We ought to go on, you and I.

The children are doing well. Kay is in neutral for the time being, always a relief to me. Have you heard anything from Gary?

Obstinately,
Brian

Nov. 28

Dear Margaret:

Again writing, not to pressure you any longer, but with a further bulletin on the saga of the tree killers. As I get the story from neighbors now (still nothing in the papers), the goons were out joyriding last night for more of their "fun and maims" when they were met by some young people who feel as you and I do.

It seems they joined battle, and the good guys beat hell out of the bad guys. Hallelujah! It happens sometimes! Our side tied the creeps to the very trees they had mutilated, to leave them to contemplate their victims overnight. And the Good Lord decided to get into the act Himself, pouring down one of the heaviest deluges we have seen in years to nearly drown the rats.

Beautiful! I thought you would like to know.

As I sit here licking my chops vindictively, I shudder to think how easily I could become a vigilante. I wish I had been there last night. How great it would have been to slam those ruffians around with my own fists! Only a letter from you would have made me happier.

Human nature!

Brian

Dec. 23

Margaret,

Season's Greetings permitted?

Brian

Dec. 26

Brian:

Greetings of the Season from our house to your house.

Margaret

Jan. 3

Dear Margaret:

Thank you for answering my Christmas card. It is the first word from you in almost three long months and, though a printed formality, it came as balm.

Do you know that your first letter to me was last Feb. 29, almost a full year ago? Leap year, you observed, as a semiexcuse for addressing an unknown man.

We didn't stay strangers long, did we? There was some chemistry between us that got on the paper despite ourselves. There is no denying that.

I want it back.

I have a broken radio on my desk that used to bring in Bach, Schubert, Mozart. I still turn the knob sometimes, forgetting it isn't working. Silence. I can have the set fixed, but how can I fix us?

I thought I meant it when I wrote about welcoming a hiatus myself for the sake of my work. The opposite is true. My work would be going better if I wasn't distracted by thoughts of you that constantly stir the sense of loss. It's become a nagging ache. I can't but believe you are having something of the same experience. We had reached too close to each other for that not to be true.

Happy New Year anyway. Up on the dateline of this letter I almost wrote the old year. It always takes me weeks into a new year before my brain turns the digit. My brain refuses to accept that I will never hear from you again.

Brian

Feb. 3

Margaret:

Another month, a longer silence. I take it that you are determined. I say again that I understand your constraint, but I cannot respect it. You know, sometimes things come clearer in silence than they do in speaking. I am very clear about us right now. There is a simple equation, and if you were a student in my classroom, I would write it on the blackboard as an exam:

A. Mr. X and Mrs. Y have a friendship that is warm but casual. They both intend that it should stay that way, because each is strongly involved with other relationships. Since they aim at nothing that could harm anyone else, and since their friendship gives them pleasure, what are the reasons they should discontinue all contact? Why in the world shouldn't they go on?

B. Mr. X and Mrs. Y have a close friendship that is much more than casual. Precisely because it is a meaningful part of their lives, ought they not to continue it? Why in the world shouldn't they go on?

The correct answer in both cases is that we should resume. Please don't compel me to flunk you . . .

I read this over and it seemed a little silly to send, but I am at a loss to find a chink in your armor. Write to me.

Brian

March 6

Lorna has written that you are in the hospital!

She gives no details, but from her tone I gather you have had a serious, a grave operation.

116   ·

Please let me know. Give Lorna your permission to tell me more, if you cannot write yourself.

I send you all my wishes, dear, dear friend. You know my concern.

Brian

March 10

Dear Brian:

I cannot let Lorna write for me what I must and want to write for myself.

First let me say I appreciate your good wishes and your concern. As you can see, I am able to use a pen, though a bit shakily still, so I am recovering apace.

The important thing to tell you is that I am ready now to accept many things that looked very different only weeks ago. I have lived through a considerable emergency, and a traumatic one. To make it short, I went to my doctor with certain symptoms with which you need not be bothered, and he spoke immediately of cancer and surgery that should not wait.

Let me add at once that, fortunately, they have reported to me that all the laboratory results are negative. My tumor, they find, was benign. (What a benign word that is.) So all I have to worry about is recovering from the operation, which, unfortunately, was complicated and will take time to get past. I feel pretty well by now, with severe pain only intermittently, but they want to keep me here for another week at least. (At these rates, I'm glad Arthur has every kind of insurance. I trust you do too.)

You can write to me here. You can write to me at home, for that matter. My dear, patient Brian, you can write to me any time and as often as you wish. It is I who made the waters murky. I suppose that was inevitable, since I am who I am, but there is nothing like a drastic surgical experience to change one's overview of life. I have certainly had some long thoughts here about the *quality* of the years I am told I still have in full measure. I have come to a Large Insight. In our circumstances, yours and mine, there is simply no relevance to "how much" we like each other. The simple answer to your exam is that we have been and are friends within the structures in which we both live. We have no thought of changing those structures, only to enrich them by knowing each other. So there is no sensible or legitimate reason at all why we should not, as you say, let it sing.

I am afraid this letter may ramble a bit because I've had pain pills this morning, but I do want to be talking to you again, dear Brian, even if a little slurry. Can you make out my handwriting? Hard to believe I once had a Spencerian hand. It is strange not to be typing. It is more personal and seems closer this way. Well, that is appropriate, it is the way I feel. I hope you can read my writing, though. Those pills have affected my fingers as well as my head.

I have learned one devil of a lot of things in these past days of pain, drugs, nurses, whispers, detachment, shadows, tears I could not control in endless nights. In my mind I have visited in caves of truth with Arthur, with Gary, with you. Caves of darkness and shadows, caves of light.

You were kind to keep writing despite my incivility. It has brought home to me how I have been taking all of my life for granted. The mock is on me for making fun of Arthur's lists. There is a final STOP sign at the end of my road as well as everyone else's. I have just had a good hard look at it in all its inevitability. Its skull and crossbones is suddenly very personal. From now on I am going to cherish every inch of the road that is left to my steps. And I hope and trust you will be one of those walking the road with me.

Yes, our anomalous situation created uncertainties, but it was not at all as impossible as I made it out to be. Let me say with no hemming and hawing—Did they give me Truth Pills this morning? —that your friendship has been more than precious. Cutting you off was like walking in a lovely garden with my eyes stupidly and stubbornly shut to the flowers. I agree totally with everything you have said about us in your last letters.

Oh, Brian, I am more of a trial to myself than to you . . .

I think Arthur has gained new perspective, too, but if he still finds it hard to accept that I wish a private relationship with you through our correspondence, that will be his problem, no longer mine. Sitting in this antiseptic room, it is crystal clear to me that I am running out of hours and accommodation. Certainly I have no more time to waste unwinding the shrouds in which other people would like to see me wrapped, for their own convenience. The truth—as crisp blue and fresh and penetrating as that good, arching sky through this window —is that I no longer give a tinker's damn what my husband (or Mother or anyone else) thinks when there is a trespass on my own space. (Note the contemporary language.)

The sky-blue truth is that my marriage is okay, but only that. It is still very much what I want, because I care for Arthur despite his lapses, and I like the comfort and security of our home and our position despite their lapses.

But, none of it is so wonderfully splendid that I will any longer pay the old prices to keep it going. They were exorbitant. That is the new lesson I have learned here beneath the surgeon's scalpels and the nurses' needles. I do want Arthur walking along with me, as I say, but I am no longer blind to the possibility that I can conceivably walk without him. That is strong medicine. Good for me.

I feel that Arthur senses and respects this new mood, this new awareness in me. I am very grateful to have him, you know. What a comfort it was to feel him beside me through every long hour of the anxious consultations, the postoperative mists, the endless cooling of one's heels waiting for lab reports, liver scans, and the rest of the medical arsenal. Waiting for those reports is much like being a defendant waiting for a judge's sentence, I suppose. I needed Arthur by my side all the way. I needed my husband in a way I did not and do not need you, Brian. That is important to say also. After 25 years of marriage there are ties between a woman and a man that simply do not exist otherwise, simply do not come into being.

At the same time, I can say that I need *you* in ways I do not need my husband! I think I could never have written that sentence if this cancer business had not intervened. I think I probably still could not write it if I were home at my desk instead of in this hospital chair.

I suspected that incorrigible fact from our very early letters. It frightened me. It was manageable as long as we were at our distance, but your looming visit was a real threat. I did not allow myself to recognize it, because that would be to acknowledge the unacceptable.

How could *I*, pillar of society, nearly 50, admit to myself, much less to you, that the letters of a young man were stirring fantasies of all sorts in me? Totally unacceptable fantasies! Impossible! Intolerable! Of course I denied them, every one. I put my hands to the serpent throats and choked them to silence and death before they could utter a first wisp and whimper of desire.

A woman like Margaret Fairfield Webb does not have such emotions or entertain such notions.

In the antiseptic truth of this room, let me ask you, Brian—when we discussed the hotel for your visit, *did* you have any thought that we might, you and I, be in love, might fall in love, make love, be lovers?

In this room, I can confess to you that it is possible for me to have thoughts it is not possible for me to think.

Oh, it comes hard for me to admit that to myself.

None of this speculation out of my pill-fogged head means I would have done anything, Brian! I am sure you know I still live within my rules. The operation has changed me to this extent, though: I recognize that my rules are not static or forever fixed. That is an exhilarating tonic, I tell you.

Ha!—promising myself a brave new world. Now who is turning cartwheels? Of course it remains to be seen what happens when I leave this truth-filled room and return to the routine of my life.

Still, my new mood, what I can only call self-determination, will last, I believe. I don't think I will again decoy myself into the placid flock. This is part of a deep experience I had a few nights ago, when I was terribly depressed. Gary was on my mind, how he has forgotten me like a pair of skates kicked behind the stairs. If I had died under the knife, he would not even know it! I hated my son for that. I wished cancer on his "Leader." It is a curse I do not take back! I was in bed, but I could see through the window, into the blackest night I have ever known. No moon, no stars, no reflection of city lights. The sky was no longer the earth's ceiling but rather the bleak bottom of the universe. Above that ponderous floor might rise golden pillars of hope and radiant heights of shining firmaments, but I was blacked out below, imprisoned in the dungeon of my illness and pain.

I was in despair, but suddenly, without any visible change in the blackness, I knew there was morning in the window. It was so faint there was not the slightest hint of light . . . it was almost as if the first dawn was a hum, a whisper in the ear. I must have dozed a minute or two. When I opened my eyes, light was racing over the world, shining like a beam through my window directly on my face. I found myself saying a prayer. It came to me in words I had never thought before. I spoke them aloud. I say them now every morning when I awake. I look across the East River, across the factory roofs, the tenements, and billboards and I speak to the new light:

"I am thankful for a new day." (I mean it with my heart and soul.)

"I am thankful to be in less pain." (I mean that with every cell in my bandaged body.)

"I will use this day as well as I can." (For only now do I know how precious are the days we have.)

Those prayers are no Sunday mumbo jumbo. They are prayers to say beneath your redwood columns, aren't they?

And they give me the only answer satisfactory to the question everyone needs to ask, and which is suddenly not sophomoric when demanded from an operating table: What is the meaning and purpose of life? For the first time I have the answer, and how good to share it with you . . .

The answer is simple: *"I am thankful for a new day."*

I intend to keep remembering that when the bandages are off and it becomes easy to forget, as is bound to happen.

Brian, I want you to know I did not overlook that enchanting thing you said about "playing me" on your piano and finding me a waltz. It is an especially happy thought in a sickbed, and I thank you sincerely if belatedly.

I am exhausted now, and anyway here comes Arthur along with the nurse bringing our lunches. Arthur joins me for lunch every day, no matter how busy he is at the office. It is so good to be talking to you again, dear friend, especially since I can now openly give this letter to Arthur to mail for me!

Yours,

Maggie again, and glad of it

March 14

Maggie, my dear:

Let me echo your last letter—good to be talking to you again! And to be calling you Maggie again! Welcome and welcome back.

Lorna was nervous that you might be angry with her for informing me you were in the hospital. Please reassure her.

I am sorry it took a nasty crisis to bring you back, but I am grateful, especially since you indicate that the prognosis is good. I assume you are telling the truth. That is a very strange thing about cancer. Not only is it usually spoken of in whispers, but there often seems to be a conspiracy among doctors, relatives, and the patients themselves to fog the situation. I know that isn't your character.

I will keep this letter on the short side because I don't want to tire you. Please don't try to answer unless you are up to it. I know how debilitating an operation can be, and hospitals are no fun, for sure. When I was laid up with my broken leg, I couldn't believe some of the things that happened in the name of "hospital care." Just as a sleeping pill would start to work, an attendant would be sure to barge in "to change the water in my pitcher" or some such nonsense. Door slammed open, a heavy tromping about, a whacking of the pitcher and clang of cover, door banging shut, and my bleary-eyed curses trailing uselessly after someone who didn't understand the language and who couldn't care less if he or she did.

I hope your "patient care" is more considerate. I wrote a considered protest to The Director on the card inviting patient comment. I wonder where those missives wind up.

Sometimes I think even doctors and nurses forget how brutal surgery is. Brutal is the word. The body doesn't know the purpose of the cutting. To our cells and our flesh, there is no difference between the assault of an ax and the stab of a scalpel.

Hold everything!

I had to jump outside again. Paul and Joan have been trying to throw a Frisbee Kay brought home. They decided the road is better than the play area. There has just been one helluva honking and squealing of brakes, along with a near heart attack when I looked out. Now both kids are upstairs crying and rubbing their behinds where I whacked them. (I agree with Gary about the back of the hand, and the latest "scientific" research backs up both up: "Some discipline spanking is good for the children and their growth.") But we parents can't win, as you have observed in other connections. To the children, I am not a good-guy Lifesaver but a bad-guy Big Goon who spoiled their fun. They are howling and moaning not because of their pain (I tapped them only gently), but protesting the injustice, indignity, and outrage of my power over them.

So have I just poured fuel into their tanks, to explode later in their lives as rebellion and discontent? Could be. Could also be they know inwardly that I discipline them out of love. I can only hope that will count more in the end than the pure hatred they undoubtedly feel toward me at present.

But I should not be inflicting this on you. Kay will be home this afternoon, and I will get on with my work.

All my wishes are with you, Maggie.

Brian

March 17

Dear Brian:

Yes, it's good to be writing back and forth again. I did miss it, too.

My strength comes and goes. It's on the wane today, I'm afraid, but I wanted to answer you, and want you to know, also, how pleased I am that you and Lorna are having your own correspondence. I have told Lorna I am glad she wrote to you about my illness. Especially with Gary still gone, Lorna has been like my own child to me through this difficult time.

Is there a geometry of friendship? If A likes B, and A likes C, then B and C should like each other! Q.E.D.?

Writing to you this way makes me smile. It occurs to me that I haven't smiled in too long. Lately, of course, it's been my discomfort here in the hospital.

Isn't pain a strange phenomenon? I felt it in a curious and unexpected fashion after the anesthesia wore off. My pain was an actual physical entity. It seemed to be sitting off on my left shoulder in the form of, of all things, a great goldfish bowl. The large bowl held a school of pretty, tiny fish motionless in clear water. As feeling returned to my body, the fish began to swim about, gradually faster, turning more and more swiftly until the water was green and roiling, and that was the Pain, mounting and whirlpooling and pulling me down to drown. I literally could not breathe. Somehow I knew I had to quiet the *fish*. I tried to call to Arthur across the room where he was reading, wanted him to take the bowl away. I couldn't get a sound out. Just then the nurse came with a needle. In minutes the fish were quiet, the water changed from murky green to yellow to clear, and I could breathe. Ah, the drowsiness and warmth of flesh seduced by drugs.

But, Brian, agony though pain is, the remarkable thing about it is that one does not, cannot, remember it later. Oh, one remembers having had the pain, but not the physical feeling itself. Interesting. But then, can we remember, say, a good taste? Or happiness? We can recall happy times, but cannot feel the emotion itself, can we? Am I wrong? Is there anything in your literature on this? Is it why life is set up as a *repeating* of experiences?

Have you ever taken drugs? I mean the heavy stuff. At first I welcomed the needles and the pills, but then found I very much disliked what they did to me. I don't take to being out of control (no surprise to you). My head floated off my body, my body itself felt, not asleep, but numb, with a sort of buzzing sensation mildly floating around inside. I seemed to be hovering outside my body, disengaged, in a twilight of gray nothingness, a disturbing deliquescence. After the first easing, it became dismal and frightening to me, especially the flabby, loose sense of slipping into a sphere where nothing matters. I suppose that is the mind-blowing and blissing-out the drug users seek, but I found it an apathetic, unpleasant state.

There was one amusing incident when I refused a shot. The nurse couldn't believe it, and insisted in any case that it was "in the order book," that Hospital Gospel. I had to argue that I had final authority over my body despite her bible. I could see she was terribly distressed, but I was proud that, although I was hardly at my best, I did refuse to be cowed. Good omen for the future.

The poor, helpful nurse could not understand me at all. "Everyone else *begs* for it," she grumbled suspiciously as she went out. As the door closed behind her, I was punished for my heroism by a surge of searing pain that reduced me to anguish and tears, but I'd be damned if I'd call the lady back.

Now I see drugs in a new light. For people to want that half-death must be a terrible admission of failure. It seems to me worse than suicide. Suicide puts the light out once and for all. Drugs leave dim bulbs that cast only shadows of self-defeat.

It occurs to me that the "bliss" is as false as it is short-lived, because I think no drug is strong enough to overcome the addict's inner knowledge of his forfeiture of life.

That's why something in me resisted the down-pull of the needles they were giving me. Though I obviously welcomed the relief, each shot brought a sharp image of my mother lying senseless after her stroke. Who can want that kind of surcease, no matter what the pressures and unhappiness of one's life?

I don't think I ever told you how shaken Arthur was by my mother's stroke. He sat and stared at her, and I could hear his mind clicking with his own foreboding. I have never seen his face so drawn, his eyes so full of sympathy. It was as if he was taking to himself the pain Mother was beyond feeling. Later he observed that the worst thing was being cut off from speech, from communication. Yes. I agree. Horrible to need to speak and to be paralyzed. It must be like being buried alive!

Arthur, bless him, has come up with a very wise idea. He and I have a pact that if we are ever stricken, we are to try *Morse code.* Usually, there is *something* one can move—a finger, an eyelid. A code card could make all the difference, couldn't it? Yet I have never heard of this simple recommendation. Have you?

I pray of course that none of any of us ever has to use it . . .

You see how lugubriously my mind shuffles if I let it go. Actually, I am quite cheerful. *Non carborundum illegitimi*—is that correct? Gary once brought home a souvenir printed on sandpaper with something like that. "Don't let the bastards get you down!" So be it.

Having read over the above, I dozed off. It may have been the medicines, but my mind wandered pleasantly into an old pastime of mine that may amuse you. It started with the little fish in my pain bowl. They were swimming quietly, now in a huge tank, and formed into a school of thousands. "School." They were all carrying little notebooks in their mouths as I dreamed them gliding to a classroom.

The connection unlatched some old forgotten oddities I used to collect when I browsed the Oxford Dictionary as a graduate student.

Schools of fish, yes, like children running together. Easy. Then a "nye" of pheasants—nye=nyde=nest=brood. Makes sense. And a skulk of foxes is clear, the foxes run to hide. A skein of ducks or geese was less immediate to my mind. Does their flight pattern suggest the shape of a skein? I don't rightly recall what the Oxford said.

But a puzzler to me: A mute of hounds. Dogs are noisy, especially on the hunt, aren't they? But perhaps in England they hunted silently. The dictionary covers both possibilities. Quiet, as with well-trained animals, or violent, as suggested by the word "mutiny."

One I'm not sure of is a "cete" of badgers. Cete is whales, isn't it? Oh, those pills! I must rest now.

Dot-dot-dot-dot/Dot-dot!
Maggie

March 27

Dear Maggie:

You haven't heard from me for a while for several reasons. Most important, I have been afraid of burdening you. I am sure this is a time you should be resting as fully as possible, both mentally and physically.

Also, I have not been at home. The powers-that-be at UCLA called me down to Los Angeles for extensive meetings to discuss the first draft of my proposals. They seem to admire my ideas. At the risk of displeasing the gods, I'll say the prospects for the appointment seem excellent. Unfortunately, some of the decision makers are away, and it will be a couple of months before they can untangle their red tape. I have my own cooling of heels to do, but I wanted you to know it does seem promising because I know your interest. (What's a fan club for if not to cheer at even the half-promise of hopeful news?)

Did my flowers ever come? I had to leave for Los Angeles in a rush, and I asked Kay to take care of arranging that. She tells me she did, but with Kay these days I can never be sure of anything.

Incidentally, you may be as surprised as I am that I was able to translate your "dot-dot-dot-dot/dot-dot." It's amazing how our brains retain what we learn as small kids. When my father went to the railroad job, he brought home an old telegraph transmitter. I became an ardent operator, real buff. Hooked up to nowhere, of course. Oh, the messages I click-clacked into empty air—times I was mad, times I was happy, times I was mixed up, times I warned of lurking bandits or attacking Indians. Nowadays scientists are broadcasting the story of mankind through the galaxies, scanning space everywhere for other planetary intelligence. I hope my pitiable signals still floating somewhere—signed "Brian Curtiss, Montana,

U.S.A., Western Hemisphere, Galaxy of the Sun and Milky Way, The Universe"—don't confuse the majestic effort.

Imagine a creature on some far planet picking up my transmissions and wondering what a Brian Curtiss might conceivably be. (Don't we all?)

Seriously, Arthur's idea is splendid, and important. It is so obvious, I would think it must be in use, but like you, I haven't heard of it before. The obvious is often the thing most widely overlooked.

Well, you signed off, "Hi," but I will be professional as befits an old-time operator . . .

Dot-dash-dot-dash-dot!

Brian

P.S. *Re* "cete." In obsolete form it meant an assembly, a gathering, so your "cete of badgers" would make sense, yes.

April 5

Dear Brian:

Yes, your flowers did come, and beautiful ones. Thank you for thinking of flowers, and please thank Kay for me for signing the card "From Brian and Kay Curtiss." I was moved by that. It seemed a thoughtful and very amiable way of saying we are all indeed friends who, if we lived nearby, would be in and out of each other's places in a most pleasant fashion. Too, it was a kind of meeting Kay, which I would truly like.

I would have acknowledged your kindness and Kay's sooner than this, but I had some sort of relapse and have been *hors de combat* again. Nor did I wish Lorna to write, because there was no point in worrying you. As you see, I am once more on the mend, and this time the doctors say there should be no more complications.

I suppose I am finding I am different from other people in many ways. I've told you about my aversion to drugs. I also have an aversion to talking about "my operation." I know with what relish people ordinarily describe the most ghastly details, but I prefer to forget the whole damnable business, put it all behind me as rapidly as possible.

The best medicine is news like yours, even if it is only half-news still. I am confident the UCLA powers will recognize your merit, Brian, though I know how impatient you must be. From my new peaks of wisdom, *I* now recommend perspective. Whatever happens with UCLA, you will after all be going on with your teaching and writing. Only remember what I have newly learned—the old wives' admonition that our health is the most important thing we own.

Things we own . . .

When I came home from the hospital two days ago, I looked at everything in my apartment with new eyes, room by room. I was comforted to be among all the things that have surrounded my life, but I see them differently since my brush with mortality. I am filled with new contradictions. On the one hand, I love my home, and want to hold on to whatever Arthur and I have. On the other hand, there is the unsettling realization that nobody really owns anything.

Suddenly I have a new envy of people who have grandchildren. It's not just a question of love, it's a matter of continuity. The things Arthur and I have accumulated through the years—I would like to see them go on to family, not be dispersed. I can visualize dealers coming through these rooms offering this amount and that (probably ridiculously low). I'm not being crass. I truly have very little concern about the money part. But now I know why I have always shivered inside a little at the auction ads in the papers saying "sold by order of the estate of XYZ . . ." and turned the page quickly. Because it's not a sale of belongings, it's the markdown of a life. In a sense the dispersal is another kind of burial, saying as loudly as the uncaring cemetery, "So what?"

Do you have a will, Brian? It is terribly important, especially since Kay's competence, like Gary's, may be something to think about twice. I don't mean to sound lawyerish, but Arthur is right. Gary is not to have full control (if he ever shows up again). Arthur has arranged for a trust. You may want to talk to your attorney. I hope you won't think this advice presumptuous. (Avuncular advice. What is the feminine form of "avuncular"? Did you read the news story of the town that changed its ordinances to call manholes "person-holes"? So absurd they had to change it back!)

I said I am full of contradictions. At the same moment as I am so preoccupied with the future of our books and jewelry and paintings and savings and sofas and Oriental rugs and silver candlesticks and Eskimo figures, I have an intense desire to be free of most of it.

Today I understand people who say that "things" seem to be

possessing them rather than the other way around. Perhaps we accumulate in the first place (aside from necessities) because we *want* to be tethered. For one thing, we make an immediate statement about ourselves by what we choose, don't we? I know a great deal about you if, entering your home for the first time, I find, say, a Maxfield Parrish on your wall rather than a Picasso—or both! The trouble is that eventually we become captives of the statement, as we often assume the style of the clothes we wear or the accent of a country we travel in. A kind of holistic Gestalt? Here is what I am driving at: Since furniture, paintings, et al., are difficult to change once they are in place, maybe that is why it is hard for people to change. Do you think I have a point? Might that make a doctoral subject?

Lately I find myself having a recurring dream. It started in the hospital, when I had the second surgery. I am in a very large, dome-ceilinged chamber, all white, floors as well as walls, and it is empty. Nobody is present, but I hear a pleasant voice, like a nurse perhaps, saying I can furnish the room any way I like. All I have to do is snap my fingers and say, "I want ————." I think it is a lovely game and begin to think of every kind of lavish luxury, but when I finally snap my hand, I find that what I have conjured as my deepest wish is a small white narrow bed, one white chair at a small white table, one small pepper plant(!), the kind that looks like little multicolored Christmas lights, and nothing else at all.

Am I telling myself I want a sweeping, sweeping change in my life? Am I telling myself that I own not possessions but clutter?

Perhaps the answer lies outside the small window I become aware of in the dream room. It is the only one, and it is high up on the wall, near the dome of the ceiling. I look around for a way to climb up and look out, to see where I am, what the landscape is like. But there is only the small chair and the table, far short of what I require. I snap my fingers and command a ladder, but the voice comes instead, telling me I have used up the power, I must make do with what I have, nothing more. So I resign myself to the fact that I can never see the outside world again. But I am curiously content in the white chamber. I find myself repeating to myself that White contains every color there is, therefore I am in the midst of the greatest possible variety and have only to imagine different shades as my changing moods may enjoy. In the same way, I can imagine any paintings on the wall I wish.

And suddenly I recognize that the voice was Clarissa's! I don't want that! I cry out and throw myself against the door. But it will not open, and I wake up pounding on my bed with Arthur trying to hold me, with a look of terror on his face. Should I have told you this, Brian?

What do you dream?

Today I read in Edith Wharton, "One would rather be the fire that tempers a sword than the fish that dyes a purple cloak." I agree. The need for meaning sneaks in the back door after all.

I looked up your dot-dash-dot-dash-dot . . .

"Finish,"
Maggie

P.S. Thank you for "cete." What about a muster of peacocks? I like that.

April 12

Dear Maggie:

Here is a picture of Kay and the children, per your request some time ago. You can't imagine how hard it is to get three fidgets like these to stand still long enough for a camera click, with even the fastest film. Well, here you have my family. I think they are quite a handsome set, don't you? Kay actually got out of chinos and into a dress—she wanted you to know she can be quite the proper wife of a proper college professor when she wants to be. Frankly, I had forgotten how nice she can look when she isn't guru-ing.

Both your letter and taking the picture turned my mind to thoughts of a will. The absurd truth is that I have simply not yet thought in terms of not being here to take care of my family. I won't fall into a trap and say it's because I am "young," but I must confess to some irresponsibility. You make me realize, too, that I have ducked the question of Kay's immaturity. I do carry considerable insurance and it should have occurred to me that Kay might not use the proceeds as wisely as might be. I would object more than mildly to any part of my hard-earned money going to some messianic bunko. You, Maggie, can be my lawyer any day. Something of

Arthur has rubbed off on you by osmosis. It sits well, and I am grateful for your interest.

I am mulling over what you said about possessions. Kay and I don't have enough stuff to worry about, but I do know and sympathize with what you are saying about grandchildren. The old clan structures of society were far better than ours in providing continuity, and with it the meaning and purpose you talk about. Even if an individual did not have offspring, a meaningful future was visible all around in the children of kin. There was also a kind of infrastructure of community rituals that celebrated the ongoingness of the group. The riches of a lifetime were not thrown to the winds, thus mocking the accumulation, as you observe. They were cherished and carried on, affirming the existence and enhancing the importance of the person to whom they had belonged. Yes, your thinking on this cuts to deep human bone.

As in everything, there was a price to pay in the clan. The individual was bound in a web of relationships always constricting, sometimes suffocating. People today are largely free. Is the advance progress? That's another dissertation.

I hope your recovery is now proceeding with no more setbacks. I have continued to be worried, not sure that either you or Lorna has been giving me the whole story. I have no choice but to believe you both, and Lorna says you are really coming along encouragingly. Good.

The children are thriving. Ditto a new article I am preparing. The subject is another aspect of my (our) preoccupation with modern youth and the subculture of these times. I am exploring how the "rites of passage" in adolescence have become "The Rights of Passage."

It is easier for me to make progress because Kay is staying home these days. She doesn't talk much about her San Francisco group any more. Maybe it's because some tatami mats they sold her turned out to have fleas. We've been picking fleas off everything, including ourselves, for a week. I hope it's the worst thing Kay brings home from her "pilgrimages," as she now calls her absences.

Obviously, I am struck by the parallel between Kay and Gary, although their Pied Pipers are very different. Kay's is not religious in any way. It is part of today's self-realization craze. I attended one "guest seminar" and was turned off by the irrationality of their puerile psychobabble. Their Great Revelation, believe it or not, is that we each have a Mystery within us! The leader is a "Realizer" who helps people Fulfill Themselves through "Penetration," in a method that forbids all speech as Unreal, and uses only body movement, chanting, screaming, and a form of karate. It seems borrowed, simplistic, and phony to me. I am unhappy that Kay is shallow enough to have been taken in. But these groups exert a powerful magnetism these days, without question. They victimize even seemingly intelligent people. Kay and Gary are among thousands of credulous ones who seem to be suckers for the wild promises of Personal Bliss. (Compare Barnum's, "This Way to the Egress.")

As a sociologist, I note for the record that I am *not* including such movements as transcendental meditation, which seem to me legitimate in purpose and content. Unhappily, Kay has been attracted to an irresponsible bunch. But they seem more zany than zealous. I am pleased that she did follow through on the flowers for you and that you liked them. Maybe if Kay had someone like you as an image of a mature woman, she would grow up faster. Funny part is that she seemed mature when I married her but seems to be regressing since. Her philosophy is to "hang loose" and everything will get done somehow. Damned if it doesn't work some of the time, but it doesn't make for confidence.

Glad to be sharing this way again.

I have nothing to top your muster of peacocks.

How about a picture of Arthur? And Gary? (I've asked Lorna for one, too, so we'll have a complete East-West collection.)

Brian

April 24

Brian dear:

The picture brings back what you said about California and children. My goodness, what beautiful, bursting joys your Paul and Joanie are! Their energy shoots right out of the photo. I can hear them laughing and shouting at their games. It brings Gary back at that age, though he was paler and thinner than yours.

And isn't Kay a delight? Once again you have fooled my imagination beyond all my imagining. I don't quite know what I did think Kay looked like, but certainly it wasn't this lovely ballet dancer, a slim princess with eyes like a fawn. She looks as if a wind could lift her away, not for weakness but because she seems almost able to fly. Is she a splendid dancer? I love her face, pert as Joanie's, but held like a queen's. She is something out of one of those old romantic movies—the fragile, seeking girl who meets a handsome man in Rome. But I know from what you have written that Kay is anything but fragile, and I can see her mind of her own in the firm set of her chin and the strong grip of her hands on the children's shoulders. What a thoroughly handsome pair the two of you make!

Interestingly, Brian, with this picture of your wife and children in my hand *you* are suddenly more real to me—more real than the man your single picture brought to me. Now I feel I know the people around you, and that adds a light that brings you forward, and closer to me.

I find it strange. I might have thought that seeing Kay would have stirred up my old misgivings. On the contrary, I now feel our friendship to be more solid than it ever was. Now I am something of a friend of the whole family. It is a firm, warm, and most pleasant feeling.

Thank you for being patient with my slowness in writing. I know my ping-pong ball has slowed way down, but I will increase the pace now that I am very much recovered. I feel almost all my old energy. In fact, Arthur is talking to my doctor today about taking me off on a cruise.

I am partial to the idea and hope the doctor doesn't disapprove. At the same time, the prospect of traveling again has brought on contrarily, something of a gray mood. You once wrote, and I thought it was most engaging, about rye and bourbon and the Whisky Divide. I perceive another Divide now. When a person is young and traveling, you are in the "hello" years—you head for scenes *you will return to enjoy* another day. But then one is in the "good-bye" years, when the prospect is a farewell to places that will never see your face again. It saddens me.

Arthur has in mind a trip we dreamed about often. If we go, we will fly to Athens and take a ship at Piraeus, magic name. I've yearned to walk places like Knossos, where Egypt, Greece, Rome, and other ancient civilizations came together. If I had my life to live over, I think I would be an archaeologist.

I have to ask myself whether that's because of a genuine interest, or only an acceptable cover for deflecting today's problems. Like Gary's . . .

We still have had no word from him, but my mother phoned last night to say *she* had a postcard! It was mailed from Toronto, but that only means Gary could be in Mexico, using a courier to throw us off the track. That was Arthur's view, and I quite agree.

It ignited the old conflict between us, though. Arthur remains adamant in saying that Gary is dead to him. When he hears me crying at night (I still can't help it sometimes), he grows angry, and scolds, "You cannot keep going to the cemetery every day!" My head knows he is right. My heart reproaches him, reminds me again that Gary is not buried.

Life is idiotic. Here are Arthur and I closer than we've ever been, since my illness. And here are our differences over Gary separating us once more.

For myself, I am happy that, whatever Gary is into, there is now enough reality in him to write a postcard. Though sent to my mother, I take it as an indirect message home. Might this be the time for action? If you think so, I would of course postpone any notion of a vacation away. Please let me know.

Maggie

P.S. Last Sunday, which was Easter again, I was remembering your early letter "under the redwoods." I had a fine image of you lolling in that hammock you described. It is hard to believe we have been writing for more than a year. I am happier about us with every letter now. Thank you again for the family picture.

April 30

Dear Maggie:

Big rush here, so this must be brief. I'm polishing the final exams for my classes and am called to Los Angeles again. They wouldn't be yanking me on this kind of yo-yo if they weren't in some earnest. The "powers" are in residence, so a final decision may be close.

About Gary—Maggie, not a week has gone by without my thinking about him. I have talked again with colleagues about the passages you sent, and we are quite sure that we recognize the language. Presumably, the strongest clue is in the incitement to hate parents. Not many groups take that specific line. The cult where it is most prominent is a "Fellowship" described in the literature I have enclosed.

This fellowship became well publicized when, quite dramatically, a respected, by-lined reporter for a major newspaper openly proclaimed his membership and specifically endorsed their credo of "Parents Are the Devil." It was arresting, appalling, and depressing.

There are two reasons I still recommend waiting, at least a little longer, hard as it may seem, Maggie. First, you need time to win Arthur's cooperation. If there's going to be an investigation, he will know better than any of us how to proceed. Second, I tend to think Gary's postcard is less a call for you than an announcement that he may be ready to come out on his own.

My advice is to go off on your well-deserved cruise with Arthur. If Gary gives no new signals within a month or two, that will be plenty of time to move. If you wish to start at once, though, I will do everything I can to help.

Kay is calling me from the car to take me to the airport for my L.A. flight. Ha! When *I* hang loose she worries I'll miss my plane!

Glad you're better,
Brian

May 4

Dear Brian:

One thing I've always admired is the way Arthur takes a decision by the horns without a lot of donkeying between bales of hay. My doctor said okay, so Arthur got the tickets, and we're off on Saturday!

What you said about waiting on Gary makes sense, for both the reasons you stated.

I may drop you a card en route, but mostly I'll save my impressions for when I get back. Perhaps by then you will know about your UCLA job. That would be a fabulous welcome home.

No point in your trying to reach me as we go, so *ciao* for a while.

Suitcase-surrounded,
Maggie

May 24

Yia son yah, Brian!

Pos eese?

That's Greek, respectively, for hello and how are you? I do not vouch for my spelling of the phonetics, especially since my own pronunciation is hysterical, as any Greek will tell you if he can stop laughing long enough.

We got home last night. I am pleasantly exhausted after a wonderful two weeks, a bumpy flight back, jet lag, and endless unpacking. But I wanted to write to you first chance, mostly to tell you how very much better things are between Arthur and me.

Sailing on the Mediterranean relaxed us both and seemed to loosen us up. The feeling of centuries of history all around made it easier to discuss our own headaches. I talked about you, more openly than ever. Arthur talked of Gary, more openly than ever. I told Arthur your thoughts about the Fellowship, and for the first time Arthur stopped his horrible notion about Gary being cast out. You can imagine how happy that has made me.

Now we will take a few days at home to plow through everything that has accumulated during our absence, and then we will see what we want to do about Gary.

I have leafed through my mail quickly hoping for a letter from you about UCLA. Let me know the minute you hear, *se parakalo* (that's "please."). *Efcharisto.* ("Thank you.")

I love the sound of Greek, at least as Greeks speak it. It's liquid and crisp somehow at the same time, much like the people we met, warm and friendly, yet strong and even spiny (hubris?) on occasion.

I find languages so difficult. In traveling I've learned the hard way not to give the impression that I speak anything but English. The first time Arthur and I came to Paris years ago, I used my Radcliffe French to ask for our hotel reservation. My accent at that moment was somehow marvelously inspired, and back came a torrent of

136 ·

French from the concierge. Of course I comprehended not one word.

"Lentement, lentement, s'il vous plait," I begged. The man responded in perfect English of course. I tried to save some face, *"Je dit un peu, un petit peu, de l'école,"* probably as incorrect as it was inane. How I envy people with an ear, like Lorna. Last year she visited Mexico and came back with fantastic Spanish after just a small go at the books on her own.

In Greece I had trouble with an important phrase, *pou eene to apohorotirio,* something like that, and it wasn't funny what with my suffering from the "Sightseers Suddens" as Arthur calls it. I could never pronounce the sentence correctly and was variously directed to a fire station, a watch repair store, and a pet shop instead of the facility I required. Do you know some Greek scholar who can tell me if I'm right in getting "apparatus" from *apohorotirio?* Have I been asking, "Where is the apparatus?" At home now I find myself saying to Arthur, "Excuse me, *se parakalo,* I am going to the apparatus . . ."

It just occurs to me that you will turn out to be a Greek scholar yourself. If so, *kalo!* (good!) and *signomi* (pardon me).

There is one experience I must share with you at once. We hired a car and driver for a trip around the Peloponnese, and before leaving Athens, we asked to stop at the site of Plato's Academy. Our chauffeur-guide was a most cultured man, but he turned to us with surprise. No one had ever requested that before, and it was clear that he had only a general notion of the location. We drove in and out of the most unlikely neighborhoods. No one could give us directions. Finally a policeman nodded and, with broad smiles of comprehension and approval, pointed the way. We soon arrived at Plato's Grocery Store.

Eventually we came to the place. It was attested by a small sign on a cyclone fence surrounding a singularly bare lot with some litter of beer cans. To one side there was a dingy shed with a green plastic roof over what seemed some shallow digging. This is the hallowed ground where so much of Western spirit and thought was birthed. It prompted me to think there is what might be called vandalism-by-omission. Pathetic. Saddening. All too symbolic.

Perhaps the Greek government has plans for some memorial but as of now, *andio,* Plato.

The Peloponnese was another wonderful story entirely. And Crete and Rhodes, and more! I am too tired to write about them now. My batteries are recharged, but energy still drains away without warning sometimes. I will write again soon.

Andio, Brian
Maggie

June 4

Welcome Home!

No, I don't have Greek, but you are a delightful teacher. I have news. Double news, as it happens.

You are now addressing Herr Associate Professor of Sociology of UCLA. It is gratifying, and a significant responsibility that I promise to discharge creditably.

What I had not been expecting has also happened. Kay has left me. Her "Realizer" and his sycophants ("Realizees"?) are inaugurating a newspaper to carry The Message nationally, and they will all be moving to Boulder, Colorado to publish from there. Fleas in the tatami notwithstanding, Kay is going along.

In honesty, Kay has tried to be fair. She offered to stay if I felt I couldn't manage the children, especially with the move to Los Angeles looming. Her offer was genuine, but I could see only disaster in it for all of us. Kay has a hard, if selfish, wisdom of her own. She is not wrong when she says she is too young to be "enslaved" by marriage. She *is* that young, unfortunately, and I am to blame for not recognizing it in time. What use can it be to rebuke her, remind her of vows, press her to stay? It would do Paul and Joan more harm than good, since Kay is driven from within to go, whatever her reasons.

Mother love? If there is such a thing, self-centered women like Kay manage to rationalize it. The party line now is: Women are better for their children if they do not allow marriage to dry them out as individuals. Well, maybe so, but I can't follow that all the way to Colorado. And certainly the Kays have never remotely entertained any notion like Kant's—that a mother should care for her children not out of a love that gives her pleasure but out of the duty that arises out of the moral imperative.

Of course the Kays have no moral imperative beyond their own impulses and satisfactions, and when I fell in love with my Kay, I neglected to inquire whether she had been reading Kant. One of the things that drew me to her was precisely the dissimilarity of our interests. She took me out of the library stacks to her discos. I needed the change then. I regret she doesn't recognize that the dancing has to end after a while. Now I almost pity Kay for missing the joy the children bring me.

The mechanics here will be tricky, even nasty, I suppose. But, as some people say, water is wet, rocks are hard, fire is hot—and Kay must leave. I can't change any of that. I will work out the family logistics somehow.

It seems strange to be summing up six years of marriage in a dozen lines or so, but the truth is there isn't very much more to add about Kay and me, and I suppose that is its own gloss and comment.

At the same time, I am giving myself the same counsel I gave you about Gary. No burning of bridges. Whether I will ever want Kay back if she should decide to return, that is something else. I need to think of Joan and Paul as well as myself.

Maggie, you once wrote that you were glad to have me at the other end of a mailbox. Let me say, dear friend, that being able to write to you today is a consolation to me. There is no one else with whom I want to discuss Kay, not even Hildie and Joe, just as you did not want to open up your Gary pain to others. Despite the distance, we are special to each other, you and I, and I am grateful.

Now it is my boat that's rocking. But I promise you it won't capsize. There is too much good and important sailing ahead on my brand new charts!

It occurs to me that you may wonder whether our friendship had a bearing on Kay's decision. Absolutely not. For one thing, Kay has been so engrossed in probing her Lofty Mystery that I doubt she has noticed our correspondence more than casually, if that. She accepted it from the beginning without any question, as I told you then. Incidentally, how is Lorna? She hasn't written lately, which I assume is a matter of her exams. Please give her the news of my UCLA appointment but not, I think, about Kay. As you might expect, I write to Lorna on a much less intimate basis than is true of you and me.

More later, and love to you now . . .

Brian

June 8

Brian:

Your news of the appointment is wonderful. Your news of Kay is disagreeable and upsetting. Despite your assurances, I know this could not have happened at a worse time for you, and I can't imagine how you plan to manage with the children by yourself. That only makes me feel the more culpable, for I am convinced our friendship inevitably had something to do with Kay's decision, whether consciously or unconsciously. I find myself wishing we lived closer, I would come by to help you with the children.

I admire your generous understanding of Kay, but isn't there such a thing as too much sufferance? You will recall my severe doubts about my having been too compliant with Gary. To accept everyone's hang-ups—is it maturity or is it surrender? In the case of your wife, doesn't she realize the burden she is placing on your shoulders just when you should be most free? You and I have seemed to agree on most things, but I disagree violently on this. Kay's place is with her husband and her children, "Self-realization" be damned!

I don't know what good this letter will do except upset you further with my own peevishness. I suppose I am so put out because I see another rat thumbing its nose at decency, coming out of the tacky, garbage-dump world you and I have deplored from the beginning.

I say it is not "old-fashioned" to insist that people should honor their commitments. Not old-fashioned of me to *despise* Kay and her ilk who run off to their self-indulgence without regard to the hurt they leave behind. You and I are not that kind of people. We understand all too well that there are times when one must simply deny one's self in the name of decency.

I had thought to write about my Greek trip, but with everything you have on your mind, the last thing you need from me right now is a visit with home movies.

> Your (frankly bitter) friend,
> Maggie

June 11

Maggie dear:

Thank you for your anger.

I might have vented some of my own steam if I had allowed myself to break dishes and slam walls, as I did feel like doing when Kay split. You may be right that my understanding is not strength but a form of weakness. I don't know, and that's the truth. One day, Kay may realize what she has forfeited, and she will punish herself. But what's in that for me? What good does it do to be vindictive? I can't change Kay, any more than I can erase the miles between you and me. The wise man accepts what he cannot change, as you've heard before, I'm sure.

Writing my letter to you helped me. Afterward, I felt loosened up enough to phone Joe and Hildie. Hildie couldn't wait to get off the phone to pack and come right on up to us. I didn't have it in mind at all, but I should have known that woman. An army couldn't hold her back, knowing the children and I are in need of a hand. I have no idea how we will work things out, but at least I will have another pair of shoulders for a while, Paul and Joan adore Hildie, so her being here will help them accept my feeble explanation that their mother had to go away on some personal business.

(And thank *you* for your offer to come over if you lived around here! I know you mean it, and you may be sure I would gladly accept.)

Joe and Hildie reacted much as you did about Kay. The word "separation" still carries a heavy charge. I confess that surprises me a little. After all, as a social scientist I can compile a thousand pages of footnotes citing studies of the contemporary acceptance of separation and divorce in our society. Hell, it has become an axiom of psychology, sociology, and magazinology that "incompatible" people should not stay together for a moment longer than necessary, even (or especially) where there are children.

Yet you were shocked and infuriated, and Hildie and Joe were "flabbergasted," as Joe put it.

Maybe my reaction should be different, but I accept my share of responsibility for what has taken place. Not that I did anything "wrong," but simply that I was or have become a personality Kay discovered she didn't want to share her life with as much as she wants to share it elsewhere. Maybe Kay came to dislike the color of my eyes, the sound of my voice, the way I walk, the prospect of moving to Los Angeles, the way I cough in the morning, the way we made love.

Of course my ego is wounded. One question is very hard to allow into my head: Do I really feel very much for Kay one way or another? Do I "love" her? If I still "loved" her, could I be feeling so little real ache at her going? I had more sense of loss when your letters stopped coming. That is a confession to you alone.

I need to keep out of the stereotype traps that surround this situation like bunkers around a golf green. "Young wife leaves, young husband grieves?" Not necessarily so, I am finding in my moments of clarity. None of the questions Kay has raised in me has an easy answer at this point. They all press hidden buttons and open secret panels and trapdoors in my head. Last night, in bed alone, it seemed to me there was a spiral staircase around my spine waiting for me to climb it to my most secret brain. But I am not ready to explore.

You asked if I dream. With a mind that creates a spiral staircase up my spine, what do I need to dream for? I am glad you told me about your white chamber, though. If you dream it again, snap me into it with you if you can.

Write to me. I do need you considerably right now.

Brian

June 12

Dear Maggie:

You will probably receive this letter at the same time as my previous one. I am writing at once because you will want to know that the situation here is looking up!

First, there is Aunt Hildie, who has taken over, with my sincere blessing and gratitude. Of course, she has her own family and can't stay, but we had a brainstorm when we talked together last night. Why didn't I phone my sister, Frances, and see whether she might not like to come out here? For a year or so now, Frances has been commuting to Chicago taking art classes. Hildie suggested she could study as well in Los Angeles and live with me. She wouldn't need a job, other than being my housekeeper in effect, and she could go to school at night.

Well, Frances loved the idea, and I danced the room around with Hildie! It turns out Frances has wanted to come West. She has nothing to hold her where she is. My father has remarried. (I don't think that has ever come up in our correspondence.) So it turns out to have been darkest before dawn and all that. Frances will be on a plane soon, and Hildie will pinch hit until she arrives. I am saved and succored.

With the family problem out of the way, I found a great change in my mood. The questions I put in yesterday's letter, about Kay and love and what my marriage has meant, do not need any answers beyond the quiet I now feel. The answer is that writing to you I am at peace. Joanie and Paul and Hildie are asleep upstairs. The house is silent except for the pleasant crackle of the small fire I have going. (Though it's June, it can still get chilly at night around here.)

I am thinking about you—my friend Margaret Webb there in New York, and suddenly you are not a continent away. I am seeing you in my mind's eyes, not even needing to look at your picture, which I have memorized. Maybe it was your saying you wish you could come over to help out, but suddenly you are very much present in this house.

It comes to me that this is the very first time I have ever been truly alone with you here. For the first time there is no Kay, or her hovering presence. I see now that she has always been, subtly, between us, as Arthur must be for you except perhaps for the times you wrote alone from the hospital.

It makes a difference to me.

I do imagine you in this room now, right here. You are very real, sitting just to the right of the fire, on the floor. You are wearing a long, homespun skirt, a tawny color. Your legs are drawn up, your long fingers are resting on your knees. You have just turned from the fire to look at me, and your lovely head is tilted a little, as if you are about to ask me a question or are waiting on one from me. The firelight obliquely catches the shadow of cheek, your eyes. Every part of your face becomes your smile, ready to spill into laughter, with that special hint of an uplift in the corner of your lips that always catches at my heart when I sit with your picture.

You fit in my room. Your beautiful face, your Aphrodite figure (yes, Botticelli), the strong planes and curves of your body . . .

I had best not continue in that fantasy.

Let me tell you instead about the room you are sitting in here. It is spare; I prefer space to walk about as I think. There is a bay window overlooking the play yard. It has a window seat cushioned in some faded red material we inherited. My desk is beside the window, where I can look out at the children, as you know. The desk is a simple functional affair. I placed a slab of redwood across two file cabinets. I have a Mexican-type chair with a cane seat uncomfortable enough to keep me alert at 3 A.M. On the opposite wall there is a (sagging) couch where I lie down when the chair gets too insistent. I do my best speculating on my back and know it's time to return to the typewriter when the springs start to jab. The only color in the room is a Mexican spread Kay and I picked up in Oaxaca in the then-happy days before we were married.

Across from where you are, on the other side of the fireplace, there is a wrought-iron table with a (cracked) glass top, on which sits an old mining-camp lamp, genuine, I think. The ceiling is (once) white plaster crossed by beams of Spanish-colonial origin. My books fill whatever wall space there is, except for my secondhand upright piano. It is badly battered and scratched outside and tinny inside, but it is in tune. Believe it or not, my mother taught me how to tune a piano! "Chopsticks" should be in tune as well as the "Appassionata," she held.

The only picture in the room is over the fireplace, a watercolor Kay did when she was pregnant with Joanie and very "tied down." She copied a postcard of the Golden Gate Bridge. When it got messy she talked about seeking a misty surrealist effect, and we both pretended it was greatly poetic.

I am going to take that down. I will put your photograph in its place as soon as I get a chance to buy a frame.

I don't need your photo to see you now. You and I are both listening to the quiet here. I don't have to speak. What I am feeling, you are feeling too. I am content with you, you with me. You are smiling. I could never before imagine you so vividly, so dear to me. I have put on Schubert's *C Major Cello Quintet,* with the heartbreaking majesty of his summing up of life and beauty. Now I have closed my eyes and leaned back in my chair, and now I am at the heights of the music with you. I think the rest must remain unspoken, unwritten. Just as you cannot reach the window in your white chamber, I am not ready to walk my spiral staircase, up or down, even with this glorious music leading me.

I wonder what you will see when you do finally reach your secret window.

Brian

June 17

Brian dear:

Your house sounds wonderful. I would like to have been real in that room you describe with such affection. Your simplicity is the height of elegance, of course. Though I never think of you as "elegant." Your photo rather emphasizes what I see as contradictions that create a strong and handsome presence—there is your athletic look contrasting with your scholarly brow, there is the impression of you being about to leap into the air, maybe playing volleyball, coupled with eyes that are looking way beyond me to Schubert and to the knowledge and thinking that set you apart. It is a magnetic combination of attributes, and I enjoy sitting with your picture, as you write that you sit with mine.

How I wish now that Arthur had some speaking engagement on the West Coast. In the past we have come out often, but this year every invitation seems to be no farther west than Chicago. Damn!

In any case, by the time you get this, you will be by your fire not with me but with your sister, Frances, as it should be. Tell me more about Frances. Your idea seems heaven-sent. How lucky it is that she can join you and the children. How wonderful and loving your Aunt Hildie sounds. I must tell you that tears came to my eyes when I read that part of your letter.

I have discussed your views about Gary with Arthur, and he agrees again that we should wait a while longer.

The Greek photos are back from development. Arthur fumed at the slowness, but he got one good joke out of it for his speeches. The joke is about a customer who returns for his prints a day after leaving them for development. When the clerk tells him they aren't ready, the man points to a sign on the counter promising "twenty-four hour service." The man asks, "What about that?" The clerk answers, "Why, sir, that means three eight-hour days!"

How true that cavalier attitude is generally.

The pictures came to over four hundred dollars! At those prices they ought to take the wrinkles out of my face!

Now I need still another lifetime to file this batch. I will send copies as soon as I select some good ones for you.

You have asked about Lorna. She has been groggy after her exams. Those poor kids study 48 hours a day, especially in first-year law.

Lorna is as upset about Gary as we are, but she has concentrated on her work. She tells me now she isn't sure how she will feel if and when he comes back. I say the more fool my son if he loses this wonderful young woman. She sends her best regards to you and promises to write when she wakes up.

Maggie

June 18

Brian!

I am writing at once to tell you we have had a letter from Gary!

It seems a little disjointed, but says quite clearly that (hosanna!) he has left the group he was with—some months ago, apparently. He has been working as a dishwasher in Oakland, living in a rented room near Berkeley.

He mentions no names, but I could not care less right now. It may or may not be the group you noted. It's enough that he writes of the experience as "a knock" and calls the head man a liar, thief, and con artist! Can you believe it? That from Gary, who bludgeoned us with the Greatness of his Thundering Teacher! Gary was never one to react by halves, whether in fanaticism or disaffection.

His letter is ambiguous about his plans, but between the lines I hear a wish he would like to come home. I have discussed it with Arthur, and he agrees with an idea that has fired up in me. I have decided to fly out to Oakland, see Gary, talk to him, assure him we want him back as long as he wants to be.

And it would also mean that you and I could finally have our postponed encounter couldn't it? That would be a separate bonus for me.

Perhaps you could meet Gary, too. I am sure he would gain much from a chance to talk with you. There are undoubtedly experiences he would discuss more freely with a near-contemporary like you than with his over-the-hill mother.

It's tentative at the moment. I'll let you know immediately as I have definite plans.

The changes in Arthur are nothing less than spectacular since Gary's letter. Of course Arthur never wanted Gary "dead," that was the twisted protest of his own anguish. I guess my illness and then the cruise made a difference. I have been surprised and gratified at Arthur's growing open-mindedness, his receptivity, the respect with which he listens to me these days, and the accord he gives to my views. It is refreshing. I can tell you, Brian, that having you in my background is greatly responsible for all this. You are part of my new strength and resolution, and the thought of you does stiffen my backbone when Arthur threatens to backslide. So thank you again, for many things.

Kalo!

Maggie, happily

June 19

Brian!

I am all set. Arthur can't leave his office, and anyway we both feel it is better for me to see Gary alone. So I am flying out to visit Gary —and you!

In all honesty at this moment I am not sure which is the more feverish prospect.

Strike that last sentence. It was the typewriter speaking, not me, of course. After all, how could I compare seeing my *son* with seeing you? I mean, I am a MOTHER first, right?

I am making fun of myself to hide my confusion. I know that you understand, and I will say nothing more. Everything is suddenly happening too swiftly. All I know is that I am charged up in every way.

Maggie

June 22

Oh, dear Brian!

Not again! What stupid, meddling, sabotaging complications! It is unbelievable and maddening, and let me tell you how it all happened.

I arrived in Oakland Sunday night. Gary surprised me in every way. It was sensational. I had expected to come upon a haggard vagrant in urgent need of mother's cooking and sock-mending. Instead, I found a healthy, clean, well-dressed young son who has never looked better. Gary summed it up to me saying his disillusion was the best thing that could have happened. "Meaning and purpose," he said quietly, "can only come from myself, not any swami, whoever he may be."

I remembered my hospital window and my prayer. Looking at my handsome son, with his head high again, I was especially grateful for a new day.

Gary's mind sometimes seemed to me full of unfamiliar angles and sharp edges like broken glass, but I sense he is past his crisis of personal identity. His detour seems to have been a good thing. There is a new look of confidence about him, he smiles in a way that spells maturity to me. Maybe it was seeing Gary alone, a continent away from our familiar place, drinking wine from a jug with my son in a motel room, but we reached each other as never before. I had a clear intimation of Gary's respect for me as a person, not just his mother —especially after I told him about my correspondence with you and how I was looking forward to meeting you at last.

Gary applauded and said he'd like to meet you, as I wished might happen.

So there we were. We planned that I would arrange to visit with you alone, and meet your children and Frances, while Gary tied up his loose ends. Then he would join us before he and I returned to New York.

I didn't try to phone you Sunday because I wanted to be with Gary, of course. After we had our all-night session I slept late on Monday, and called your house a little after noon. At the prospect of hearing your voice, my heart thumped so hard it shook the phone.

When it was your sister who answered, I assumed you were on campus, and I asked for your number there.

That's when I learned the idiotic news that you were away!

Frances told me you had had to leave unexpectedly for a Los Angeles session with your new dean.

I could have ripped the phone out in my disappointment! Frances sounds a dear, sweet person. You must have told her nice things about me because she sounded as cruelly upset as I was that you and I had passed in the night again!

Our personal Jinx didn't even permit me to reach you in Los Angeles. I left messages with your hotel but apparently you received them too late to contact me before I had to fly back to New York. I would gladly have come down to Los Angeles, but when I phoned Arthur, he insisted (and I think he was right) that I bring Gary back before he changed his mercurial mind. Then we got Lorna on the phone, too, with everybody talking at once, and my domestic priorities flew me home. I had no choice. And from what Frances said, you were having wall-to-wall meetings anyway.

So here I am at this mocking typewriter again, the same old 3,000 miles away, after having been next door!

It is a huge and incredible shame. I do not know what god we have offended, but he, she, or it is a total and unfair scoundrel!

Still, let's keep our focus on the Important Stuff. Frances says you are moving the family next week, so congratulations are in order again. You have found a house in Los Angeles, apparently. Don't overlook sending me your new address.

As ever, it seems,

Evangeline

June 26

Dearest Maggie:

What can I say after I say I echo your frustration? It was miserably wicked misfortune that we missed again.

I am happy to hear the good news about Gary. I was reasonably sure he would be one of those who see the light.

It's good to know that the tensions are eased on all sides in your house. You deserve a calm harbor after the spells of bad weather. As for me, I am over my head in worms, selling the Marin house, closing on a Los Angeles house (damned fortunate to find it, too), and learning where the men's room is on the new campus. I would be utterly lost without Frances, especially since it looks as if Joanie has selected this week to present the first symptoms of what may be the mumps. Frances has an SOS call in to Hildie, just in case. No word from Kay, of course. We will manage without her, but if she were here right now, amid all the cartons and crates and poor Joanie's discomfort, I'd enjoy punching her in the nose. Princess, indeed!

Lorna has written a note, but please explain I simply don't have time to answer. I'm sure she will understand.

Best to all of you,
Brian

June 30

Dear Brian:

I hope it isn't the mumps, and if it is, that it's mild and that Paul doesn't catch it, though that's inevitable. Were you able to get Aunt Hildie? I can imagine how hectic things must be. I am so terribly sorry it is happening this way when your move to Los Angeles and UCLA should be a joyous and rewarding occasion.

I won't take your time with a long letter. Just wanted you to know your fan club is still cheering.

Maggie

July 5

Dear Brian:

July 4 again! Another reminder of how long we have been corresponding, now quite incredibly into a second year. Absence makes the pen grow mightier.

Things are easier here, although for a critical interval I was on edge again. Arthur moved right into the sticky area of Gary's intentions about law school. "A man needs a substantial career under his feet in this world" and so on.

A year ago I would have been squarely on his side but, as I've told you, I have changed. It is clear to me that the decision should be Gary's, not Arthur's, and without carrots or sticks.

The big news is that Arthur stopped and listened to me when I asked him to. He stopped and listened to me when I said this was too sensitive a time to tangle with Gary.

As it happens, the matter has not ended with that. There is a truce between my husband and my son, but there is a new conflict in me. You are the only one I can discuss this with . . .

As I was arguing Gary's case with Arthur, I suddenly saw myself in the same mirror. What do *I* want? I wake up thankful for the precious new day, but what do I do with it? I must tell you that this has come upon me with an unexpected urgency. At first I dismissed it as the Near-Fifty-Itch (adult smallpox?). But it has stayed with me in the form of a very sharp challenge: Surely there is a better way to use my time than my charity work, my shopping, and bridge, and counting the laundry when (and these days *if*) it comes back.

I have even half-considered returning to school to escalate my ABD to the Ph.D. I started. But what kind of career would be open at my age, assuming I got my doctorate at all? On the other hand, "hobbies" are no answer. My singing is good for nothing but swallowing moths. When you haven't got it, don't flaunt it. How I envy the blessed who have both a call and the gifts to fulfill it. They are the luckiest people in life. When aptitude, talent, desire, and opportunity come together, that is my definition of Heaven.

To have fierce desires and no gifts, that is a good definition of Hell.

Why does God give people aspirations beyond their abilities? It is tragic to keep reaching for what is forever beyond your grasp. That is worse even than the curse of Sisyphus.

I know I shouldn't invite the wrath of the gods with my complaints. After all, most people would envy me my home, my husband, my social circle, my security—and my cherished friendship with Professor Brian Curtiss.

And maybe I am putting myself down too quickly. Once again, writing out my thoughts to you is helping to sharpen and focus them. There *are* things I could do with a Ph.D. Am I ducking because I'm afraid I'd look silly in a classroom of young people? I would. But so what if it's something I want to do? Actually, I could specialize in the problem of illiteracy, for one thing. I did considerable work in reading disabilities, and Lord knows illiteracy is seriously on the rise. I don't know if you've seen them, but official figures say that more than one out of two American adults over 17 cannot readily read the labels on grocery shelves, or look up a telephone number! Many high school graduates cannot fill out a job application! I could aim at working with one of the corrective programs going forward locally or even nationally.

Why not? What do you think? This is not to be shrugged off, by either of us, as "menopausal." What a tinny word that is!

I am saying nothing of this to Arthur at this time. He takes a dim view of women having interests outside the home, which won't surprise you. All I would accomplish is another confrontation, pointless and untimely. It will be different if I bring him a decision I have already made by myself. That, with what I hope is your encouragement, is where I am heading now. Wish me good fortune, and let me have whatever advice you can send along.

Frankly, I don't know why this hasn't come to me before . . .

Looking for a job!
Maggie

Part Five

July 24

Dear Maggie:

Sorry I haven't been able to get to the typewriter for over two weeks. The campus is alive with summer classes, but my time is filled with meetings and the drawing board. I am very pleased with the atmosphere. Not only the faculty but most of the students care about excellence, from what I can see. There is a minimum of campus wise-guyism and the anti-intellectualism that I half expected in so large an institution. Gratifyingly to the contrary, I find things upscale, in an atmosphere of academic distinction, indeed, the "Harvard of the West" (with your father's permission).

The family is pretty well nested. We are in a house reasonably near campus. I will be mortgaged to the end of your husband's life tables, but a new friend in the economics dep't firmly advises the wisdom of borrowing as heavily as possible when inflation looms. "You pay back in cheaper dollars. . . ." So I am a financial wizard *malgré moi.*

The children have adjusted like rubber bands. It wasn't the mumps, thank God. There are lots of instant friends for Joanie and Paul all about us, and children are gregarious animals. The young faculty here is in the midst of a population explosion of its own, despite the pleas of Planned Parenthood. There is a well-recommended nursery only a block away. Frances is giving us full time for the summer. I will never be able to repay her. Nor will I ever be able to repay Aunt Hildie who, believe it or not, rushed here to help us unpack and get moved in.

The fly in the ointment is the house itself. It's one of the recently built affairs I've always thought of as the quick slum-buildings of tomorrow. The surface cosmetics are impressive, a great-looking kitchen, etc. But the workmanship is obtrusively shoddy. The plumbing is a prayer, the walls and floors aren't true square, everywhere I see where corners were cut. We are becoming a country of jerry-built junk. It's hard to remember we were once a nation of pride in craftsmanship and accomplishment. Some trades, like plasterers, are becoming extinct.

It's not just inflation, the expense of materials and labor. It's not just featherbedding practices. Basically, it's not caring. The developer, the builder, the workers—nobody gives a damn except to take the buck and get out. Whether it's houses, or a sewer system that has to be ripped up, etc. It's another kind of vandalism, and one we will all pay for heavily. It goes beyond the physical rip-off. It celebrates shoddiness. The built-in decay poisons the atmosphere. When shoddiness is the norm in housing and so many major products today—including cars and tires that have to be recalled, the appliances that fail, and repairmen who rob customers blind—how can we expect anything but cynicism and a corroding resentment about everything in our society?

Oh, I am overstating the case, I know. I suppose it is part of my annoyance with Kay, who has turned out to be a shoddy, jerry-built human being. There are still some well-built homes, fine cars and appliances, honest repairmen, and the rest.

Let me get out of the sucking mire to tell you some of the really nice things here. We have all sorts of magnificent flowers outside and blazing flowering bushes I still have to identify. It's beautiful and colorful, but I can't get used to the trees. They are some variety of palm, slender and bare almost to the very top, so very different from my redwoods. In a way, the difference reflects the change of pace I feel. The furniture is in place, but I am not. I suppose I will get to feel at home in due course. I am struck again by how quickly and easily Joanie and Paul have fitted in. Right now they are in our yard with a gaggle of their new friends, playing some hide-&-seek games I haven't seen or heard before. Joanie is piping out:

I hold my little finger,
I thought it was my thumb,

I give you all a warning,
and here I come.

One of the other kids had a different rhyme:

Charlie over the water,
Charlie over the sea,
Charlie caught a blackbird and can't catch me.

Fascinating. I wonder where these game rhymes come from? As an English student, did you ever look into that by any chance? Just now they are yelling another new one:

Ally, ally, onker
My first conker
Quack, quack,
My first smack.

Upon which Joanie apparently wins license to punch Paul on the shoulder. It may be a good game for defusing rougher battles. But I think she is taking advantage of her new stock, Paul not being old enough to match everything she is picking up, like:

Five little sausages, frying in a pan,
One went pop, the others went Bang!

Whereupon Paul receives another bang on the shoulder.

Several of the nearby families are from England, and I suspect these children's games originated there because I've never heard them before. Let me know if you have any clues. I may put a student to studying games and rhymes as they reflect local social relationships, backgrounds, and customs. This is right in line with my interest in cutting across the disciplinary fences, as you know.

I have spent some time reading over your recent letters. I suppose it is the unsettled feeling I have here, but I am grateful I have you to turn to as an old friend. I have found deep pleasure and comfort in your writing; it is almost as good as if we were able to talk.

One thing that struck me was your observation about people who keep pushing for a goal they cannot possibly reach. It's the tragedy of a one-armed man being obsessed with the violin. The answer is tough but unarguable. He must accept that he can never play. His obsession must be meliorated; limitations must be accepted and borne. On my own gravestone I'll be content with, "He didn't do bad/With what he had."

I don't mean to be flippant by any means. I deeply respect your wish to do more than "count the laundry." It is part of what I mean when I say you are not "old."

I enthusiastically applaud your positive thinking and would make only one suggestion. Before you enroll for more academic work, consider whether you don't already have sufficient background and experience to move right ahead. For example, quite serendipitously, there is a friend offstage here who may well be slated to come on for a central role. Let me do a magic act for you that may pull not a rabbit out of my hat but a possible job for you. The prestidigitation goes this way:

—You may recall my mention of a second mortgage on the Marin house. That help came from a great friend of mine. His name is Charles Henley. He is about your husband's age, a fine chap in every way, a wealthy man not content to sit on his laurels on his boat or in his Malibu estate. He was doing business in San Francisco when I first met him as a student in two of my night courses, which was unusual enough. We drank beer together after class and had first-rate bull sessions.

—With my move to Los Angeles now, I had to contact Charlie about the mortgage red tape. He is generously helping me again with this Los Angeles house. More important for you, I waved my magic wand during our recent conversations and learned that

—Charles Henley has just developed an educational device aimed foursquare at the field of your interest. It is an aid to literacy for both children and adults, using a minicomputer, photographs, texts, and so on. Henley raves about the test results to date and

—He expressed genuine interest when I waved my wand to reveal you waiting in the wings, ready, willing, and able to help him!

Orchestral flourish? Well, it may be too soon to take a bow because obviously there are a lot of questions to be answered. For one thing, Henley knows the bloom is off the educational market, but he (sincerely) cares less about making more money than in helping if he can. Over our beers he told me he has been looking for a partner to provide continuing expert input. I took the liberty of giving him your address, assuming you would like at least to explore the possibility.

So keep an eye out for the prospectus Charles Henley is putting in the mail to you.

Let me give you my assurance that Henley is genuine, and a splendid gentleman in every way. The only flaw is that he is a handsome widower, and your husband is more than enough competition for me (thanks for the new pictures) without anyone else entering our scene. I know that Charlie is planning a New York trip and I would hate to think that, after the way you and I have muffed every planned meeting, it will be another man who will buy you that drink!

I don't recall the name of the fellow Evangeline could not find in her search, or I'd sign his name instead of

Brian

July 28

Dear Brian "Merlin" Curtiss:

I didn't know you numbered Magic among your talents, but you certainly wave a golden magic wand! I have received the material sent by your friend, studied it, and am quite charged up about meeting Charles Henley. I never dreamed when I sent you my "laundry-list letter" that wheels would start revolving so quickly and so promisingly. Of course there are scores of questions, and I am reasonably sure nothing will come of it, but your magic act is intriguing at the least, and I will audition for a part, as long as you promise not to dress me in spangles and saw me in half.

Seriously, I do hope things work out, because Henley's project promises a more direct and meaningful way to make use of my background than I had dared anticipate or hope for. (I remember your observing that while we plan and calculate for the future, everything happens by chance.)

Arthur's reaction was amusing, really, except that he was dead serious.

"Who is Charles Henley?"

"Brian's friend."

"Who is Brian?"

I was exasperated. "I have told you everything about Brian Curtiss!"

Arthur, the lawyer: "All you know is what Brian Curtiss has chosen to tell you."

"Oh, come off it, Arthur."

"Isn't that true?"

"I trust Brian implicitly!"

"Answer yes or no!"

"Arthur! I am not on a witness stand, you know."

"These people could be any kind of common bunkos!"

"For God's sake, Brian Curtiss is a professor at UCLA!"

"I didn't see his name on the faculty register!"

Of course Arthur would check.

I told him you had just been appointed, but he persisted. "I don't like you dealing with all these strangers."

That offended me right to the bone. "Brian Curtiss happens to be the *best* friend I have!"

"Through the mail?" Now Arthur let fly the arrow I knew he has been holding on a drawn bow a long, long time. "It's a damned strange relationship, if you ask me!"

Well, so do I think it's out of the ordinary, but I am not conceding that to Arthur.

He adds, "This fellow Henley sounds like an adventurer to me."

My answer is one he won't deny. "Well, I have the best lawyer in town to protect little old me from wolves in sheep's clothing." (Note my only half-sarcastic acceptance of the credo that a woman needs a male to protect her in money matters.)

Arthur puffed a cloud of peace-pipe smoke. "One sure thing, Margaret. No swindler ever comes on like one."

Brian, are you a swindler? Have you been corresponding with a poor aging lady to set up a Scam and A Sting? Isn't Arthur absolutely ridiculous!

Can't stay at the desk any longer, must get going. We have been invited to a friend's place in Vermont for a couple of weeks. It will be wonderful to breathe the country air. My love affair with New York becomes strained in the heat and mugginess of our summer. I have a lot of packing and things to do including, happily, buying a new bathing suit. I have been losing weight! I ought to confess to you that I started going to a gym when you first announced your possible Princeton trip. Vanity, vanity, all is vanity.

We will be back before Labor Day, in plenty of time for me to meet Charles Henley regardless of Arthur's gross insults. I have written

Mr. Henley directly about my keen interest in his project. Thank you, Merlin!

You will want to know that Gary seems fine now. He and Lorna are both working this summer as "paralegals" in Arthur's office. They've agreed it's a sensible way for Gary to check out his interest in law, or lack of it. It is so good to have my son at home this way. Even Arthur is walking around with a smile, when he thinks no one is looking.

Lorna, for her part, has decided that Gary has sowed his disquieting oats, and they are back in their old relationship as far as I can tell. I don't probe, of course. I only pray that it lasts. Nothing would make me happier than to see them married—and give me the grandchildren I crave. I think time is on my side.

Maggie

P.S. Every time I think of dieting, I mean to ask whether you have ever come upon studies that might confirm a theory of mine about the Universal Weight Problem. Let me bounce it off you.

It is my hypothesis (it really doesn't rise to the dignity of a theory) that modern man's difficulty in losing poundage is *a legacy of the hunting stage* in our development. Before you call the men in white coats, consider this:

When tribes had to go without food for unpredictable intervals, the survivors—who are obviously *our* ancestors—somehow enjoyed bodies and chemistries that *stored and hoarded* what ever came their way. Starvation and death struck first at those whose metabolism did not build and save fat against the lean days.

But the metabolism of the survivors is precisely adverse when food is plentiful, as today. Our bodies still store fat against hazard even though it is far less necessary for most of us to do so!

When Arthur and I are on his banquet circuit, we eat and drink constantly. It is impossible not to. As my weight climbs, I console myself with the thought that I am descended, *ipso facto,* from the strongest and healthiest of ancient mankind!

Probably not worth a second thought, but it's an appealing idea.

About those children's rhymes—which I found delightful, of course—no, I know nothing of how they get started or whence they derive. I have often wondered the same about common jokes. Who makes them up in the first place? Do you know anything about that?

July 30

Dear Maggie:

I trust this will reach you before you leave for Vermont. I have a message for you from Henley. He has had to fly to Canada on a business emergency, and he asked me to thank you for writing to him. He also asked me to clarify a point not yet discussed. He would like it understood at the outset that what he is offering is a partnership participation. He wants a person with more than an employee's interest, especially since he intends to concentrate his own time on other matters. This means an investment, the size of which he would discuss at your meeting if you still want to proceed.

I enormously dislike the feeling I now have of being in the middle. I am the magician-friend and don't want to see this get sweaty on either side.

I suppose the investment angle will convince Arthur that Curtiss and Henley are fortune hunters. (I have sometimes wished I had a Henley-type dynamo instead of my bookish blood. It would be easier to pay for the orthodontia I am told Joanie will need.)

Have a great vacation. I am looking forward to fall classes with great satisfaction in the new horizons all around me this year. Your Fat Theory is delicious and probably absolutely accurate!

The masked bandit,
Brian

Aug. 12
From Vermont

Oh, dear Brian—

Of course Arthur is convinced I am heading for trouble. He is only partially reassured by my promise that I will not see Mr. Henley without him.

I find it all quite diverting but, you know, I can understand Arthur's skepticism. After all, haven't I myself been asking you steadily what on earth keeps a brilliant young California professor writing to a totally undistinguished housewife? In candor, we have never satisfactorily answered that, have we? Shall I tell Arthur we are "letting it sing itself?" Oh boy!

I have been dreadfully unfair in writing about Arthur. It's true that he is prickly on occasion, but he is also warm, and often very charming in his fashion. I write too much about the quarrels between us, which are after all true of any marriage, and not enough about my happiness with this good man. Why didn't I tell you, for example, that last month Arthur set up a fund to buy musical instruments for poor children in Harlem? Isn't that a fine thing?

Maybe it is being in the country, but I feel expansive about Arthur right now. We walk together in the fields. I love the country here. Space in New York goes straight up and down. The heights bear down on one sometimes. Here in Vermont the space is spread out, more congenial, so to speak. Our friends are directly on Lake Champlain, and the proximity to the water washes the air crystal clear. I especially enjoy the shift from day to night. The blazing sun is hot on my skin until, abruptly, there is a breeze at dusk.

It's a sharp and welcome contrast between the drowsy heat of bees, cows, and the daytime pastures and the night's shivers. Even in summer there is an early morning cold here that reminds me of what I myself never experienced but read about so often when I was a girl —the way a pioneer woman descended a frigid staircase with her arms wound tightly across her thin chest for warmth, as she hurried to light the kitchen stove and put the kettle on while children upstairs washed with chattering teeth out of icy water in porcelain pitchers.

There is such a pitcher and bowl up in my room, but it is only an antique showpiece.

Few of those children grew up with Gary-problems so far as I know. Something you once said stays with me. Is advance progress?

Large stretches of Vermont are bucolic and idyllic in this area. I can walk for miles forgetting progress. I wander for hours in fields, along streams, around ponds, seeing nothing but cows and birds and an occasional deer peering at me doubtfully from the surrounding woods. It bounds off wagging its white-flag tail like a finger scolding me for disturbing its feeding.

Arthur often goes off to play golf with our host. When I walk by myself I think of you, sometimes talk aloud to you as I go, though in a whisper so the cows won't think me too eccentric. I remember, with pleasure, your writing about the cattle on your farm—they were red and white, you said. I had forgotten the breed, and asked my friends here. They were intrigued by my interest in cows. They told me—"Herefords, probably." That sounds right. I'll go back to your letter and check it when I get home. The cows here are black and white. "Holsteins." There, I am an expert on cattle.

How my mind skates and skitters. Montreal flashes into my head.

I always recall the geography here with a start of surprise. I *know* that Montreal is only an hour's drive north (down?), but it doesn't seem right that a foreign country should be so close by. It adds to the enjoyment of being away from the routine. I suppose people living in southern California have the same sort of feeling about Mexico.

I am saddened when I think of the divisiveness between the French and English population. It seems so unnecessary. I can't help but remember what you said about how, if men could find no other reason, redheads would scourge brunettes, etc. Yesterday, passing a farmhouse I saw a man bullying a boy mercilessly. The child, no more than seven or eight, had no way of fighting back. It was unmitigated cruelty. As the man walked away into his barn, I heard the boy, beaten to the ground, call softly, "Some day I'll kill you! I'll kill you some day!"

How right you are, Brian. Where does that boy's great anger have to go but to fuel an inner engine of hatred? He will never kill his father. He will forget his threat because it is too impossible to entertain in our society. So I saw one of your candidates for social violence in the making, and as you say, it isn't always or even mostly a matter of slums or poverty or geopolitics. Maybe the repressed anguish I saw in the boy will drive him on to be governor of the state. Let's hope it's that rather than a mugger, or a hijacker. Or cult leader . . .

I didn't mean to strike another sour note, but while I'm at it, let me ask whether anyone has written a thesis on "Incidence of Sexual Passes under the Guise of Social Dancing in Upper-Middle-Class Society."

At a weekend party here, one guest was a macho tycoon type. He was impressive, I must admit, over six feet, a well-preserved figure, a bronzed young-looking face under a stark white mane. An attractive "Who's Who" success, and aware of it to the last strand of his carefully sprayed hair and his assured smile.

Excellent dancer, too. Macho led me like Fred Astaire. I was no Ginger Rogers, but it was unexpectedly enjoyable. *Until,* after some drinks, he danced me to a corner of the terrace and began what I took to be a new step. I tried to follow and then realized what he was trying.

Brian, I am not an innocent. Even in Boston I had my share of the Leggies and the Gropies, in school and out, but this man so brazenly cupped my breast that I was absolutely stunned. Maybe it was the drinks, but I decided to treat it as accidental. He took my uncertainty as encouragement!

My question, Brian, is not why he then did his other things. I can accept it that a man, any man at all, might consider any female fair prey, at least to the extent of "trying." *My* question is why this man was so smugly sure that I would not (a) haul off and smack his face, and/or (b) scream my resentment out loud, and/or (c) yell for my husband (who was a boxer in college—I don't think I've ever told you that)?

Well, leave out (a) and (b) above on the assumption that Sir Lothario assumes I am so housebroken that I won't embarrass my hosts. But doesn't this ape consider that my husband might object? Apparently not, and I believe I know the shocking answer. This man truly believes that women do not find his assault unpleasant. He believes women even welcome it.

Brian, am I a freak? What does your Sociology say about this? What *I* did was run off to the garden shed to cry. He had actually dared to force my hand down to touch him. Expecting me, Female, to swoon with surging passion.

Brian, tell me another thing. Do women ever do that to a man? I'm not talking about teases, or nymphomaniacs. I mean your garden variety, reasonably sexed, "nice" ladies like Margaret Fairfield Webb. Does such a woman ever touch (or even consider touching) a man's crotch the way this boor touched me?

I feel as stupid as a schoolgirl—everything I always wanted to know and was afraid to ask, of anyone but you.

How can I tell you how good it makes me feel to be able to be so open with you?

Later I saw Don Juan kissing his wife, and it brought to mind my mother once saying, "When a man keeps kissing his wife in public, I doubt he kisses her much at home!" I don't know where she got the line, but I'm sure it applies to this lout.

You can write to me here,
Maggie

Aug.17

Dear Maggie:

Unlike Arthur (man of many surprises!) I have never been a boxer, but I would gladly have taken a swing at that son of a bitch "dancer" of yours!

No, Maggie, most men are not like that, certainly not after they've grown a bit. For kids, "copping a feel" is par for the course, sure. It's a way of learning about sex when there's really no other chance for experience (at least until recent years). But unless a man is sick in the head, he doesn't go around molesting women, on the dance floor or off.

Still, I suppose I shouldn't be so dogmatic. I read recently that Mexico City is planning separate subway cars for women because during the crush of rush hour "things happen." The "things" must be endemic to require separate cars!

I would like to write at length but am still avalanched. I depend on you to understand.

Anything new in your thinking about Henley? The one aspect that concerns me is that—assuming the money is no block—you don't let your enthusiasm lead you to bite off more than you can chew. Lorna writes that you are still looking pale. (That was before Vermont sun.) As you once told me, health is our most important possession. Please keep watching yours.

Love,
Brian

Aug. 21

Dear Brian:

Thanks for your note. I do understand. It's almost September and the start of your seminar. Up here it's easy to forget the fast turning of the wheels outside. Including those of Mr. Henley.

It was coincidence that you wrote about my health. It is fine, but at the same time it is a consideration. Arthur and I have been reviewing the whole Henley idea, and I have been entertaining second thoughts. It is easy for me to get carried away by the excitement of "having a career," but the more I think about it the less sure I am that I would not just be spinning my own wheels. I don't know that I truly want the intensity of an outside commitment. And Arthur is not wrong when he observes that at this stage of his career my place is at his side.

I don't know where Mr. Henley is at the present time, so would appreciate your conveying to him that I see no point now in our meeting. I doubt he will be too disappointed. Doubtless he considered me in the first place only at your urging. I would think he needs younger blood.

Please know, Brian, that this is my decision, not Arthur's. That is important to me.

I am glad I have settled my mind. I am sleeping better without the apprehension of plunging into strange waters at this time of my life.

> My thanks in any case,
> Maggie

Aug. 25

Maggie, Maggie!

I am rushing this off because I think you are making a devil of a mistake. I am enough your friend to presume to scold.

At worst, you can disregard this and tell me it's none of my business. At best, it can help you examine the ruts you are allowing to slow down your wheels for no good reason—always assuming your health is not the issue.

Other than that, what remains is my feeling that you are allowing your husband to push you around again. You write that the decision is your own, but it doesn't sound like "the new you" at all. You had come too far in your honest enthusiasm. If you give up this project without trying your wings, there will always be a residue of resentment, which must be corrosive to your marriage.

At the same time, permit me to say I do not think you give Arthur enough credit. Yes, he comes across as sometimes antediluvian, but he is after all a man of experience, he has his own maturity, as his picture clearly shows, and you have already written several times of

166 .

his new regard for you as a person. Don't take that lightly. Your letters have reflected a new simmering in your marriage, good changes brewing. It isn't my place to play marriage counselor (as perhaps I should never have played magician) but it seems to me you ought to build on Arthur's new respect, not turn the heat down.

If you waffle, Arthur naturally assumes he knows best. If you waffle, it may be because you want him to assume he knows best.

There is only one way I can be wrong here. You must answer this for yourself. *If Arthur were not involved, would you be turning Henley down?*

I am writing this way because I felt more of you coming alive. I sensed a fresh electricity between the lines of your letters. The fact is that your background *and* your maturity would make you a more valuable asset to a project like Henley's than the "young blood" you still have such a confounded fixation about!

A woman cannot satisfy her husband by diminishing herself! If I had my way, those words would be part of every marriage ceremony. Both ways, of course.

Maggie, I think I know you as well as anyone in the world, even though we haven't met. And I say that no woman like you should turn herself into a ukelele, accompanying her husband's life with a few dingy chords. "My-dog-has-fleas" is no way to tune a life!

Not for any person, much less you.

My aggravation reflects how much I care for you. I am risking a great deal by writing in this unvarnished way. You may be offended. But friends sometimes have to be unpleasant with each other, or they are not living in a real world.

I am placing my own bets at this point. I am betting that I, for all the distance between us, know you better than you know yourself.

Now you can send me packing and tell me you never gave me license to write such a letter. If I have overstepped, I apologize to Margaret Fairfield Webb. But to Maggie, I beg, please give prayerful consideration to what I have said today out of my deep affection for you.

Brian

Aug. 29

Dear Brian:

All right, your letter has given me pause, if that is any satisfaction
to you.

Let me say this: In your own way, you are pressing me much as
you say Arthur has done. The fact is that I do see myself very clearly
right now in my life with my family. I have lived well with my
portion; it has been generous. I have thought about the limitations,
sometimes bitterly, but I accept that in any case we are all of us cogs
in a machine bigger than we are, a machine that often has different
directions than what I might choose if I were not built into the
confounded contraption.

But I *am* built into it, by my parents, by society, by God, by
Whoever and Whatever. It's where I find myself. It's "my space."
My gears are cut and ground and shaped to fit with precision into
the wheels of my marriage, my circle.

There are big gears and little gears, weights and counterweights,
wheels and sprockets, bells and whistles, all turning, ringing, blowing, around me, above me, below and beside me. I am rotated on the
most powerful transmission shaft in the world—all the images and
codes and pieties I have absorbed since Day One.

I don't need psychoanalysis to comprehend that the shaft revolves
me. It does so through my "wife" cogs and "mother" sprockets and
"social" ratchets and "caste" cams. They are all officially greased
and oiled for smooth turning, to the greater glory of the socially-
licensed machine.

It occurs to me that the only time I ever *set myself in motion
independently* was the day I first wrote to you.

My point is that I am not about to monkey-wrench the works. In
the abstract, there might have been other patterns to my life, but that
is moot. As I am now, I am not unhappy where I find myself. You
do not seem to grasp that fundamental, Brian.

At Gary's age, and Kay's, one has time and energy for exploring
and seeking. At my age there is acceptance. I repeat that, within
reason, I am satisfied.

Don't answer, "So is a cow!" That would be a cheap shot. I have
done as well as I could with who I was, where I was, what I had to
work with. *It is not antifeminist to make a good home, help a husband
succeed, and pray to be a loving grandmother.* It is very human,

perhaps the most human aspiration of all!

I believe in my heart that the family is the most important single dynamic in our society. From everything you have said, I would expect you to agree emphatically that without the family the world as we know it would fall apart.

Dear Brian Curtiss, I know that my cog is not of heroic proportions. I think we women will all do better if we accept that fact, and keep our parts of the machinery working as well as we possibly can. That in itself is a rewarding challenge and responsibility, without more.

Surely we need fuel and oiling, care and repairs sometimes when things break down, as they do for everyone born of Adam. But that is very different from bombing the works just because they don't function as we would like all the time.

I appreciate your concern. I appreciate your honesty. Far from sending you packing, I tell you I love you for caring about me as you do. But as of now it would take some kind of earthquake to shake me out of the decision I have reached.

Faithfully,
Maggie

P.S. My Vermont friends have been intrigued by my "California letters." I started to tell them about you when *Arthur* took over and observed, quite proudly and possessively, that you are "a friend of the family"! How about that!

Sept. 2

Maggie:

If you were a student of mine, I would point out that it is one thing to agree on the centrality of family but, just as axiomatic to me, the family need not be a woman's only significant preoccupation.

And I don't enthuse over your description of yourself as a cog. Hell, Maggie, we all accommodate to our condition, but that is far from voluntarily bowing the neck to a subordinate role.

Indeed, I argue the opposite—that in order to contribute to the whole, each person must insist on his or her total integrity as an individual. If I am a wheel on a big bus loaded with people, I had better make damned sure I am not about to blow a tire.

Well, I must be satisfied that I tried to get you to change your mind. I think you are unreasonable, benighted, pigheaded and short-sighted, my dear, but I also know in my heart that it was no "cog" who wrote that first letter to Brian Curtiss, and it is no cog to whom I am sending my love now.

Brian

Sept. 5

Dear Brian:

It would be my luck to fall in with an exasperating character like you. Your letters on the Henley Caper have upset me. Not that I haven't meant every word I wrote. But you said one thing that got under my skin and has been a burr ever since, about a woman not being a ukelele accompanying her husband's life with a few plunks now and then. What an outrageous way to describe any woman, much less me!

Last night I dreamed I was looking in a mirror after my bath and saw my body as a large Ukelele! My hair was braided to make the four strings. A man came into the room with a large plastic pick (never mind its shape) and plucked away until my scalp ached. And no sound came out.

Easy enough to interpret. I am telling myself that I am still, when all is said and done, a silent instrument.

Since your ukelele-letter, I have walked through the day wondering whether you may be right after all. What you are too polite to say, except between the lines, is that I am a coward. Maybe that's true. Maybe I turned from Mr. Henley because I am afraid of anything really new (including *you*), and I have rationalized my anxiety with a holier-than-thou celebration of Family and a Woman's Real Place in Life.

I badly need to get honest with myself about this, and about you. Am I truly so irretrievably stuck in the old rut that I am *scared* to get out?

The more I think about it, the truer I see that may be. I was able to get excited about Henley when the proposal was just a notion, and as distant from me as you are. But when I held the actual prospectus in my hand, and realized I might well fit into it, the reality challenged me too threateningly.

So I ran from it. (As, maybe, in some larger life design than we know, *I* have somehow been the cause of our not meeting!)

Methinks I have protested too much. Am I bovine, after all, despite my protests and pretexts?

I don't like myself very much this minute. I don't like this bogey you have made me look at. Am I really so afraid of change? That would be horrible to admit, because my own personal definition of Old Age has been precisely that—it is the moment when one becomes afraid of change!

I am thinking aloud on paper again with you. As always, it is helping me sift and clarify. I don't dismiss my misgivings, they are real. But I am bristling to say they are without foundation. Why in the unblinking world shouldn't I at least give myself a chance, as you say? (What is the female form of Milquetoast!)

Brian, I am going to phone my husband at his office this minute, before the impulse leaves me. Surely he can't object to my having at least one meeting with Charles Henley!

Brian, after I typed that last sentence, I did get out of my chair to go to the table beside my bed for the phone. I felt keyed up. I was halfway through dialing when I slammed the receiver down, furious with myself. Not because I am changing my mind about Henley, but because I hopped like that to call my husband. Why did I have to speak to Arthur? Why couldn't I just keep on with this letter and write to you that I have changed my mind (*I* have changed my mind; I *have* changed my mind; I have *changed* my mind; I have changed *my mind* . . .)?

I ask you now to get in touch with Charles Henley wherever the devil he is, and ask him to contact me when he comes to New York!

I do not need Arthur's permission for that. Or for anything else!

I do not know how far this will go, if it goes at all, but at least I am not going to trip over my bound little feet before I start! Brian, thank you for reminding me that I am . . .

. . . nobody's damn ukelele!
Maggie

P.S. I suppose you noticed the postmark is New York again. I never got to tell you that I saw Señor Don Juan trying his sex act on my hostess before we left. She handled him the right way, bless her wise heart. She pretended to stumble as the music played on and came down hard on his open-sandaled foot with her spiky heel. He danced no more.

The vacation was fine. Now I need a vacation to recover.

Sept. 10

Brava Maggie:

Brava, brava!
Another shot heard round the world.

I called Charlie in Edmonton as soon as I got your letter, and he is as pleased as I am at your turnabout. You will be hearing from him directly. Whatever develops, this itself is positive for you.

Of course you are no ukelele. You are your whole own symphony orchestra, as is everyone who tunes up and listens to the inner instruments.

Now hear this: Princeton is considering another panel, for the spring. If it materializes, I am sure the Eumenides wouldn't be ruthless enough to interfere a *third* time. But let us pretend I've said nothing, and I'll whisper if it becomes definite.

My recent letters have been short to the point of curtness, and I haven't had a chance to tell you much of our new lives here in Los Angeles.

I miss my redwoods mightily, and it's not easy to get used to the flatness. There are mountains around Los Angeles, of course, but the city itself spreads like a pancake (too often sizzling). I miss San Francisco's ups and downs, and the water. I keep looking for at least glimpses of the ocean or the Bay. Up there I always had a sense of water nearby, and it was somehow refreshing. I don't have that here at all, although the Pacific isn't far on the freeways.

Those roads are everything incredible you have ever heard. The cars dart on and off the ramps like fish fleeing sharks. It is quite true that one wrong turn can finish you for a day. I take it to be the Los Angeles metaphor for life: Keep Alert For All Direction Signs, At The Risk of Losing Your WAY!

So far I have stayed close to campus, so I haven't goofed, but Frances tried for a beach the other day, and she had the children halfway to San Diego before she realized she had gone wrong.

I haven't even had time to do the sightseeing rites in Hollywood-Beverly Hills. The children couldn't care less, but Frances would like to see Who lives Where. (If I go along, it will be for purely sociological observation, you understand.)

The star phenomenon does fascinate me, both personally and professionally. One aspect is the hero worship of a society starved for dream images. Another, which offends me, is the magnitude of the acclaim given to The Entertainer as against The Artist in our world. A concert violinist requires immeasurably more talent and lifelong effort than, say, a rock star. But the popular kudos and dollars are more easily won by musical illiterates with wiggling pelvis and thumb-to-nose lyrics (if intelligible at all). They may work hard, but they come nowhere near the dedication of, say, a Beverly Sills, a Sutherland, a Marian Anderson, an Isaac Stern, a Horowitz, a Tureck.

I am not an elitist. I caution my classes to avoid invidious comparisons. An apple tree can't be compared to an airplane; a Sinatra is to be understood in different terms than a Pavarroti. But ultimately, much as I may admire a Sinatra, I can't escape a value judgment that Pavarroti's contribution as a singer is more vital, more worthy of society's support, recognition, and rewards.

Sticky questions, as well left for my classrooms, where there aren't any answers either.

Paul and Joanie are thriving. To them our move has been more of a lark than anything else. They miss Kay, but they have accepted Frances easily. There is even a kind of dividend for me in Kay not being here. I recognize now how much time and energy went into wondering when she would go and come. It's more tranquil this way, though I do not deny there are ways, which I need not spell out, in which I naturally miss her. I am glad I can write that to you without constraint.

As for Kay, I realize she permanently lives temporarily. I suppose people like her are the contemporary counterparts of the gypsies who exist in every society.

Well, what is temporary and what is permanent? When I watch with my own eyes the space shuttle Enterprise on its historic first flight, I see mankind clearly on its way to the eventual colonization of space, even in my lifetime. Our old parameters simply do not hold generation to generation, and the pace of *seminal* change is accelerating to the point where Temporary is becoming the only Permanent.

I did discuss with colleagues your Don Juan question, which I have not yet replied to. I don't recall the literature like Kinsey or Masters & Johnson, et al., discussing "party wolves" specifically, though there may be scientific surveys, and of course Don Juan has been with us from the beginning. Indeed, it would make an interesting project. One problem is that the data depend on interviews, and they can be questionable (no pun intended). People lie both ways—not just in denying kinky sex, which is to be expected, but in admitting and exaggerating what never happened. It's another way of getting kicks, I suppose.

As between you and me, I have to admit my wish that our relationship wasn't as exotic as it is. We are too much like the orchid plants that root in air. It is wonderful how far we have come on just our letters and pictures, but we need planting, you and I, though I have not the faintest notion of how that can be accomplished beyond these letters, our messengers and surrogates.

Meantime, let me get on to the important announcement that my daughter was an Exalted Six Years Old yesterday. Six is a milestone, I need not tell you, the way shifting into teens is a metamorphosis after twelve. There is an immediate new loftiness in Joan's treatment of Paul. *He* is still only a "kid," you see. And she does not wish to be called Joanie any more. "Joan" is more to her now-mature taste.

We did the zoo in the morning, then a birthday party for what seemed all the children in Los Angeles. Frances and Joanie had spent the weekend putting up decorations, and it will be another week before Paul is washed clean of tape, flour paste, and shades of ice cream your Medford grandfather never dreamed of. Kids are not easy on the nerves. Would you add to your collectives a Pandemonium of Children?

What really shook me was Joanie losing her first tooth last week. Frances wondered whether I, the sensible professor, approved of the Tooth Fairy ritual. She was as delighted as Joanie when I soberly assured them that of course and beyond all doubt there exists a Tooth Fairy. How could there be any possible question! As if I would deprive my child (and my sister) of that felicity.

Joanie, I mean Joan! is in pigtails. She is pure Little Girl at this stage, though still managing to play telephone repairman. Yesterday she climbed a pole, and Frances had to call the fire department to rescue the two of us!

As you see, we are doing splendidly without Kay.

Discussing with my sister the shock of finding *my* daughter at *school age,* Frances told me a funny story. It is about a mother who bursts into tears as she presents her child to the teacher who is registering for first grade. The woman weeps, "So young, so young . . ." The teacher looks up, surprised. "Why, madam, she's the same age as the other children." "Not her," the mother cries. "Me!"

Given your hang-ups about age, I suspect you will get a chuckle out of that. Arthur may be able to use it in a speech?

Fondly,
Brian

Sept. 14

Dear Brian:

Given my hang-ups about age, you inadvertently rubbed my nose in it very unkindly when you spoke of how you would see space age colonies in your lifetime. I have no doubt you will. I have no doubt I, unequivocally, will not. Enough of that.

I enjoyed your letter as if we'd gotten the chance for another of our ghost walks. I am glad you wrote about Joanie, I mean Joan. (I take that very seriously.)

I disagree that we are "rooted in air," though I like being compared to orchids. Arthur and I visited a fabulous orchid garden in Hilo when he lectured in Hawaii a few years ago, and I was simply overwhelmed with the beauty and variety. I think that having our photos and writing as we do is genuine "planting" for you and me.

And herewith more photos of me and Arthur in Knossos, Lindos, Rhodes, Athens, Olympia, et cetera. The problem for me is that I can't take too much sun these days, so wear a wide-brim hat. Arthur fumes he can't photograph my face properly. But if I take the darned hat off, I squint. As between being invisible and being snapped looking like a quince, I prefer the former. (I have never seen a quince; why do I assume it is a wrinkled fruit? It does sound like it, though, doesn't it? My apologies to quinces if I am wrong.) But Arthur is handsome in my snaps of him, isn't he?

Thank God for the governments and foundations that are preserving the antiquities (I don't mean my face). There is so much modern building going on everywhere that the wonderful ancient world would be lost, like the immense archaeology lost beneath major buildings in Mexico City, as I am sure you know.

It's a world of colliding interests, isn't it? When Arthur and I drove down from Vermont, we saw so many housing developments chewing up the farms. What's to be done? People must have homes. But if we transform all the farmland, how are we going to eat?—quite aside from losing the precious sight of the wide landscapes, the rolling hills, the white farmhouses (not jerry-built), the red barns, the silos flaring their aluminum in the sun with light so bright it dims the sight.

Dilemmas of our "advanced civilization." Wasn't it Spengler who predicted all this in his *Decline of the West*? Do you read him in your classes? I think it is a seminal work, though at college it was fashionable to pooh-pooh Spengler as a pessimist and (often incorrect) pedant. Today I fear he was only too, too clear-sighted.

When is Paul's birthday? And Frances's? *And* yours!

You will have noticed I have made no mention in this letter of the possible P- - - - - - -n t- -p, though you would think the F- - -s would have something more important to do than keep eavesdropping on you and me.

I have heard from Charles Henley again. He will be in New York soon, though the date is not certain. I haven't told Arthur yet, but we will definitely be meeting.

Planted, not in air,

Maggie

P.S. Brian, has any sociologist or psychologist ever studied why so many people walk around with toothpicks sticking out of their mouths?

Sept. 18

Dear Maggie:

What a great lady you are! Joanie is simply enchanted with the birthday doll you sent. She eats and sleeps with it and has named it Peggy. I enjoy hearing your name spoken in my house, aloud, and by my daughter. It is almost as if you will come in from the next room.

Looking at your Greek pictures with me, Joanie wants to know why you live in such strange places, with houses all collapsed, and "all that old-looking stuff." But she thinks you very beautiful, as I do. You have exaggerated again. The sun hat doesn't hide as much as you said, and you certainly don't look like any quince, whatever that looks like, and I don't know either. Frances says it is a perfectly respectable-looking fruit, a sort of pear. Maligned only for its name . . .

I am struck again by the one thing you keep denying, the youthfulness that comes across abundantly from everything your photos show. I am sorry I ever mentioned space-age colonies. Consider instead the eager turn of your head that shares your enjoyment with me. Frances points out the way you stand poised, like a dancer, as if you have been walking fast and stopped suddenly to say hello to us. And your smile, it's a magnet for all of us. Joanie has said it best —simply, "Peggy makes me feel good."

I am angry all over again, angry at the times we missed each other. I am growing tired of knowing you only with the taste of postage glue on my tongue. I suspect you have the same reaction about me, and I am praying that P-------- does not fail us.

When Joanie got your doll and asked if *you* were the Tooth Fairy, I explained you are a friend of mine. She was puzzled and wanted to know why she never saw you, as she sees my other friends. When I told Joanie I have never seen you either, she erupted in giggles. Are you a ghost, she wants to know?

Damn it, Maggie, after all this time, you are a ghost!

In the end, it tickled Joanie mightily that I have a friend who is manifest only in photographs. She confided that she has invisible friends, too, friends who also now appear only in pictures. The ones she misses most are the Big Trees. She tells me they were her guardians in the dark, especially when Kay wasn't home. As I put your photographs away, Joanie wanted to know, "Can Peggy be my friend, too?"

I told her you are indeed.

It is a particular blessing that you thought of the child because, believe it or not, Kay did not. That is abandonment. Still, Kay is notoriously lax about dates, so a gift may yet appear from her.

Kay has sent me the first issue of her group's paper. At the risk of giving offense, the only proper description of it is Total Bullshit. It carries a banner headline: WHAT DO YOU WANT OUT OF LIFE?

What, indeed? That question has become the litany of a fat generation. Self-realization, "personal fulfillment," etc., are *luxuries* seldom before possible in history. In the past, people have been too busy "realizing" food for empty stomachs.

We are the first generations to have any significant energy left over after survival is taken care of. These children forget that all of Alexander's mightiness could not buy him an airplane ticket.

Should Alexander have spent his life stamping his foot and bellowing that he *wanted* to fly?

You once said how painful it is to wish for goals beyond reach. Kay's headline question is basically phony in just that sense. One can only "want from life" what life is prepared to give, assuming thorough preparation and hard work. Anything else is self-defeating. I would paraphrase John Kennedy. Ask not what your life can do for you, ask what you can do for your life. To me what Kay is doing is quixotic, not visionary; chimerical, not imaginative; futile, not rhapsodic. This kind of spirit is not audacious, but insolent; not robust, but feverish; not salubrious, but unwholesome.

To ask a stupid question with great sincerity does not make the question less inane. (Teach sophomores some day!) The tragedy is that posing phony questions as if they were sagacious leads to fruitless explorations and wasted lives—like Kay's.

Before too much of my biliousness shows, let me report that I spoke to Charlie Henley this morning. He is leaving for New York in a day or two and will be staying on Central Park West, which I take to be near you. I am sure you will enjoy each other. Charlie is as pleasant as he is high-powered, not a combination you find often. I commend you to good hands, though wishing they were my own.

Brian

P.S. Toothpicks! My answer is pure speculation. If it were mostly poor people who sport the toothpicks, I might conclude that the fellow wants to show the world he can afford a meal. But affluent people also chew toothpicks just as uncouthly. Perhaps they are harking back to when they were poor. Or they may be affecting a mucker pose to identify with the lower classes. Or it may be simply (complexly?) Freudian orality. Observe that some folks use matches rather than toothpicks, and the answer should cover both conditions. What a Ph.D. effusion that would be! "Incidence of Public Tooth-Picking by Income, Age, Sex, and Place of Origin."

Really, Maggie, you are quite incendiary.

Sept. 22

Dear Brian:

Call Joan "Joanie" in your letters to me if you wish, but call her "Joan" at home as she requested! That is an order.

Tell Joan I am not invisible, and hope very much to prove that to her some day. I am delighted that she likes the doll.

I have now met your friend Charles Henley, and he is as impressive a man as you said. Before I report on developments, let me preface this letter with a reassurance I am sure you do not require:

As compared with Charles Henley, you, Brian Curtiss, are far better looking, more attractive, and beyond question more my style in every way. Not that Henley is disagreeable, but he does have a California manner I don't sense from you, just a little breezy for my taste, a touch too informal. I find Henley charming, yes, but he makes me slightly uncomfortable, as I am never uncomfortable with you. On the contrary, with you I am my most comfortable self of all.

There, that should quiet your jealousy, which of course I have found very flattering—as, too, your overkind comments about my pictures.

There have now been several meetings with your friend. The first, held in Arthur's office, was stiff and all business. It came to me that I had never witnessed Arthur in professional action. It was a revelation. He, who seldom smiles, was one big smile. I have never seen so much of my husband's teeth. But it wasn't the half-shy smile I have loved from the first night my father brought him home. This was a plastic grimace. I remember that a show of teeth is an animal way of displaying hostility. I was afraid Arthur's face would crack if he changed his expression.

I take it to be a gambit that puts opponents off in an adversary proceeding, eh? The "Arthur" nods and smiles you into a sense of false security, and when you are well lulled, he wallops you over the head. Still smiling.

I must say, Brian, I do not like Arthur-the-lawyer too well and am glad he is a much nicer person around the house. I found the whole episode disturbing, and I saw that Henley was quite put off. I could not blame him, and I accepted at once when he later asked if I would meet with him alone at the apartment where he is staying. At this point I want to thank you again for not letting this project get away from me. It is decidedly my cup of tea and has very promising potential in terms of both personal satisfaction for me and the possibility of profit, to which I am not at all averse.

Our business discussions to date can be summed up in an exchange of fortune cookies served in a Chinese restaurant last night. Mr. Henley's read (I swear): "Person who makes waves sails on new tide."

Mine said (I swear): "Person who makes waves capsize own boat."

Confucius need to make up his mind!

And so do I.

Because I do confront a bigger wave now than any of us anticipated. And it is quite likely to capsize the whole deal. Charles Henley wants $50,000 as an investment! Frankly, I never contemplated anything that pricey. I assumed he was thinking of a token amount.

I haven't spoken to Arthur about this yet, but it is bound to confirm every doubt he has had, justified or not.

If I *were* to consider going it alone, it would take almost every dollar my father left me, and, frankly, I don't find that too agreeable a prospect. I understand Mr. Henley's wanting a full partner, but I do wonder why, since he is wealthy, he has named such a high figure. Maybe $50,000 doesn't sound like much to a Californian, but it's a great deal of money to a Bostonian living in New York.

I did have to laugh at myself, Brian. When I went alone to Mr. Henley's apartment, I felt guilty, as if I were cheating. Cheating not on Arthur but on *you*. When Henley offered me a glass of wine I felt even worse. That should have been *our* drink. It seemed traitorous to be having it with someone else. Still, in a way it was appropriate enough, since Henley is my contemporary in age.

Yet meeting Henley has been like catching a sensation of you, the way a messenger carries something of the vibration of the sender. Or, rather, being with someone who actually knows you makes you suddenly more real in the real world than before.

It made me sad, because it's you I want to meet, and not any courier, pleasant and my contemporary though he be.

Brian, you still owe me the list of birthdays.

And I can't help but inquire whether anything has come for Joan from Kay.

My regards to Frances, love to the children, as I find myself hoping, even more now, for word of P- - - - - - - -!

As always,
Maggie

180   ·

Sept. 25

Maggie dear:

I am making sure to call Joanie "Joan." Your scolding was entirely in order, and I am grateful for it.

Attached is the birthday list. Thank you for wanting it and for having become a member of the family. It is the best gift any of us could have.

There has been no word from Kay, and I believe it is just as well. It would only stir up new questions just when the children are accepting the household as it is. I cannot psychoanalyze Kay, but she must be terribly afraid of love to prefer a pinchbeck life to what she could have here.

American women seem to be in trouble. A recent study shows some *20 million* women into drugs and abuse of medication-and-alcohol! That is about one out of every five women. Just count off, sitting on a bus, or standing on a supermarket line. It's hard to take in, isn't it?

And this reflects only the observable abuse, the problems visible enough to become a statistic. We can reasonably expect that the number of afflicted women is greater than the data show. And how much distress, beyond that, is reflected in other responses and syndromes the contemporary woman displays, like Kay's eternal fidgeting, to say nothing of extramarital affairs, marriages à trois, à quatre, à cuckoo . . .

I'm not saying this to get mired in a Spenglerian swamp with you again, but to view Kay as part of a general malaise rather than a "wicked woman" herself.

I don't have data on men, but I'm sure they would show similar unhappiness.

The meaning for us, for you and me, is to enjoy our lives as well as we can. That cannot be urged too often.

I have had a note from Charlie, and my worst suspicions are aroused. Not only is he enthusiastic about the prospect of having you as a business partner, but he thinks you are one of the most attractive women he has ever met. As I so well know.

I am consumed with pangs of jealousy.

Your bosh-and-quibble about our ages continues to plague me. I wish you would lay that bugaboo to rest once and for all. Maggie, I feel a closer bond with you at this point than I ever felt with Kay, except at the very beginning. I can put it no other way. We have grown very near, you and I, and it is simply indecent of you to keep throwing unnecessary rocks in our path.

Incidentally, let me give you another reason for joining C. Henley Enterprises. It would give you an excuse to come to Los Angeles and visit here tax deductible to boot!

However, I too am given pause by the $50,000 requirement. Charlie never discussed details with me, and I am in no position to comment one way or another. I am confident you will make the decision that is right for you.

I have held the bad news for last. The Princeton seminar is doubtful, according to the latest word. It's not canceled entirely, but it's fading. There is some problem about funding. My own guess is that, though you and I have hardly whispered, our Nemesis got wind of the possibility and dropped everything else in the universe to throttle it! You win some and lose some and lose some and lose some . . .

Dammit!
Brian

Oct. 3

Dear Brian:

It's been a long week since I wrote last, with things in a jumble-and-tumble here. For a while I was thrown off balance, and right now I am not at all sure of my thoughts or emotions or decisions, except for a consuming rage at Arthur.

I am writing this from Charlie Henley's apartment, where I have been staying the past few days.

I would have gone to Lorna's but Gary is living there now. That is a separate headache for me. All I can tell Gary and Lorna is that they should not take my resigned acceptance for approval. Apparently, there is simply no longer any concept of guilt in living together without marriage. Frankly, I did not expect it of Lorna and am disappointed in her. Yet I suppose what is happening in morality is much like what has happened in art (and I am not sure which came first!). Today, as I enjoy Bartok, Webern, Berg, I recall that Stravinsky stirred a riot in 1913 with *Sacre* in Paris. To modern ears there is simply no such thing as dissonance. It seems that to modern youth there is simply no such thing as immorality.

Let me take it from the top, as Charlie would say.

It started with Arthur balking when I told him of the $50,000. I can see his reservations about the risk involved, but that wasn't the sticking point as much as something else that shocked me totally. Arthur is openly jealous of Charles Henley! He as much as accused me of being interested in Charlie as a man as well as a partner! You should have seen Arthur's face when I spoke of the traveling Henley and I would plainly have to do together. My husband appalls me! After all these years he does not trust me! His suspicion of me is *genuine!* I cannot conceive it, I cannot believe it, I cannot and will in no way accept it!

Some wives might feel complimented. I feel hollowed out!

In any case, for whatever his reasons, Arthur presented his final decision yesterday. He will not put up a cent for me.

I told him that, very well, I would invest my own money, and that was *my* final decision, and there wasn't a cheeky, bloody thing he could do about it because he had not the faintest claim of control over what my father had left to me.

I felt very set up indeed! I thanked Father, for the first time, from the bottom of my heart. He who had stolen my independence had given me the financial means to assert it. That is a lovely poetic justice for me.

But my husband responded, incredibly, "It is *not* your money!"

The air dribbled out of my balloon. Had those two lawyers maneuvered some trick to cut the ground from under my feet? I spluttered that I knew my father's will, there were no strings attached to my funds, I wasn't some dimwit knucklehead Arthur could pull the wool over the eyes of!

Now Arthur was shouting. "It is not your money without strings because your father meant for you to use it prudently. Your father would have forbidden this crackbrained investment, and I stand in his place as his surrogate and fiduciary to protect the intent of his bequest!"

I couldn't credit my ears. Even Arthur must have known he was speaking hysterically, as either attorney or husband. I had not realized how insecure he was! He could only be raving so grossly because he had a fear of our marriage at its center! What a revelation to me!

One part of me actually felt sorry for the man. He was biting his pipe so hard he broke the stem. Another part of me felt not just anger but—yes, I can confide it to you, Brian—contempt!

But then Arthur topped himself. His face got red as a fire truck as he threw down the gauntlet. He lifted his right hand with his first finger poked up in the air histrionically—for all the world like some Shakespearian actor about to declaim—and declaimed.

An Ultimatum!

An Order from the mountaintop of his authority over little me, now supposed to be cringing and bathed in tears of remorse and self-reproach. Arthur proclaimed: If I went on with Mr. Henley, I was never to return to him!

Voice of doom, thundering the earth with his authority over me, my liege lord paramount!

I yelled at him, a fishwife for the first time in my life. *"You don't own me, you know!"*

Arthur's answer was flabbergasting. "No wonder Gary went haywire!" I suppose that kind of irrelevancy confuses witnesses in court, but I was not about to be switched off my new track.

I got even louder (my throat still rasps and hurts), and I threw at Arthur every single slogan from every women's book and magazine. "I am not just your cook and bedmate, you know!" (That sounded feeble, even to me. I need feminist slogans of my own, Brian!)

Arthur got control of himself. More lawyer-strategy. When you goad the witness to yelling, you calm way down to a whisper. Now he came on with a patronizing smile and a bland sigh. He said, "I don't understand you, Peggy."

Ha! Brian, listen hard to what I am about to write. It is terribly important for a sociologist to know about, and very few people who are abused this way are aware they are being attacked, much less able to mount a defense.

One of the strongest cudgels in the world is that unholy phrase: "I don't understand you."

Those four devil-inspired words were used as a weapon against me by Arthur from our first date.

The beauty of using those four words as a sword is that they undo the victim every single time whether you are right or wrong.

They always put me immediately on the defensive. My automatic response was a headlong dive into guilt. If the great mind of Arthur Webb did not understand me, the fault obviously had to be mine. I had been (again) unclear, stupid, incomplete, obscure, vague, and imbecilic. So *I* would go searching for the fault in me, instead of telling Arthur to go fly a kite!

Charlie says the "I-don't-understand-you" technique is widely used in the business world, with malice aforethought. He believes some executives do it relatively innocently, but that most are calculating, particularly in dealing with subordinates.

Does sociology get into this? That phrase is nothing less than a mental switchblade!

When this came to me in a blinding flash, I shifted roles! I came off the wall at Arthur! Instead of hastening to explain myself abjectly, as always before, this time I shouted that *I did not understand HIM!*

Arthur was so taken aback, he found nothing to say. He stared at me with eyes that looked like two poached eggs.

Eggs. I know why that figure of speech got associated right here. Because I have spent my life walking on eggs with this man. Do you know, if I had something to say that might upset Arthur, I would actually rehearse my words first?

That is quite a different picture of my marriage than I have let you see before. It doesn't mean the memorable good times are not true. It does mean I have too long closed my own eyes to the underside of this relationship.

Blinders and earmuffs—I wore them constantly in the interest of peace, in the interest of Gary, in the interest of my mother and my father and all my ancestors right back to the first amoeba. I did what they all expected of me.

To save what? This afternoon I was reading a letter of the poet Pasternak to his friend Mandelstann: "Everything is covered with hardened layers of accumulated insensitivity, deafness, entrenched routine."

That is a too-true definition of my marriage.

And it's my fault, too. Kneeling is a posture from which it is difficult to command respect.

The woman Arthur Webb has known only as his wife lives in her own skin, not his. She can and will now make her decisions, and make her mistakes. For the sake of her very soul.

I wound up our marital battle with an ultimatum of my own. I walked out on my husband. Not as I did over Gary, the time I went to Lorna's. This is in earnest.

I moved to a hotel, but Charlie is quite right that I ought not waste money when he has the use of this huge apartment where I have separate rooms of my own.

This time I *was* Nora, quite consciously so I might add. When Arthur realized it, he dropped his pride. As I moved to the door, dressed and suitcased to leave, he called to me—I could hear the disbelief and shock and pain in his voice, and I wanted to turn back to him and kiss the top of his head and tell him there *is* old love in me for him as well as my new anger.

But I went straight on out. This time nothing he might have pleaded could move me. I have done pussyfooting with that man!

I did leave a note in the bedroom, which I assume he has seen. I have told Arthur I don't know what I will yet decide about our future, but I must have time for myself now. I intend it to be considerable time.

Brian, I am finally becoming a contemporary in action. I can't believe I am off "in my own space." I have a new regard and respect for myself that has nothing to do with Arthur Webb or—let me be totally candid—nothing to do with Charlie, or even with you.

Now you will be pleased to hear this, Brian Curtiss: I have never felt so YOUNG.

I am sure it is no accident that when I dreamed my white chamber last night, the window was larger and had moved down the wall. It is still too high, but it is coming within reach.

The first thing Charlie and I did this morning after depositing my check to the account of Henley Enterprises was to buy *two* tickets to Los Angeles.

I am coming West! (Tax-deductible, as you said!) To start a new career *and,* finally and hopefully, to see and visit Brian Curtiss! I am saying it aloud, shouting it! No whispering now about anything, because things are going to be my way for a change!

So . . .

Brave new world for Margaret Fairfield. (I am using my maiden name in the business.) Who knows what the future now holds? A week ago my life was as predictable as Arthur's charts in the medicine chest. Today, let 'er rip! Life begins at 50!

I've waited too long!
Maggie F.

P.S. I have told Charlie I want him to hang back when the plane lands in Los Angeles. I want my first sight of you to be just the two of us. I would never have had the audacity to plan that before. I hope you admire the new me as much as I do. I leave in a week, will send you details before then.

Oct. 6

Maggie:

Fantastic that you are coming out here.

Thank you for thinking of asking Charlie to wait. It does want to be a private moment.

By coincidence, Frances is taking Joan and Paul to Illinois to visit my father, who is ill. I would have liked to go along, but my classes have started. Fortunately, it isn't anything serious, but makes a good excuse for the trip. The children haven't seen "P-Pop" for too long. So the house will be ours alone, unless you will be more comfortable in a nearby motel. You can decide after you get here.

Impatiently,
Brian

P.S. Don't think I haven't noticed how quickly you have moved from "Mr. Henley" to "Charlie." But I'm joking. That is exactly as it should be. Charlie doesn't stay Charles for very long to anyone he likes.

Oct. 9

Brian:

Just a quick note, fingers crossed, to say that, though Charlie and I have had to delay for a week, we will be on our way and *nothing* will interfere with my meeting you this time, I promise.

I have talked to Gary and Lorna about Arthur and me. It is to laugh! Or groan. They understand freedom when it is for them. They aren't quite so sure it sits well for *me*.

They are both deeply troubled by my separation from Arthur. They have to say they understand, of course, but I see their puzzled, even hurt, looks. I tell you it is nothing less than theatre of the absurd to see Gary frown when I say I don't know when I'll be back from the Coast.

I won't write again before we take off, too many loose ends to tie up here. See you soon! Can't believe that I am . . .

Evangeline no longer!

Part Six

Oct. 18

Brian—

It was the most beautiful thing that has ever happened to me. And the most impossible.

I do not regret that it happened. It must never happen again.

Brian, it takes two to love, three is unfaithful. That is not for me.

I have refused to take your calls because I cannot trust myself with you, as I proved too clearly in your home.

Still, I owe it to you to let you know that I am all right. You will have seen by the postmark that I am in Malibu. I am staying with Charlie.

I am very seriously considering returning to New York. A woman my age should not be traipsing around. In any case, it is cruel at my age to be made to feel young again.

I cannot handle the contradiction. I am not transformed, I am mangled.

I beg one favor of you, dearest Brian. If you love me as you say you do, please do not write to me again. It is too painful. This is my last letter to you, and this time there will be no changing my mind.

With my love always,
Maggie

Oct. 21

Maggie:

It was the most beautiful and perfect thing that ever happened in my life too. And the most absolutely right.

I will, if I must, respect your wish that I never write to you again. Can you truly want that? Let me share what is in my heart.

We both knew, didn't we, that what happened was inevitable from the moment you came through the airline gate. I suspect that inwardly we both sensed it long ago, from almost the very first letters.

Of that night, what stays with me is how ageless you are. It is important for you to know that I have never experienced passion like yours. I never knew a "young" woman who loved so completely, gave herself so totally and so beautifully. You brought me to a sexual passion I did not know was in me. You lifted me out of myself. You took me into a world I long ago dismissed as romantic illusion, not real in prosaic life.

Knowing your "puritanism" so well, I should have been astonished when you came through my door with your eyes shining for me, your lips turning for mine, and your arms opening for me.

I was not astonished.

I turned to you the same way, with the same profound knowledge of our love for each other, our need for each other.

The woman who moved into my arms was not the one who had written letters from New York. I held a new person, free, uninhibited. You wanted the magic and transport between us as I did, and you did not hide it. There was nothing to separate us, no miles, no years. There was only the love we had both tried for so long to call by other names, or to deny entirely.

We said not ten words at the airport. Henley saw how it was and made his considerate quick excuse to leave. It was as if you and I had always been together. There was nothing to say, only the hunger for each other we shared beyond speech, beyond thought. We needed no wine or music, only the enchantment of my hand on your shoulder at last, and the smile of your willing answer.

Everything floated together in a dream, irresistibly, all silently taken and given the way waves come to shore and recede, in vastness, in passion, finally in peace. We had traveled across space and time, reaching for each other with our paper words for so long. We had strung our paper dolls across the country pretending it was only a game, pretending because it was so vastly and profoundly not a game with either of us. Isn't that true?

It is why you and I had finally to lie on a shore of our love together, as naturally and simply, as innocently and perfectly, as sea and sky exist.

I am different now and can tell that to you for both of us. My lungs are new, the air is fresher. I see brighter colors in every street, every field, each leaf and petal of flowers. I know what you have done for me. Before you, the world was written in invisible ink. Your love has evoked the world in joy, radiance, and new beauty.

But not hope?

Now you are denying me, us, hope. I wish I were a poet instead of straining to make you hear. I fear all you are hearing is the strain in me and not the music I cannot free.

Knowing your love has stretched me, Maggie. I live in a new, wider space. I am out of a sleep I did not know I was drowsing in. *I* was the one becoming old, dear love. Old in my academic pride, the measured respect of my students and colleagues, my dignified future assured in my world. You, who have so unmercifully scourged yourself with years, have brought me back to untenured youth.

Of course I understand why you ask me not to write. Everything has happened too quickly, too turbulently. Suddenly you are out of your familiar shell, not only into a career, but into emotions that nothing in your life has prepared you to contend with.

This private earthquake of ours has shaken me too, me and whatever may be left of my marriage. I am not sure how to deal with this wonder either. But we must not turn away from it because we can't see how to fit it in! You and I stand at the threshold of a magnificent mansion, with unexplored rooms inviting us in every direction. It is an enchantment, yes, but the mansion holds only more beauty, not trolls and witches. I promise!

You are shaken, Maggie, and so am I, but we need not be afraid. Listen.

For myself, it has become clear now how this should be resolved. It is simply wrong for people who love each other as we do to be apart. It is a waste of happiness in a world that owns too little happiness. That may be the most unholy sin of all.

I remember the piercing prayer you taught: *"I am thankful for a new day . . ."*

I have not always been able to say that in my life, but I have said it since you.

192   .

Your prayer, so true and so challenging, gives me the right to answer our dilemma in the only way it can be answered. There is only one resolution for us. I am asking you to marry me.

This is no impulse, no rebound of a cast-off husband, no effusion of a moonstruck juvenile. It is considered, responsible, and beleaguered.

Margaret Webb cannot answer me, I know. But Margaret Fairfield can. Let me be a Herr Professor for a moment to plead my cause, Maggie. This is so difficult and so momentous for us that nothing less than the perspective of Death itself can help me. The philosopher Heidegger stands at my shoulder, telling me to remind you that "Death is the last possibility."

Isn't that an eye-opening way of defining *life?*—because it teaches that life is *"the renewing possibility,"* the opening up of the greatest range of meaningful possibilities, which for us, so happily, is love.

I've said it clumsily, as a professor would. I am not at ease in declaring love, in wooing you. I risk frightening you further off.

I know you have a thousand good reasons why "it would not work." Of course those reasons exist, and probably more. But they weigh less than a feather against the gift we have together. We have a right.

Maggie, we should at the least see each other again. We need only talk, nothing more. But it is a crime to cut us down just as we have come together. I beg you to reconsider. The thought of looking up and seeing a passing plane that might be carrying you away is more than I can bear.

Please answer me.

> We do have a right.
> Brian

Oct. 24

Brian:

Although I said I would not write again, your letter touched me, obviously. You are right that it is not fair of me to leave without another word.

But please do not misunderstand my writing now. This is *not* to resume our relationship, the old one or the new one. I mean it when I ask you never to write to me again, and I truly intend it when I tell you this is the last you will hear from me.

It is really simplicity itself, Brian. We went too far. What happened in your home was not what I intended when I left my husband.

Let me say quickly that I am not blaming you, not in any way. You are right that I do want to be with you. I want that more than I . . . the only way to express it is to say that for the first time in my life I know what the word "want" means. You are right that it was beautiful and joyous, glorious.

And it was of my own free will. I want you to know that beyond question, and I never want to forget it, myself.

I want you to know, dear Brian, that I am glad it happened, not sorry. Happy for it with all my heart.

That is just why I do not want to go on. It would make everything tawdry and common instead of the glowing jewel I now possess.

Marry you? Oh, Brian, how many ill-starred lovers through all the years have bemoaned that they were not born in the right time, did not meet in the right place? You and I are disconnected in too many ways. I know you are sincere, and I love you more for it, but one night together does not burn through all the bindings that tether me to my old life, despite that traumatic quarrel with Arthur.

The truth is I am giddy with confusion, with this split in my personalities. I think this must be the reaction of a zoo animal that has gotten out of its cage by mistake. Exhilarated to be free, but bewildered at the absence of bars. Bars are not just constraints, they are safety, too.

And I am still in a state of shock. Laugh at me if you will. In these liberated days, sleeping with a man not your husband is supposed to be no big deal. But it is not my character. I am encapsulated in guilt, Brian.

I am pleased about one thing anyway. I can write all this with total honesty to you, including the truth I have been struggling to face—what frightens me most, Brian, is the great joy I knew with you. You write of my awakening *you*. Oh, my dearest, I have been such a wooden wife! I live the night over and over, learning how much I have been cheated of in the years of my ignorance. With you, I learned what I have never believed of the whispers I have occasionally heard. I always thought they were exaggeration, gossipy effusion. I was content with what I had.

What you taught me terrifies me. Oh, my beloved, being with you was like driving a speeding car that suddenly skids violently out of control. There is nothing more harrowing for me. It happened to me once, actually, and I will never forget the awful helplessness when the telephone pole rushed straight at me. The crash sprung the door and I was whipped out. The great beast of a car kept ricocheting on the icy road, nearly crushed me a half-dozen times. I was in pure agony lying there immobile before those monstrous wheels.

That terror came back to me last night in a dream. It is your bed that is the icy road where the juggernaut will destroy me.

Brian, don't you see that for me even to remotely consider *marriage* would be insanity, going totally out of control? Accuse me of being helplessly cemented in middle-class-itis, I will agree. Tell me security and habit are splints keeping me from dancing, I will agree. Tell me our dream mansion holds real treasure for us, I will concede. But you have yet to learn the hard lesson I now know too well: There is some harness impossible to remove after it has been worn too long. Yes, listen—in some terrible way I don't even want to take it off, even though I champ at the bit when the iron chafes my mouth, as my marriage has chafed it.

The irony is that I might be able to go on with you if we cared *less*. It is just because we have turned out to be such a churning, cataclysmic Vesuvius that I must escape. You are threatening every slope of my life. To call it love rather than threat is bravado, not courage.

I know how desperate you feel, because I feel desperate too. I know your loss because it is mine. But that is no excuse to compound our mistake.

I must face it, Brian. For one thing, and bluntly, I do not see myself as a mother to two small children. Besides, Joanie and Paul deserve a mother young enough to deal with their wonderful energy, a woman young enough to grow with them. You know in your heart and in your head that I am right. You know, too, that the future must hold such a woman for you and the children, whether it will be Kay again or someone new. In either case, I surely must not be in the way, must not be a block. Whatever else is confused, this one paramount and overriding consideration is absolutely crystal clear.

Oh, how hard it is to write this, but the arithmetic of our lives *is* malevolent and cross-grained to our love. Brian, you need no pencil to know that in ten years Joanie and Paul will be in their teens, and I, *60*—fine for a grandmother's holiday visits, but not for the mother they will badly need every day at that age, as I know so well from my experiences with Gary. And how can we blink our own birthdays, my dear? In 20 years you will be young and vigorous at about 50, while I will be 70—with all your good wishes, hardly in my prime.

Maybe, if there were no question of the children, we might nevertheless claim the years we could enjoy together. There are many such marriages, of course. And those years might well be worth everything else. But the equation still has to deal with my own marriage, and Arthur.

You turn away from that too easily by saying we have "a right," our love has "a right."

Life is unfortunately not that neatly wrought. I recall a verse my father used when he taught me to drive. It told of a driver who insisted on his right of way when another car was clearly violating a red light . . .

> *He was right, dead right,*
> *But he was just as dead*
> *As if he was wrong!*

I have never forgotten that, you see, and it is apposite now. It is not enough to be right. I am not a swooning damsel, no tender Evangeline. You and I are surrounded by real red lights, Brian, and loud warning sirens on all the intersections of our lives. I don't want, for either of us, a smashup that would leave people as injured as if we were wrong.

What else can I say to you, my dear?

That I am weeping as I write these damnable words at you. Should I tell you the typewriter clacking under my ears sounds like gunshots? It does. Will it make it easier for you—or harder—if I tell you I am drowning in my love, freely confessed, for you? Easier or harder if I tell you that as I sit here this minute I ache for you, yearn for your touch, your kiss, yes, your flesh. I don't know myself, don't recognize myself, don't own myself. I am bold and brassy enough to confess I am on fire with the memory of your hard young body. My skin feels your strong arms and I want the hot lightning you sent coursing through my mummied husk waking me, waking me, bringing me to that full joy for the very first time in my life. I did not know what it could be. I did not suspect.

I want you again that way. Oh, so much, so incredibly much. Too much! and that is why it cannot happen again.

Brian, I wish I were different. I wish I were one of the free spirits (I think there are fewer such women than are made out to be!), but *I* am *not* free. I can propel myself toward the future but I am also and always a creature of my past. I don't believe in transformation, in metamorphosis. I am in a constraint that cannot be shed. I am not an insect.

My stepping away from my husband has been a good thing, and wise for me. There *are* changes I need to make in my life, want to make, am able to make. You are not one of them. I have not foreclosed that there can and should be a sensible accommodation between Arthur and me, about my work, about my privacy.

Oh, how stiff and cruddy that sounds! As if I am trying to have my cake and eat it too. But the bottom line (to use a phrase of Arthur's) is that I remain bound by my nature. Maybe I wish I had some other nature. I may curse myself, but I cannot change the color of my eyes. Life doesn't round things off, unfortunately. It leaves splinters and sharp corners and shin traps. Call me hopeless. My skid in your bed has made me a more cautious driver, not more reckless.

Ever since that night I have been listening to myself, hard. I am still getting back mixed-up signals. Perhaps I am my own conspiracy of defeat. Perhaps I connive with myself in a complicity of deception, like walking in a hall of distorting mirrors, but this hall is the only house I really know. For me, I suppose, it has to be enough to live by the amenities. Didn't Freud say that what we *do* is what we most truly wish to be doing? Then I most truly do not wish to be with you.

I wish this was not so painful for both of us. I am full of anger and resentment. I have tried to follow the Instruction Sheet of my life for all my years, only to see again and again that the directions are garbled, twisted, misleading. God is worse than the most stupid manufacturers. At least with their products you can guess what part is missing, what errors need to be corrected. God's pattern seems only frustration.

I don't say this with self-pity, but with self-disgust. How I do wish I were one of those who can knife across doubts, dismiss confusions.

Let me share one last thing with you, Brian Curtiss. This honesty hurts! It is hurting me terribly. I have more pain than when they cut me in the hospital.

And if we were to go on trying to write to each other, as we did before, every letter would only be another scalpel slicing away.

I don't want that, and I don't think you want it, either.

Please. Let us remember the joy of us and not continue this wrestling. We were given a gift, as you have so well and dearly said. We can cherish it. Even the one night was more than we might have expected, given all our circumstances. We can be grateful rather than melancholy.

I am glad that Charlie wants me to travel about for a while. (Alone.) Keeping busy will help me, it always has. I will be going up to Sacramento and down to San Diego, and that will keep my mind off you.

My mind. Not my heart. If there is comfort for you in that, I say it happily.

Now there is nothing else, except . . .

> Goodbye,
> Margaret Fairfield Webb

P.S. Do you know John Donne's, "A Valediction: Forbidding Mourning"? It is beautiful, Brian, and needs now to be true for you as well as it is true for me . . .

> *Dull sublunary lovers' love,*
> *(Whose soule is sense) cannot admit*
> *Absence, because it doth remove*
> *Those things which elemented it.*
> *But we by a love so much refined,*
> *That ourselves know not what it is,*
> *Inter-assured of the mind,*
> Care lesse, eyes, lips, hands to misse.
>
> *Our two soules therefore, which are one,*
> *Though I must goe, endure. . .*

Even so, dear Brian, let me goe, and let us endure.

Oct. 28

Maggie:

I am sending this care of Charlie, hoping both that it will reach you and that you will relent. I have to take the chance that you will not throw it into the wastebasket. It is miserably difficult for me to accept your decision. John Donne's poem of renunciation is lovely and mollifying, but it isn't persuasive to me. Neither he nor you can forbid me my mourning at my loss.

I have a recurring dream now. I keep climbing stairs in a building, but as I rise new stories are constructed above. How am I ever to reach the top? Then I dream of a man in bed who finds that if he pulls his blanket high enough to warm his neck, it is too short to cover his feet, so he cuts a piece off the top to lengthen the bottom. That is the state to which you have reduced me.

Would it help if I took back my precipitous proposal? I can understand your feeling marriage to be rash, premature, unsuitable.

It was a measure of my desperation, my aching fear of losing you.

I had it in mind that things would-could work out somehow, with Frances staying with us to look after the children. But I suppose that could only be a temporary arrangement, so you are not wrong on that score. But only on that score.

Would it save us to live another day if I retreat to "Can't we be friends?" or—what was that sociological locution?—"companionate lovers"?

Still hopefully,
Brian

Dec. 21

Dear Margaret Fairfield Webb:

You win. I have no way of knowing whether you ever saw my last letter, but your silence for over a month says it no longer matters. I find your silence a physical assailant, a killer. It stands like a murderer over my bed when I sleep. It accosts me every morning when I awaken. It bludgeons me when I am lecturing before my classes, it scatters my papers when I am working on my book, it blinds and deafens me when I try to be with the children and Frances.

I think only of you. At times with a granite anger. I never wanted or intended to love and need you as I do. I never wanted or intended to give any other person such a weapon against my life, especially after Kay.

All right. I have thought about all of this unblinkingly now. Last night I lifted a glass in a toast to our friendship, to give it a decent burial. Notice I have written "friendship," not "love." If you loved me, you would not find it possible to slaughter me with your silence as you have done.

We could have worked out the complications. You chose to let them overwhelm you, and dry up our lives, because you are the fainthearted coward you always said you were. I may love you, but I do not like the coward I find in you.

I regret ending our correspondence and our relationship on an embittered note. I ought to thank you for memories that will enrich me as long as I live, but that would be a lie. I am full of hurt pride, vindictiveness, and rage. I have learned, thanks to you, that there is something worse than missing Paradise, and that is a short trip through it. Only the Devil works that way.

You once said you believe the Devil walks the earth these times.

Are you the Devil, Margaret Fairfield Webb? (With everything else in our time being feminized, how has "Lucy-fer" been overlooked!)

For one night I thought I knew who you truly were. To that wonderful woman, a sad good-bye, then.

Brian Curtiss

P.S. Just to complete the record, if anything I do in the future should happen to stir another "unabashed fan letter," you may be sure it will, decidedly, go unanswered by me.

Part Seven

Christmas Day

Dear What-Shall-I-Call-You?

I hope this reaches you somehow, with holiday wishes from all of us.

I miss hearing from you, sorely. I don't blame you for not writing, since you have never received my retraction (my last letters have been returned to me by the post office; prayerfully this one will not be). What I have tried to tell you is my realization that my talk of marriage was ill-considered.

Can't we still write to each other? I have no thought now that things can be as they were, but there is a gaping hole in my life without word from you, and I suspect the same is true for you.

I happened upon Longfellow in the library and read *Evangeline* again, for the first time in years. To my surprise I find it a powerful and moving work. The name of Evangeline's betrothed, that I could not remember, is Gabriel.

Gabriel Lajeunesse, make of that what you will! I needed no help in identifying with the young man to whom destiny denied his love until too late.

Joan, Paul, and Frances join me in wishing you a Merry Christmas and a Happy New Year.

Make mine happy by writing.

Brian

Dec. 30

Dear Brian:

I find I can't be withdrawn during the holiday season. Charles did forward your greeting to me here in San Diego, where I am seeing people on business. I suppose it was the Christmas envelope that led Charles to disregard my instructions. Well, I was glad to get it in a way. And sad. Because there is still nothing more that I have to say. I hope you find that as time passes it is easier to forget and turn to the future. That is coming to be true for me.

It is especially true because I have now heard from Arthur and have just completed a letter to him. It is my first since I left home. He has been too stiff-necked to write, and I have been too occupied with business and more to the point, too uncertain of my own mind.

Brian, as time begins to fade out my lapse, I find that I want more and more *to* forget. Because I am ashamed. Whatever else you and I have said and felt and rationalized, in my deepest self I am ashamed of my conduct—not because of my father, not because of Arthur, but because I am the way I am, as I have had to say to you before.

This circles us both back to the fact that I cannot change my spots. Even if I would like to, it is impossible. My sense of shame circulates with my very blood, accusing and accusing with every heartbeat.

As I have said, I am sure that many women and men would think me foolish for such agonizing about what so many take so casually these days. I think if I were one of "the enlightened," you would be the first to turn away.

Perhaps the only way to make you stop writing is to show you the kind of turmoil with which I am trying to make my peace. I have a letter from Arthur that confronts me with the dilemma I have created, and I feel that it is addressed as much to you as to me. Rather than try to paraphrase Arthur's sentiments, I have decided to send you excerpts of what he has written. Here they are, as received just after Christmas:

... As your husband, I must say it is impossibly strange to be writing a letter to you this Christmas morning instead of being with you at our tree, opening the family presents as always, taking our holiday drink together.

The shock of your incomprehensible act in leaving me has worn off a little. It is now 87 days since you walked out. I am assuming you are still

working with Mr. Henley and that this will reach you through his office
. . .

Gary and Lorna came over to the apartment last night, but there was no Christmas spirit here, no lift in decorating the tree. It was always you who put the family angel on top, the gilt cardboard figure that Gary made long ago in kindergarten. Gary didn't want to touch it. He, too, felt how incomplete, even grotesque, the evening was without your presence. The tree was an empty gesture in an empty holiday. Lorna finally went up the ladder, but as if mirroring my feelings, the arms of the angel tore off. Gary patched it with tape and set it in place, but I couldn't help but see the broken, forlorn, lusterless angel as symbolic of what has happened to all of us . . .

No one knows what to do about my Christmas presents for you. How can gay packages look so dreary? I'll store them in your closet . . .

I am concerned about you, Margaret. Gary tells me the Henley project is showing signs of life, and for that I am pleased of course. No one would be more satisfied than I to find the venture fully legitimate and even lucrative. But I am worried about your health. You have tried to make light of your surgery and its aftermath. That is admirable in its way, but you should be here where Dr. Douglas can check up on you . . .

Margaret, I submit that this undefined, irrational, nonarrangement between us must be clarified. I would have thought that after 27 years of marriage you would in the first place have had more consideration for me than to stalk out of our home as you did. Your note was unfair and unwarranted, even conceding fault on my part. If I was in an excess of temper it was for your own sake, and to protect you . . .

But I am not writing to blame or scold, or denounce; on the contrary, to concede that I was at fault in being peremptory about your use of your money. Yet, it must be said that from my point of view I would have been derelict as both your husband and your attorney—and your father's— had I not cautioned you as emphatically as I did. You might have appreciated my sense of obligation instead of taking umbrage . . .

I had no reason to believe you were so unhappy with me, as must have been the case to cause so violent and out of character a performance. I considered our differences to be no more than the run-of-the-mill marital disagreements. Your untoward reaction shows again how little we know of people we think we know. It is another proof, I might note, that an attorney can never be too careful in probing witnesses, his own as well as his adversary's. After many years of professional observation, I have concluded that surfaces are *always* deceptive. No one should be surprised when life presents the unexpected, no matter how smooth the veneer may have seemed.

That goes for my own personality as well. This admission may raise your eyebrows, Margaret, but it is entirely possible that you know me as little as I apparently have apprehended you.

To all outward appearances, my conduct bespeaks an individual who is well adjusted and contented with his days and his life-style. If you had stayed to continue our discussion instead of storming out, some eye-openers may have emerged, on my side as well as yours.

For example, you ought to know that I do *fully* understand your impulse (what I find incomprehensible is that you would *act* on it). What you were reflecting in your tantrum is normal enough at our stage of marriage. It's no news that relationships grow stale, people get an itch for something new and different. If it hadn't been Mr. Henley's chance proposition, it would have been some other trigger. Perhaps your correspondence with your California professor would have stirred things up.

No sensible person would find this too surprising, for marriage is always a balancing act. One side of the scales is weighted by our old-shoe familiarity. That counts a great deal for people of our age. But on the other scale is the *cost* of that comfort. I, too, recognize that people pay a considerable price in personal freedom for a marriage's sake. As a lawyer, I know even better than you the inevitability of one partner or the other asking one day what the marriage is worth . . .

Well, you have been having your adventure. I am frank to say that I admire your gumption.

But what can I do to bring you back now, Margaret?

It would not be true or fair to say I miss you passionately. I am not a young swain, and you would recognize the hyperbole.

Passion has not been our long suit, and I have not been getting younger or more ardent, I know all too regretfully and regrettably.

But we have had a great deal together aside from "romantic love." Need I catalog a marriage counselor's checklist of the many happy and positive things between us? Most important, I have concluded there is no reason why you should not continue your business venture. Actually, the stimulation of your outside activity should enhance our life together rather than diminish it. This is the counsel I give my clients. My obduracy at home has been due to my suspicions of the transaction. I am glad it seems I was wrong, and I ask your understanding and pardon.

There is also Gary to consider. While he seems stable and independent at this point, it would help if you and I were in a more normal pattern.

Still, your decision must obviously be based on what is best not for Gary or for me, but what is best for you.

I mean that. It isn't just soft soap.

In closing, I must, in fairness to myself, add that the anomalous situation between us is not best for *me* and ought to be resolved as soon as possible. So please let me hear from you. Meantime I send you my very warmest holiday greetings. It will be a Happy New Year for me only if we are together again.

Your husband,
Arthur

Brian, as you may imagine, I have taken this letter of Arthur's very, very seriously. The best way I can explain my reaction is to let you see what I have written in response:

... I can't say I'm all that glad you wrote, but I am not sorry either. I can't disagree when you say it's time we decided where we stand. The end of a year is a good hour to put old shadows to rest and see where new light may come in.

I shared your distressed feelings about this Christmas, especially when I was sending presents to Gary and Lorna. It was the first time I had not sent gifts to you, and it did seem very strange. (I was going to write "the first time in my life." That's how hard it is to think of any time I wasn't married to you.)

Maybe that's what is wrong with marriage. It swallows a person up whole. It siphoned the marrow out of my bones. It wrapped me in a cocoon. Never mind my mixed metaphors—I was a Jonah in a whale, and I wanted to be spit out to see the world before being digested entirely. One thing this means is that it wasn't so much *you* I needed to escape, but the whale ...

It was sad for me too not to share the tree on Christmas Eve, and I'm sorry the angel is showing its years so badly. It was pretty far gone last year, I recall. I'm glad Gary was there to fix it. There is no way it can ever be replaced ...

Christmas was particularly strange here in the sunshine, the palm trees, the blue waters of San Diego. It is so far away in every way from snow and cold and the northern hustle-bustle. Here, with pleasure boats on sparkling waters wherever you look, one lives in a perpetual holiday world. It's relaxed, and pleasant, and easy to laugh ...

We needed to laugh more, Arthur.

In these 87-plus days many things have happened to me. Some have been ordinary, some extraordinary. All have been private. If I return, that will have to be understood and agreed.

To me, this separation from you has been something like—like the intravenous feeding I received when I was in the hospital. There was nourishment coming into my body though I wasn't eating as I ordinarily do. Much of this new experience is like that, and the nourishment is real and good, and tasty.

That doesn't mean I don't miss my old life. Certainly I want to see Gary, and in my own way I miss you too. No matter what else happens, you can never be entirely out of my life, Arthur. How could that be? There has been a connecting tube running between our blood systems for too many years now. I may have other relationships in my life, but I recognize the special, even primary bond that exists between you and me.

If you hear a difference in my language and my thinking, it's because I have been opening my mind to many new ideas. I may not accept them all for myself, but I am much less sure of my old dogmatism. I feel tons lighter in the head. People should diet intellectually as well as for their figures. The phrase "fat-headed" can be taken quite literally . . .

As to coming home, I do have it in mind. But I am considering that if I do, I should stay at a hotel, and you come courting, Arthur, as you did once. Who knows what may happen if we try really *de novo?* But I am still not quite decided. I need more time by myself and will let you know when I am clearer.

Well, Brian, there is the record, and it speaks for itself. I have taken you into my fullest and closest confidence because I do owe you this much. But now I must repeat what I said to Arthur. I need more time by myself, away from both of you. I mean to have it. You will do me a great favor if you do not complicate this interval by insisting on writing.

Margaret

Jan. 7

Dear Maggie:

I appreciate your sharing Arthur's correspondence with me. For better or worse I have become a part of what happens or doesn't happen among the three of us. I have a new, though not unexpected, insight into the conflicting pressures on all of us. You have written so powerfully about your continuing sense of guilt. Do you think I have none? What you said about dissonance in music is apt but I, too, have not become attuned to amorality. I have been walking in my own landscape of guilt and moral distress, there is no other way to put it. And, clearly, Arthur is not wrong to remind you—to remind *me*—of what you owe to your marriage.

But that is no answer at all to the other question we face, you and I. What do we owe to our love?

Maggie, I am sure that somewhere in school you had the experience of lightning striking the brain, when some book or teacher brought you up sharp with a blazing truth you had never recognized before, although the insight was self-evident once contemplated. That happened to me in an ethics course. My then-sophomoric view of ethical values was a more or less straight line ascending up the scale from lowest (most animal) to highest (most human), from selfish to altruistic, that kind of thing. Then I came upon Nicolai Hartmann, a German philosopher of the 1920s, who opened my eyes. He saw morals "in the round," so to speak. He emphasized that two values on the same level of human desirability might be *opposed*. Justice is a virtue of high order, but so is mercy. Two values of the same order of merit, importance, and desirability often collide, can often be in conflict.

I realized at once that I had known this inwardly all along, but it was a revelation (the kind one hopes education is all about).

I am sure I don't have to belabor Hartmann's point with you. It leads to impasse, for me as well as for you.

In the end I suppose you are right about ending these letters. Especially after your last letter, and Arthur's, I see more clearly how crooked our road is turning out to be. I hear more plainly your story of the time your car skidded.

It may be that, yes, the cold circumstances of our lives have iced our way so wretchedly that not even the fire of love can clear a safe route. It may be so.

Miserably,
Brian

Jan. 10

Dear Brian:

This time I have no hesitation in answering. Your letter only proves again what I have known from the beginning. You are a fine and a wise person. You have said everything much better than I have been able to. There is some solace, at least for me, in seeing our dilemma as not just some flailing about but in the moral perspective you describe. The truth is, I suppose, that the moment I admitted my love for you we became mortal enemies, stalemated on a battle line of guilt. Nothing has happened to change that, and I see no alternative but retreat.

Unhappily,
Maggie

Jan. 14

Dear Maggie:

All kinds of things going on here, and I thought you would want to know about them.

At five o'clock this morning there was a pounding on the door downstairs. For one crazy, wild moment I thought that, somehow, it might be you. Perhaps you had come to Los Angeles unexpectedly, needed a place to stay (it was storming), or had changed your mind about wanting to see me, or ——

I jumped all the stairs going down.

It wasn't you, of course. It was Kay.

The rain was fierce and she was drenched, had been walking for some time, I could see. She was utterly bedraggled in torn sandals, tattered chinos, a ripped sweater, and a filthy scarf wrapped over her head like a pirate.

When she smiled at me as if I should be delighted to see her, there was blood in her mouth, two teeth missing. And she smelled bad. I was reminded of what you once told me of Gary.

Kay. My wife. The mother of the sweet and sweet-smelling children whom my sister had had to bathe and powder and put to sleep because this vagrant at the door had defaulted on us all. I hardly recognized her. I nearly slammed the door in her face.

But of course I didn't. When I got her cleaned up and to bed, I had a disoriented feeling. *She* was the stranger who did not belong in my bedroom. She was the trespasser where my true wife had been —you.

But I must not think that way any longer. There is too much pain in the hopelessness.

In the morning, I sent Frances out with the kids before Kay woke up. I called in sick and stayed home from classes (I *was* sick to my stomach). Kay and I needed to talk.

I wasn't much surprised by her tale of pilgrimage, adventure, and woe. Kay's man turned out to be a fancy-speaking pimp, in plain language, though he wore the mantle of a teacher of some sort. His "school" in Colorado was a front for a harem of runaway girls, mostly younger than Kay. Under the guise of establishing a "World Order of the Realized" or some such crap, The Leader forced the girls out to work as waitresses, bartenders, clerks, and often outright prostitutes. That turned out to be too much for even Kay, when it finally penetrated her ingenuous loyalty. She says she left when he pressured her to join the others on the streets. Until then she had been a sort of housemother, apparently. Do you know, I believe her. Kay is unconventional and credulous, but she always had a strong sense of, as she put it, "belonging to herself." It was one of the things that made marriage difficult for her. She would be incapable of prostitution, I am convinced, though God knows her disreputable appearance is no reassurance. Nor is her story that she lost her two teeth last night fighting off the last truck driver who gave her a lift.

Yet I believe her, as I say. She sat with me and cried all afternoon about how much she missed me and the children. She said she had planned presents for our birthdays and for Christmas, but the Realizer had stolen her savings. All she wants now is to be forgiven and to return here "where she belongs."

Can I truthfully say Kay does not belong here? She has some right to the children, and they have considerable right to her. Always dilemma.

There has always been something about Kay that gets to me. I think it is a ragamuffin quality, not quite real, that reminds of the time I myself was a child ready to dash this way and that, eager for any game anyone could dream up. She is a curious combination, Kay. There is her total self-centeredness, again much like a child's. At the same time there is an artless quality in her—the princess quality you felt in her picture—as if she has only to turn her head to discover the treasure everyone around her has proven does not exist. That's it. Kay always seems ready to believe in or be part of, the next fairy tale. Maybe it reaches something in me that would like to be back to when I was a child, before everything fell apart.

So I find myself ambivalent about wanting Kay to stay, although I really have no choice. How can I send her away from Paul and Joan, at least until I see what her promises add up to?

Kay has spent the day promising me the moon, of course. She will:

Straighten up.

Fly right.

No more drinking.

No more marijuana.

No more coke. (My God, I didn't know she was into cocaine, and where the devil did she get the heavy money that takes?)

No, no, no, she will redress all her awful mistakes. Sorry-sorry. Crazy-mad to have left such a great, wonderful, super husband. She hopes and prays that I will understand what she did, needed to discover inner space, outer mind, mystery of life and death, God and non-God, and the "eternal circle of nonpurpose in its becoming the purpose of both personal and world realization." Memorized, robot talk. Now she has learned her lesson, knows it is All A Load Of Phony Shit out there everywhere. (Her language.) Happiness own backyard. Should have known all the time. Sorry, sorry (more flooding tears, genuine). It hurts her that she has hurt and disappointed me. I always so fine, reliable, gentle, sympathetic, a scholar not a bum, always so good to her in every way, great father, and so great in bed, too. She doesn't deserve. Will understand if I kick her out. No more than she deserves. Only, please, let (weep) stay (weep, now clearly phony) long enough (weep, weep) to see her children one moment (weep, weep, weep). East Lynn. Just allow her a look at them through keyhole (East East Lynn Lynn). I am so outraged at her that I am tempted to invite her to play the keyhole game and push the pencil through!

Genuine and false at the same time. That is Kay. Princess and Witch.

Now she is in bed having another nap. She looks like a rag doll. Her vulnerability still tugs at me. But now it's thin pity for a nondescript bird with a clipped wing. I don't think I will buy it. But for the sake of the children . . . ?

I hear the car in the driveway. Frances is back with the kids. I needed to write this to you. Never a dull moment. In my mind's eye

I see you reading this letter over there in Malibu, and Kay asleep here upstairs. It's all wrong! I hear the children racing to the house. They'll wake Kay. I had better prepare them to greet their mother.

Yours,
Brian

Jan. 17

Dear Brian:

I am glad you wrote the news. I have always had a feeling that Kay would return. Of course she belongs with her children. And with you. Certainly she is owed a chance to keep her promises. I applaud you for granting that, and I respect you the more for it.

My own crystal ball predicts Kay will be different from now on. I think she *has* learned her lessons and is ready to appreciate what a splendid husband and father you have been indeed. I see a long and happy life for you both. There is nobody in the wide world who does not have much to forgive. You in Kay. Arthur in me. I in Arthur. We can only live together by focusing on the good and blurring the less good, at least as long as there is more good than bad, which only time ever tells. That sounds like my mother, but it doesn't make it less valid.

It's true we have to place most of our bets blindly, but we can try to stack the odds through forgiveness, understanding, and extending the same charity to others we would like for ourselves.

End of sampler sayings . . .

I used the gambling figure because Charlie has just brought me back from Las Vegas. It was a special celebrity party and, as Charlie wisecracked, "Everybody who is nobody is here!" (I also like what he said about the new television programs this year, "They had no place to go, and they went there.")

I thank the Lord and you for Charlie Henley. He is a brick, and a gentleman in all our dealings. He keeps everything businesslike, as I wish it. I enjoy an occasional outing with new friends on his boat or dinner at one of his clubs. It is casual and undemanding, a much-needed neutral and stabilizing environment for me.

You'll be pleased to know that the reason for Las Vegas was the celebration of the first big contract I landed. San Diego came through! When I got the actual check I almost fainted with excitement and elation. Real money!—not just talk or encouragement or promises. My father used to say, "When *strangers* pay you, you'll know you're doing a job."

Since you were "the finder" in this deal, I ought to pay you a fee out of this check, but Charlie says you would only send it back, so accept my thanks instead.

I have learned so very much from Charlie. Selling is an art, a profession. I now have a structured presentation, with all my selling points—and "Answers to Objections"—prepared in advance. Fascinating! I never had an inkling of how complicated a salesman's job is. I suppose I half-looked down at salesmen. Believe me, I now have a new respect. The courses Charlie has been leading me through are quite on a graduate-school level, very professional publications.

So I have swapped my ABD for a $$$, and glad of it! I am even developing a killer instinct for "The Close." I am feeling good about this part of my life anyway.

In an important way, Kay's return home lightens me now even more. As I read your letter I could feel my mood altering. I was glad to be hearing from you again, and I could admit it without too heavy a jolt of guilt.

I think we are both taking still another turn in the road, and especially since it is not heading us toward each other, perhaps we can at least wave back and forth as we go on our ways. Why play ostrich? Kay is with you. I will probably go back home to Arthur fairly soon. And I am enjoying my new career. Mightily, I might say. It may be time for us to stop seeing ourselves in a dilemma.

I seem to be given to these swings of conviction about us, but I think that may be over finally. We won't be letting anything sing itself, but there is no reason why we can't at least communicate every now and then as the old friends we have been and need not deny.

So love to all,
Maggie

Jan. 18

Dear Maggie:

New road, indeed! How I wish it were. People should not promise what they don't have to give . . .

Kay, of course.

The first days after she cleaned herself up, you could not conceive that she had ever been anything but model wife and ideal mother. With time out only for the dentist, she sent Frances away to sketch all day, and she did the cleaning, ironing, washing, shopping, cooking, mopping, and played with the children. She even washed the windows herself. Unheard of before!

It's beautiful how quickly children accept answers, though I always have to wonder whether they aren't masking some reservations behind those uplooking, trustful eyes. I think they hide their doubts the way chipmunks cache nuts in their cheeks.

To me, Kay's presence has been troublesome. As she settled into domesticity, she also settled back into the role of a wife in other ways. I was sleeping on the couch in our room, leaving her the bed, but she came over to me. I cannot write about it to you, except to say that I was glad when Frances moved out the next day to a rooming house down the block. (Frances has never liked Kay too much, and Joan and Paul are better off with "one mother" in the house. Fortunately, Frances had no trouble getting a quick job as a waitress nearby.) I shifted into the vacant room, leaving Kay the bedroom to herself.

In truth, I was not entirely clear. Your letter did seem sensible, grounding both of us firmly where we were at the time we started writing. If all you and I are ever to be to each other now is people "waving back and forth" occasionally, then I, like you, had better decide where my ground really is. I admit that one night I was tempted to go across to Kay's bedroom. I am not sure what held me back. Some instinct for self-preservation, perhaps. Whatever it was, I am grateful for it in the light of what transpired next.

Aunt Hildie phoned to ask a favor. Cousin Carl had a promise of a job in Los Angeles, he was coming down for an interview. Could I put him up for a couple of days? She didn't say they were short of money, but I know Joe has been too sick to work for a month or so. Hildie minds the stand. In any case, how could I refuse either of them anything? I could move back to the couch in the bedroom and let Carl have the room Frances had used.

Ah, Carl. We took a long walk the next afternoon, reminiscing about old times. It was with false warmth on both sides, as people will pretend on such occasions. Carl had grown fat since I last saw him. He sported a large moustache that hung down the sides of his mouth with a gross look, as if his last meal had never been entirely cleaned off. As you see, I didn't like him any more than I ever had. But he was my guest and I was helping Hildie and Joe, so I would be as pleasant as possible for the few days.

On our walk Carl was as full of promises as Kay had been. His old wildness was over and done. He knew the score now, wanted to settle down, maybe with a nice girl he might meet in Los Angeles if he got the job. (Did Frances or Kay have friends?) He wanted to apologize for all the lousy things he had done to me. I half-thought of asking if he had tampered with Gentle's gate, but decided I didn't want to hear either a lie or a truth. Carl's martini-colored eyes held pale tears of regret and apology. His mouth was pressed together earnestly. His new sincerity trotted at his heels like a visible little dog panting with its loyal tongue hanging out, its tail wagging. (I remembered the piglet he had grabbed, its tail coiled tightly in panic.)

I found it was all nothing to me.

Carl has neither the brains, the heart, nor the grace to know humility. He came on like a three-dollar bill. I decided that not even for my aunt and uncle would I keep Carl around my family for any length of time. There were enough window-scratching vibrations going on in my home as it was.

"I'm going straight," Carl said.

Well, there's an old farm saying that a straight tail on a hog means a sick animal.

Thursday night we had family dinner, with Frances joining us. Damned if Kay didn't turn out a first-class roast. Something good had come from her Colorado sojourn—she had learned to cook! With a jug of wine *Carl* bought, we had a surprisingly fair time. I let Paul and Joan stay up to enjoy it. I liked their liking the sense of a larger family. It has been missing for too long. I began to think Carl might finally have grown up, at that.

Maybe it was the glow of the wine, but as I looked around the table I thought it might just be possible for me to accept Kay more than formally. Life with her would be very imperfect, but everything in life is good old compromise—as you and I know too well.

It's like the adage that people have to eat a peck of dirt in a lifetime. With today's inflation, make that more like a ton. But, I told myself, might as well get it down with as little gagging as possible.

That is what I repeated to myself about 4 A.M. Friday morning when Kay had not yet come home from the dance to which Carl had insisted she go after dinner. (Discotheques are no longer for me.)

Then the dawn, and found Kay snoring drunkenly in her sleep when I woke up to go to my classes. I had piles of paper to mark that day, so didn't get back home until after five. Carl was out. Paul was alone at the television. He informed me that Kay was upstairs bathing Joanie. Good. All tranquilly domestic, and the house smelled invitingly of a mouth-watering stew on the kitchen stove. All exceedingly pleasant indeed. My spirits began to unsag.

Paul leaped at me to frolic. He yelled, "Daddy, can we do Funny Wrestling?"

"What's that?" Kay might have brought home a game I'd never heard of. "Did Mommy play it with you?"

"No. With Carl."

"What?"

"I saw them playing it this afternoon."

I was sure the lightning splitting my head must have come from a sudden storm outside. There was no way that what I was imagining could possibly have happened, not in this house, certainly not where the children could pass by and see!

My little son was going on. "I was outside with Joanie and needed peepee, and I saw Mommy with Carl upstairs." He told me, giggling, "You have to bend like a pretzel and you have to make funny noises, like you can't breathe . . ."

My God, he began to imitate the "funny noises"! I changed the subject, you may believe!

When Kay came downstairs with Joanie, I planted both kids in front of the TV, for which device I am sometimes thankful, and I hustled my wife back up the steps.

No, I did not strike her.

First she denied it strenuously. Then she broke down, buckets of remorse. But not her fault (sob), Carl made her (sob, sob), as much as raped her, and not her fault, he being *my* cousin!

What I could not believe was that I suddenly felt nothing. As indifferent as if Kay had told me she and Carl had spent the afternoon crayoning coloring books. I simply did not care. I'd have felt more anger if I were watching a movie of infidelity. There existed nothing in the situation I could identify with, because Kay was NOT my wife.

What Kay was and is is a slut. Everything else I have ever said about her has been a rationalization to salvage some of my own self-respect. I never admitted that I knew in my gut what Kay was doing "in San Francisco" all along.

But with her children in the house!

I searched Kay's face for some clue to make myself wrong. I could see her eyes measuring my expression like a ruler, with her fear marked off in the dark lines of worry that showed she knew she had gone too far.

I didn't know I could speak so softly and so loud at the same time, but that's the tone in which I told her that I am divorcing her.

Kay had the grace to hang her head and remain silent, not even to pretend to cry.

Let her go back to Colorado. Let her go to Carl. Let her go to hades. I want her out of my life. Out!

And that, Maggie, has nothing to do with you.

Carl came back for dinner, believe it or not. He brought more wine for me, and his martini eyes were shining with honesty and good fellowship, and his little dog of sincerity was panting at his heels. I had to smile at his brazenness—my Jewish colleagues would call it *chutzpah,* a wonderful word the world requires in more languages than Yiddish. But, then, Carl has always been scrupulously oblivious of anyone else's feelings.

I proved mine to him at once. Though he has height and heft on me, I punched him groggy and bloody until he was squealing like the pig he is. Kay had the good sense to keep the children upstairs. I wanted to murder the lout, not because I give a damn about Kay, but because of their insolence, their violation of my house. Their vandalism.

I thought of your sauntering rat again.

And with that I had a crushing thought. Who was I to be so enraged? Doesn't your husband have as much right to want to kill *me?*

Oh, argue the difference between love and funny wrestling, between discretion and swashbuckling. Still, I would not like to be explaining to Arthur, would I? It depends on who is wearing what shoe, doesn't it? We are back to—who is ever to judge anyone else?

But I am glad these civilized considerations did not occur to me the night I fought Carl. I would never want to miss the joy and delight of my fists sinking deep into that fat, beer-bloated belly, my sheer ecstasy at hearing Carl gasp for breath, my satisfaction at seeing his eyes cross with surprise and hurt as he doubled over. I beat him for everything he had ever done to me and mine and to his father and mother. I beat him savagely, I am delighted and proud to say.

Because *I* know the difference between you and me and Carl-Kay. Kay and Carl are beneath contempt, but I *honor* you and me, Maggie, because there is a universe of difference between their lust and our love.

What has happened has helped me open my eyes again to what I was prepared to put out of my sight. I love you. I love you, Maggie. And I refuse to blind myself against it, and I will say it. I love you. Maybe that will smash everything again, but I must say truth!

You will also want to know that Kay is gone and Frances is back home. The children are curious, cranky, aggrieved, but that can't be helped for a while. I don't know whether they will heal fast, or slowly, or at all, but like the rest of us they must learn realities. Unfortunately, no age is spared.

I have started the divorce. I have an attorney recommended by our law school. There is no turning back. It's a dirty mess right now, but I have an almost relieved feeling too. I suspect no one man can ever satisfy Kay's (sick?) needs. Better to face it, then, while the children aren't too hurt. God, how could I do my work at the college if I had to be wondering whether every class bell was ringing another stud into my wife's bed!

Inelegantly but profoundly, a student I overhead in the cafeteria said it all just this noon. A friend of his was apparently urging him to steal his father's wallet to buy drugs. The fellow answered, really angry, "I don't shit where I eat!" Deplorably, Kay does.

How little I have known of Kay. I confess to you that unsettles me and calls my capacity as a man and a teacher into question.

I have a new typewriter with an ingenious white ribbon for correcting errors. If only one could backspace in life, and white out one's mistakes.

I am sending this to the office since the receptionist there told me you and Charlie will be back from Sacramento in days. Phone me if you can. If you are not going to New York right off, please let me take you to dinner. This time it is me who can use a friend.

Brian

P.S. How about "an equerry of cuckolds"? I just made that up.

Jan. 22

Brian, my dear:

How perfectly terrible for you! I find myself sharing your outrage with Kay, though I am in no position to throw stones. Still, in your words, there is a profound difference between her act and ours.

As I've said before, I have admired and respected your patience, your readiness to understand and accept Kay as she was. It was never my place to say so, but from your first mentions Kay made me bristle. Before I saw her picture, I had the impression of a cheeky, spoiled brat. I felt, though, that a man as sensitive and knowledgeable as you are must see qualities that far overbalanced her weaknesses. Or, who knows, perhaps it was her very weaknesses that appealed to you. That's often true.

Your cousin Carl is sleazy, hideous, and contemptible. I almost wish you hadn't told me, it makes me sick to my stomach. But of course I want to know. I want to know everything that happens to you.

Brian, I want us to find a way to resume our friendship despite our own indiscretion. I do want you in my life, as you want me in yours. I understand too well what you are going through now. No matter what everyone says—that divorce is no more significant than a hang-nail these days—the word itself still gives me willies, still spells ugliness, failure, blame and, somehow, even shame.

That is a heavy shadow over my own head now as I rethink my relationship with my husband. My thoughts and emotions about him keep turning to powder. I can't solidify them into a shape that holds long enough for decision. I don't really know what to do about my marriage, what I should do, what I must do.

I keep remembering my husband as he issued his Command about Charlie Henley's business proposition. I haven't told you this, but I was *afraid* of Arthur then. He was a person I had never known. His eyes were stony, his cheeks were literally twitching. His mouth was sucked in, an awful mask without lips.

I was infuriated as well as scared. For the first time I saw myself as I looked to Arthur, with all the surface civilities of modern life stripped away. I saw not a caveman but a tyrant, who viewed me as nothing, ultimately, but the servant of His Castle. We could both pretend a wife was an equal, but when the chips went down, it would always turn out morganatic. He is Boss, Chief, Satrap, Big Mogul.

Oh, he is an enlightened, even benevolent Sultan, who mostly goes through all the motions of sharing. The flag of democracy is duly raised and saluted in the home, but decisions will be His in the end because that is The Natural Order of Things.

I have never understood how deeply *that* male-female modality is etched in our bones. I keep hearing echoes of our quarrel that night. How taken aback Arthur was when he did not find me the accustomed docile, circumspect, submissive wife ready to keep walking one step behind him. How he thundered at me as his disbelief grew . . .

"My wishes should be respected in this house!"

I asked why his wishes should be respected more than my own.

"Because that is the way it's supposed to be in a marriage!"

"Where is that written, Arthur?"

"In the vows we took, dammit!"

"I don't recall any vow about not investing my own funds as I see fit!"

Arthur cannot stand my standing up to him. He is beet-faced and swelling. He doesn't shout, he bellows. "A wife ought to listen to her husband about matters she does not understand, follow his advice and counsel!"

I reply that I am not a law case to be decided on precedent.

Oh, I don't want to remember any more of that insufferable contest. Some people may enjoy locking horns that way, I do not. As you see, every ugly word was burned into my head, and each word widened the gulf between my husband and me. It comes to me—now that I have the perspective of time, distance, and meaningful outside interests—that I gave myself as a meek hostage to a marriage. I submerged my own personality, my brains, my wishes, and, yes, my heart. And classically, I never even suspected what was happening to me! Until I moved away from my marriage (in so many ways!),

I never guessed how deeply I myself was notched with Father's damned codes and my husband's. Run me through a computer and nothing would come out but *their* Gradus ad Parnassum.

I am not blaming Arthur, or even my father, I suppose. Arthur is only spouting what I acquiesced in for years. It was in the air we both breathed, in the common language we both tongued. In trying to rule me, Arthur honestly does believe he is acting as a *good* man, in the best interests of his family. That only makes it harder for me to penetrate his atmosphere. I feel like a spaceship hovering for an open place to land, somewhere, safely. But everywhere I look is spiny, forbidding rock of one sort or another.

What I have to consider now is this: If my husband's computer is programmed so inflexibly and murderously against me as a separate person, then let me say what only minutes ago seemed unsayable. Let me say this impossible discovery of mine to the one man whose strength supports this explosive revelation—

I am no longer afraid of divorce.

I see that it isn't Arthur I have to divorce, but my old self. I see that marriage—as you once wrote about distance—is a palpable force in and of itself. I have felt it bend and twist my will like a giant wrestler. But I am finally stronger!

Don't misread me, Brian. I don't *want* a divorce, and I am not considering one at this time. But I repeat that I am not afraid of it any longer. Finally it is a word I admit into my vocabulary.

I have in these past weeks declared my own sovereignty to myself. The rope that tied me is fraying. And that restores my power to weigh the positive aspects of my marriage in the scales. Oddly enough, now that I am no longer petrified by the very word Divorce, I think it is much less likely between Arthur and me!

New decisions are possible, but they won't be hasty. As of now I still do not know where my spaceship will put down.

I hope you have some peace of mind in the fact that your decision is made about divorcing Kay. I know you have a bad stretch ahead, that is inevitable. I hope it is short. Meantime, yes, please do take me to dinner. I would like it now.

Love,
Maggie

P.S. I am sure I don't have to add, *just* dinner, Brian.

Part Eight

Feb. 7

Dear Brian:

Another new postmark, back in New York City as you see.

Many new wheels have been turning since we had our dinner date in Los Angeles. Before I tell you what is happening here, let me thank you again for that most pleasant evening. I had wondered whether I could be relaxed with you, but it went so easily. I enjoyed our being just friends, and am grateful that you chose a restaurant where we could rubberneck and talk about the TV and movie stars instead of our personal complications. I think one reason I like being with Charlie so much is that we almost always are talking about business, seldom anything personal.

Truth to tell, I had feared a heavy confrontation with you. I appreciate your not pressing me. It was sensitive of you. It helped solidify the ground under our new friendship. I hope you feel the same way, for this is what makes it possible for us to continue.

Now about the turning wheel of fate . . .

I returned home following a letter from Arthur that convinced me I could not longer continue irresolute. I was right to delay as long as I did, but this letter moved me fiercely and opened a new view of everything. I send this copy on to you in all good conscience for, once again, you are centrally involved and intimately concerned with what my husband has so eloquently brought home to me:

> . . . I believe I have been more than tolerant in not forcing the issue that we face. A wife's leaving her husband's bed and board is a desertion, legally speaking. You have written to me of "the differences between us." I do not know of anything I have done now or through the years, by commission or omission, to justify the unfair accusations stated and implicit in your conduct . . .
>
> You have acted and written as if you consider me to be a wooden stick without feelings. You protest "stereotypes" (beyond endurance, I might add), but you proceed on a whole series of unexamined assumptions about "a man." "A man" is *naturally* to be strong, silent, unemotional. To start with, that is an incredible hypocrisy. I do not take my satisfaction in life only from going to my office daily. In reality, too often that means only that other people sap my energy, consume my brains, my training, my vitality in causes which, shall I say, are not always the most gratifying. In this sense, Gary is not entirely wrong about what it means to be a lawyer.
>
> And these days, I return home to an empty apartment. I am not referring to petty annoyances like having to prepare my own dinner or dine out more often than I like. I am talking about having to make a life with only half of myself . . .
>
> Margaret Fairfield, you have been the other half of me since the night I first saw you in your father's house. If you don't know how I have loved and cherished you from that moment to this, then nothing I can say now will reach you.
>
> Don't you think I am hurt? Do you think I just smile blithely when I go into our empty bedroom, toss in the cold bed, get up without the sight or sound of you around me?
>
> Have I been only a breadwinning machine to you?
>
> Perhaps the fault is mine, in that I have never expressed my innermost feelings about our relationship as it affected *me*. Maybe it is time, Margaret, for women like you to pay some overdue attention to how marriage looks and feels to the husband.
>
> *You* persons endlessly complain about society imprisoning you in roles that bind your souls the way the Chinese once bound girls' feet. Certainly that is wrong, *but* what about the way society cripples the male?
>
> Do you know what happened the day *I* was born? My feet were not bound, but *a ring was placed in my nose*. A ring stronger than any used on bull animals. It was forged of my parents' voices, the most powerful metal in God's world. It became a whip cracked by teachers and preach-

ers. It slashed at me morning and night, searing its commandments into my flesh, my bone, my muscle, my blood, my brain, my soul—the whip of conscience:

Lash: A boy is to become strong, is to take care of others, is to make a living, is to prepare to bring bread and bacon to a woman and to the children they will have. (*And* a boy is made of puppy dogs' tails, not of sugar and spice or anything nice!)

Lash: A man is to pay rent, to build a house, to provide shelter from the elements, and also jewels and fur coats and toys and hairdressers, for a wife and children.

Lash: A man is to provide medical care and dental, vacations and automobiles, music lessons and college tuition, insurances and assurances of every kind, movies and television sets, and bail as needed for a wife and children.

Lash: A man is to be stalwart, brave, dependable, broad-shouldered, resourceful, courageous, self-denying, disease-resistant, *responsible* above all, and a leader in all things. A man is to build a solid career, be a stalwart citizen, give to charity, be mannerly to his fellows, make a lasting contribution to society, and pay taxes, pay taxes, pay taxes.

Lash: A man is to be a hero, to fight in defense of his country, to die for honor, to offer his body and mind to be wounded, torn, maimed, to protect a wife and children.

Lash: A man is also to be gentle and understanding, strong and tough, cautious and alert, prudent and provident, wise and kind, tender and forceful, a guide, a student and teacher. And of course help with coats, hold doors open, and give up his bus seat to ladies though he have an aching back.

Above all, a man is to tame his natural drives. God may have fashioned him with passions, but the man must throttle them and live out his life on the narrow path of righteousness in a straitjacket of denial.

Oh, he is to be permitted a safety-valve now and then, a night out with the good old boys lest he explode with the suppressed pressures. A game of poker, a swig of beer, a visit to the track, and even—though always surreptitiously—he may on rare occasion seek the sex that must regrettably be acknowledged to make its inconsiderate demands. It is even whispered that some knavish louts, reprobates, and ingrates may actually feel sexual attraction from women other than their wives, despite the marriage vows and the Holy Commandments. No decent man, of course, could ever stoop to entertaining such a desire.

Let me suggest that the lenience of the so-called double standard is largely a fabrication. Certainly it does exist, but most wives do uncompromisingly expect and insist that their husbands be faithful. That is my experience as both a lawyer and a man. Wives plummet into a bottomless abyss of misery and recrimination if they ever learn of an outside episode, and that goes for a great majority of the women who pride themselves on being modern. The casual views displayed in motion pictures and on television are not, to my observation, reflected in real life, certainly nowhere near the extent we would be led to believe.

Nor, commonly, is a husband relieved of his duty to be faithful even if his wife is never sexually disposed, or after she has "dried up" emotionally and/or physically. I purposely put it inelegantly because I have heard so many falsehoods about it in divorce litigation. What is a man supposed to do with his sexual appetite in such cases? The woman would not ask her husband to stop eating just because she decided to fast. But he is supposed to become sexless when she withdraws from sex.

Oh, not sexless, since that is patently impossible, God being such a clumsy Fellow. The trick is for the man to sublimate his unacceptable desires, to take up jogging or playing the flute, practice the recorder or become a Sunday painter, do crossword puzzles, or write a Beethoven symphony . . .

Let me recall to your mind, Margaret, an incident you have undoubtedly forgotten, if indeed it ever got past your reflex rejection of things outside the pale. Last New Year's Eve, when we were coming home from Betsie Matthew's party, we were waiting for a cab on Park Avenue when a car of young people stopped for the light. A gorgeous, happy young blond reached her hand out to me. I smelled a ravishing perfume. The girl was laughing the way I'd forgotten anyone could *enjoy* life. Astonishingly, she invited us to join them. I remember her exact words, "You're my type, lover!" She said that to *me,* Arthur Darby Webb. Of course she had to be drunk or stoned. How could she mean that about *me?* How could old ice-bucket Arthur Webb, Esquire be for the likes of her?

Let me confess to you now, my dear wife, I would have given anything in the world to leave you and to leap into that car with the girl and her friends. That shining girl could have taken me anyplace. It would have been sheer heaven. You know, I can still smell her scent. Her eyes really wanted me. I don't know why and don't care. Maybe she has a neurotic father fixation. For me, she was a delightful and wonderful gift of the gods.

But you, dear predictable wife, did the expected. You yanked me backward so hard (though I hadn't moved an inch) that I nearly broke my spine sliding and slipping on the icy sidewalk. I made a joke of it, embarrassed and as frustrated as I was, and I called Happy New Year to the golden young woman as the traffic light changed and she drove off. I recall that I turned to you and slumped back into our frame of reference at once by saying, "Dumb kids, drunk as coots . . ." Damned traitor that I was! And you frowned your total Beacon Hill disapproval of anyone breaking The Rules, even if it was New Year's Eve.

You know, Margaret, I dream of that beautiful, tempting, luscious, nubile girl sometimes. And do you know, Margaret, I am still sorry I did not, could not, was not permitted to, join those sparkling, fornicating kids! Not that I could ever have let go, but my point is that it never *occurred* to you that I might have the desire to do so! Talk about your encoded mores! *That* is ring-in-the-nose!

So, my dear wife, *you* tell *me.* Where has my freedom been all *my* life? Why, perfectly clearly, in hock to you and Gary!

You write and act as if you are the only one in the world who has discovered that we have only once around the track, *tempus fugit,* and all that shallow profundity. Do you know what is most significant? That it would genuinely shock you to learn the same is true of and for me. Yes, Margaret, I too live by the same relentless and fated clock. I too hear the lesson of the quotidian tolling of the bell that Gary's clever toilet poem referred to.

There is a dark image in my head that you have never suspected. It never leaves me, morning, noon, or night. I will say it is my fault that I have never discussed this with you before, but, then, you must ask yourself whether there has been something in you that discouraged this kind of confidence between us. I am speaking now of the moment of my father's death, in the hospital room where the end came. I was alone with the attendant, whom I still remember as a repulsive pasty-faced, fat fairy. I saw my father's figure go still. I asked, "Is he dead?" The man shushed me. "They can still *hear,* you know!" With which there came a gasping breath from the bed. I felt I had committed a monstrous trespass. I still shudder with horror at the memory. I think how it would be if, lying paralyzed myself one day, I were to hear you or Gary ask, "Is he dead?"

But that is not what I started out to tell. What I can never forget is how the attendant a few minutes later lifted the sheet and tied a cardboard tag by a string to my father's big toe. The man tied the string around my father's big toe (I remember the nail, so pale and very long, needed clipping), *with a tag like a laundry ticket, a baggage claim check, as if my father were a duffle bag.* To me, that awful tag, not his gravestone, marks my father's death. That little rectangle of cardboard, not his cemetery plot, asks why and how he lived, why and how he denied himself for my mother and for me and my brothers and sisters.

Was my father right to deny himself? Am *I?* Can you understand, Margaret, that *I see that ticket being tied onto my big toe every time I put my socks on every morning of my life with you and Gary and my law partners . . . ?*

You feel free to correspond with a strange man behind my back, and tootle off across the country with your Mr. Charles Henley, but *I* have never been free to take the tiniest wayward wobble off the straight and narrow, certainly not without being made to feel (by myself if no one else!) traitorous and iniquitous. Have I ever wobbled at all? Let that be one of my privacies as you wish yours. I can tell you this: I have earned more Brownie points than I have ever received for all the wobbling I have *not* done that I might have done! When am *I* permitted to lament the temptations I have denied myself, hobbled as I have been through the ring in my nose?

Yes, society permits a young man to sow his wild oats, but preferably out of the sight of decent folks, and only on the understanding that he will settle down later.

Of course there is compensation, society makes haste to observe. In return for the nose ring, the man is given the pleasures of the conjugal bed, the comfort of a homemaker, and the solace (?) of children . . .

We men buy all that church-sliced baloney and swallow it while wearing the hair shirt of marriage and career without a whimper of protest. It is incredible, incredible, incredible how we allow ourselves to be conned! The clergy act as God's haberdashers and fit our hair shirts with ceremonies of pious noises and solemn musics. And the ring slips not on the finger but into the nose.

Perhaps people cry at weddings because they secretly understand the truth, the bloody truth. They are not in a church but in a slaughterhouse.

I am not thick-headed, Margaret, and not a fool. I am not saying these things to accuse you, or the so-called Women's Movement, or to deny that you all suffer equally painful restraints, even more painful in some ways, yes. But my question persists. My challenge increases. When are You-Persons going to recognize that We-Persons are in the *same* social shredding machine? I want as much equality as you want!

If women and men both accepted this truth, marriages would work better and last longer.

As for the two of us specifically, I am infuriated by your bland assumption that I will simply go on sitting at home with my ring in my nose until you take a fancy to reappear.

That is why I am telling you, flatly, that I have temporized as long as I am going to. At this point I am unfurling my own Lib Banner, saying *I* am through!

If you don't come home within one week after receipt of this letter to at least discuss our future, I will institute divorce proceedings. This is no placard on parade, it is no bluff. I am out of patience with you, Margaret, out of tolerance, out of sympathy, out of everything but a consuming anger. I want your ring out of my nose. I expect to hear from you at once!

Your husband?
Arthur

P.S. You might like to know that the license number that night was 6X7X4! And this year, alone on New Year's for the first time since our marriage, I went back to stand on that corner, remembering and hopefully waiting. Too much champagne, of course. Nothing happened, of course. But it wasn't the girl I missed. It was you.

Brian, I am sure you agree that is a letter to ponder. I have read it over many times, with a churning of many feelings, old and new. I do believe that if Arthur had been as open with me in the past we would have had a different and a happier relationship. How could I help but respect what he says about his own capitulations to marriage and his assigned roles? How could I deny his right about our need to talk?

Now that I am back home with Arthur, it comes to me that a marriage like ours is something like your redwoods. One does have to consider most prayerfully before taking an ax to it. Arthur and I are going to try to be more tolerant of each other in every way. I have learned much and so has he.

You will be interested to know, incidentally, that, without my saying anything, *Arthur has taken down all of his actuarial lists!* You know, when things go poorly they tend to avalanche. When things move well they spiral up. My reunion with Arthur promises an upward spiral now. We both wish to try.

Charlie and I have agreed I will work in the New York area for the time being, so I seem set and settled for a time at least.

Now for some separate news in closing. It concerns Lorna. You may recall my mentioning her interest in Indian history. She is assisting a study of certain West Coast treaties believed to have been violated over the years, and she'll be doing some of the research in your university library. Gary is out of sorts about my proposing that she look you up. He taps your picture on my desk and jokes about your being too handsome to trust. If he knew how true his mother knows that to be! Don't have *too* much fun with our redheaded young friend!

I must take another minute to tell you something really amusing, Brian, even though this letter is overlong. When I got home, I found a jar of some mysterious black powder in my refrigerator. It turns out to be a discovery of Arthur's. It seems he tried to make himself a stew one night while we were separated, and he set the oven far too hot. The casserole split and the meat flamed to a crisp before he discovered anything was wrong. Rather than dump it, my ever-prudent Arthur decided—shades of Charles Lamb discovering roast pork when the house burned—that he had invented the best (and most expensive) charcoal flavoring known to man. He chopped up the scorched beef and I'll be salt-and-peppered if he hasn't turned out to be 100 percent correct. It's a delicious seasoning!

It occurs to me that there may be some obscure symbolism in this story as it relates to all of us . . . a culinary victory plucked from kitchen disaster.

I must quit this epistle (it can't be called anything less than that). Arthur has made an appointment for me to have a medical checkup, and I'll be late if I don't run (though the doctors keep one waiting for ages after you've rushed to be on time.) I really don't need this examination rigmarole, but it will please Arthur, so . . .

I'm off,
Maggie

Feb. 19

Dear Maggie:

What a delight it has been to have Lorna here! She is even lovelier and livelier than I remembered from our brief encounter in New York the time you had to go to your mother in Boston.

I have never seen hair like hers. When we walk out together she literally shines in the sun. People stop and turn, even in this Hollywood land where glamour is a dime a dozen. Lorna is indeed special. I think it is the contrast one does not expect. She radiates her intelligence and her unadorned honesty at the same time as her beauty captivates the eye. It's in the way she moves, talks, tosses her long hair, and gestures so earnestly with her hands to make her Portia points. You see that I am much taken with her. Gary is a fortunate young man, indeed.

The children adore Lorna. Oddly, as you may have noticed from the photographs, Joanie—Joan!—bears quite a resemblance to Lorna. This morning when we all went weekend shopping at the supermart, people took us for one (big happy) family. It was a pleasant experience.

Yesterday afternoon we all went sailing on Charlie's boat. We talked mostly about you. Of course I did not let Lorna guess how I feel. I see what you mean about gaining a daughter. She admires and loves you as if she were. She told me you and Arthur are getting along well, if tentatively. Charlie is your fan, too. Listening to the two of them saying nice things about you brought you close to me again—but I won't speak of that. You and I have tacitly developed a kind of truce, haven't we? A kind of no-lover's-land we must not cross . . .

Charlie praised your work highly. He added that things are going well for your business in the East, so everything seems to be falling into some kind of place.

My own pieces have moved into the divorce court formally. Kay has returned to Colorado. I receive an occasional letter, saying little, reminding me of a mouth idly chewing gum. I don't mean to be unkind, a waste of time in any event, but I have very ungenerous feelings about Kay. They aren't helped by the fact that legally here she has to get half of what I own, at the least. She does not deserve either the money or the trouble I now have to go through. I don't want to sell the house, so will have to borrow. I suppose the bank won't look too kindly on my income. I don't like asking Charlie again, but may have no choice. I think I once mentioned that I had to ask him for help with the house in Marin. I was startled by his first answer, until I thought about it. He told me he didn't have a liquid cent much beyond his living needs. That's what it means to be rich. Every dollar is out in overalls working away for more. Charlie came through, of course. You know his generosity. He sold some stock and bailed me out. He has taken a similar second mortgage on the Los Angeles house. If I need cash for Kay, though, I will try to manage some other way. You are the last person I want to burden with the thorns Kay has scattered around here. What's important is that the children are fine, and Frances is able to stay.

Right now, what depresses us all is that Lorna is leaving in less than a week. She has been sharing Frances's room, and they have become fast friends. The chemistry was right and quick (as you and I happen to know can happen). I am deeply impressed with Lorna's competence. I have half a thought my department might invite her out for a future lecture series on Indian affairs. The legal dimension is an important specialty, and Lorna is more than receptive to the idea. So your fan letter turns out to have opened up many kinds of possibilities, some quite unpredictable, for others like Charlie, and Lorna now.

I am going to cut this letter off before I start telling you once more what I must not say again about you and me. One truth I have learned. Emotions do refuse all reason. Emotions hang on until you are done with them, or they are through with you. For me, it comes to the same thing. I live with an emptiness I cannot fill. Allow me to say that much.

My love to you, Maggie.
Brian

Feb. 26

Dear Brian:

The weather here is snow and ice and a brutal wind that slams one down. What happened to sun and palm trees and gentle breezes? I can't believe I was ever in Malibu or San Diego or Los Angeles, except that Lorna returned yesterday bringing it all with her, especially in her enthusiasm for you. You surely have made another fan! Lorna went on and on about how brilliant you are, how wonderful with your children, what an amiable sense of humor you have, how greatly respected you are on campus. If Gary hadn't kept clearing his throat she would not have stopped. I was almost sorry when she tapered off because Lorna's talking of you almost brought you into the room for me, and I did enjoy the sense of being close. Now that the stream of my life is finding its bed here again, I can look back over our two years with new eyes. Plainly, I had no idea that my first letter would lead anywhere near where it did or I would never have written it, as you know. I would say that I am sentimental about everything that happened, except that "sentiment" to me is like writing a check on a phony account—there is no emotion in the bank on which it is drawn.

That is so very much *not* true for you and me. I remember so well what we said as I left you after our last dinner together—that it would be stupid and impossible to pretend that you and I were not drawn together, have not been deeply and wonderfully in love. Let me write that down now, as well as having said it then. To exorcise it by plain speaking.

Exorcise it because for us it is devilish, because for us life is this contradiction. I want to keep the happiness of knowing you, and I don't want the unhappiness of missing you. The alternative, if you can call it that, is to slide out of reality altogether, into Clarissa's Santa Fe. That is not for either of us.

So I am making my peace with you, more and more every day. I hope the same is true for you.

I am finding it easier to write to you without stirring up a hornet's nest of misgivings and cursings of Fate. I honestly believe we can enter a new phase. I expect it is going to be even better for us, because now we no longer have to be anxious about what might happen. It has happened, we know what it means and doesn't mean, and we both are handling it.

I have been thinking about you—about us—day after day, hours on end. What has come to me, finally, is, of all things, recollection of a drawing class when I was, oh, 11 or 12? We had to do vanishing points. Remember that? I found the concept beyond comprehension. I could not square the logic of never-meeting parallel lines with the perception that such lines touch visually. Something in me rebelled at that contradiction, rebelled so violently that I was almost paralytically prevented from drawing correctly. My eye, my hand, my brain went separate ways. Even after I saw roads and railroad tracks from the air making their ineluctable statements, it was not just difficult but *painful* to take in.

This has very much to do with you and me. Our letters have been like parallel tracks in the landscape of our lives, seeking a destination, a vanishing point. Until we actually met—until we came together—we had no horizon to *place* the world we were traveling. That night settled a map for us, provided compass points, even if the directions were forbidden. We knew then that our earth was flat and that we would fall off if we went over the edge, but at least we knew where the edge was.

This is what makes it possible for us now to live apart yet together. I see us as parallel lines simultaneously reaching to the vanishing point that joins us on our private horizon.

This eases the tension for me. I no longer feel I must cut you off, forget you. This way is so much better. The regret I live with now is a small price to pay compared with the sorrow of locking myself away from you entirely. Didn't you write once that the price of caring is the risk of disappointment? And that the price of not caring is death. I have learned so much from you.

I hear the front door. Arthur will be in in a moment. But first— Brian dear, if you haven't borrowed from Charlie, please let me know what you need. Nothing would make me happier than to lend you whatever I can. For one thing, it would be a concrete proof that I am now a genuine career woman! (Incidentally, I will be giving a major presentation in Albany soon—details to come.)

Arthur just walked across the bedroom to my desk and bent down to kiss my cheek. I am glad he is watching me type this. I am glad I can so easily look up at him as I am doing now and smile when he says, "Give Mr. Henley my regards," and *I* can casually and openly say to him, "It is not Charlie Henley, it's Brian Curtiss." Arthur blinks a moment at that. I can see him start to speak, then think better of it, and his answer becomes a smile. It is still uncertain like a shrug on his face, but with a companionable gesture, not an angry one. He is getting used to the new me. He watches where his shoes end and my toes begin.

He's gone into the bathroom to wash up, and it's time for me to stir our martinis and get on with our dinner. I'm finding it fun to be cooking again. I once took some of Michael Field's courses and learned to whip up a few interesting dishes. He was a dear man, and an intense teacher. I won't forget the time, incidentally, when Field's son came by to sniff at the delicious pots on the stove, and asked his chef father, "Can *I* have a TV dinner?" Poor Arthur apparently lived on them while I was away. The freezer was full of nothing else when I came home.

Love and home cooking,

Maggie

Feb. 28

Dear Maggie:

Today is a holiday for us, and I have a gift for you! It's exactly two years since your inaugural letter. My present is that we are going to be able to toast this anniversary in person, together, if a few weeks late!

It's not P- - - - - - - - this time, but N- - Y- - - U- - - - - - - - - -. I am to be on a panel to discuss my (fairly unpopular) views on ethnicity. So we will have another meeting, as the friends we have now become.

"Friends," you and I . . .

Well, I suppose we have traveled a kind of Hegelian spiral at that.

We started with Acquaintanceship, circled through Friendship, on around and up to the Love (you so properly described as "deep . . . wonderful . . . and devilish"), and another turn (upward?) to the Bond for which we have no meaningful word. It is a return to the beginning, but at a higher level.

You will remember Hegel's point that each stage of the spiral of experience includes what went before and is enriched by it as the final stage becomes a flowering of its own, containing all.

I was always impressed with Hegel's concept of dialectical history, and I suppose it is my response to your statement about our love running on parallel lines to a vanishing point. I cannot get much clearer about us, either, but I have to agree there is no other answer, at least at this stage of the spiral. Maybe it does end here because it has no further space to move in. So we will meet as "friends."

It occurred to me that Lorna might like to attend the seminar, too, and I am dropping her a separate note. Then we can all drink wine and argue my thesis that today's thrust toward greater ethnicity is negative for our society. I am as aware as anyone of the importance of group culture, history, and roots. But the world pays a very high price for a few dances, crafts, costumes, cuisines, and customs of "the old ways." Ethnicity, as it is *exaggerated* today, runs counter to hopes for universal brotherhood. In the name of roots it uproots commonality and celebrates differences rather than samenesses. It turns us back to tent enclaves and stockades, and arms us with old weapons of distrust, alienation, hostility, and lies about each other. It is as *tribes* that nations justify and make wars. I take the position of Orlando Patterson, the Harvard sociologist, that ethnic pluralism is not only divisive, but that it obscures real issues like unemployment and poverty. It is a chauvinism without significant content, "for the roots are simply not there," as he says.

Come to my session, bring Lorna—and Gary and Arthur, too, for that matter—and let the fur fly.

Looking forward again!
Brian

March 4

Brian dear:

Every time I get comfortable here, you stir things up. Of course I want to see you. Of course I don't.

My peace with Arthur is possible because I am succeeding in fading you back into your photographs and stuffing you back between the rollers of my typewriter where I don't see your eyes or hear your voice or feel your hands, your lips. I can handle that.

But the prospect of being together again brings everything home too dauntingly. You and I must know what will inevitably happen. Georg Wilhelm Friedrich Hegel's dialectical spiral is not going to halt conveniently where you point on our dial. I know that because the very thought of being with you brings all my guilt flooding back.

I have rebuilt the stone fences of my life here, and now you are banging my head against them. I feel this almost physically. It is painful. Brian, I do not want to go through the wringer of our spiral again! I don't care whether it's weakness or strength, foolishness or wisdom, cowardice or courage. I am simply too old for this wrestling and seesawing.

If you come East, fine—see Lorna, not me!

I have come to understand that I can manage my feelings for you when you are a continent away, but no closer. It isn't any accident that my typewriter came up with that vanishing-point esotericism in my last letter. It is a subconscious metaphor that declares precisely what we ought to do. We ought to vanish out of each other's lives in order to stay in them. It sounds like a paradox, but it is true and right and realistic. Just think about it, and you'll agree.

I dreamed my white chamber again. You are right about the window. Last night it came down low enough for me to look out if I put the chair on the table. I did just that and was climbing to the window—electrified with suspense—when the damned chair broke and sent me crashing to the floor.

Please let's not do this to each other any more.

Maggie

March 8

Dear Maggie:

You ask me not to bang your head against your fences. They are *your* stockade, not mine. But no one can live in a state of perpetual frustration, outrage, and indignation. You are brilliantly perceptive about Hegel's spiral not stopping conveniently. For the simple reason that it has not reached its apex.

I have been trying to evade the truth. For your sake. For my sake. I don't know for whose sake any more.

What I know is that we belong together.

You and I. Brian Curtiss and Margaret Fairfield.

The apex is for us to be together, no matter what it takes to bring it about.

We belong together. That is where the spiral takes us. Anything else is wrong, backward, destructive. To be together is not wanton. For us to be separated is wanton.

I know now there is no possibility of compromise. I don't say anything will be easy, but there is no possibility of compromise. We have tried compromise and it doesn't work.

I am coming to New York for you. The panel is a handy excuse; I would come without it. I am going to see you, and you are going to come back with me. You are not going to Albany, you are not going to worry about Arthur's charcoal or frozen dinners. Let him learn to cook himself, as I have.

We have both given too much thought and consideration to others. I know you must have the same sense I have of being cheated. I repeat what I have told you. In a world where there is so much ugliness, we owe a *duty* to beauty. Yes, in damned near a Kantian sense! We are the opposite of the one-armed man and the violin— we have been given the instrument of love and the arms to play it, to make its music beautifully. It is *sinful* to throw away our gift. I need to keep shouting that because I know you have your palms pressed over your ears.

Of course there will be problems, including my children. But who does not have problems? The difference will be that we will face ours together in the happiness of our love, offered us so miraculously. Most people are not so fortunate.

I will not let you turn from this. I know all your "reasons" better than you do.

We have tried to be more than fair to everyone, except ourselves. We have given ourselves the test of separation. We have each tried, in our own way, to deny what life has brought. We cannot stop that life, cannot stop our love. I am coming for you, and you can give me only one answer.

I love you with all my heart . . .

                                                                Brian

March 11

Oh, dear Brian:

So now it's you telling me I must not go to Albany, and commanding me how to feel about Arthur's frozen dinners, and I am laughing so hard at all of us that there are tears in my eyes.

I think the rest of this letter is going to surprise you as much as my laughter, so hang on as The Spiral Moves . . .

My dream came to its fulfillment last night, and now I know very clearly what I have been trying to tell myself ever since I left you to come back to Arthur.

When I entered the white dream chamber, the window I had tried to see out of was gone entirely. I was in a panic of claustrophobia. I ran to the door, but it was locked and there was no one to answer my pounding. I heard Arthur's voice in the distance beyond the door, but he could not hear me because he was shouting at some witness, "Answer yes or no! Answer yes or no!" Over and over again.

In despair, I sat like a child on the little chair (all repaired) at the little white table, and started to count the Christmas lights on my pepper plant when, suddenly, there was the snap of shades flying up. Miraculously, there was not just the one window before me but a whole section of the room was open glass, clear as air, through which I could see the place I was in.

I stood up in awe. It was the most beautiful garden imaginable, Brian. I cannot begin to describe it. As you once said about us, the English language does not have enough words. It was a garden in spirit, is the only way I can put it, for there were no flowers in the familiar sense, no lawns, pools, trees, walks, trellises. There was the *sense* of all of them hovering just above the sweet-smelling ground. Like the flowers in a Monet canvas, they were there and not there at the same time; they dissolved into the pure beauty of the vision. Petals were not petals, paint was not paint, everything was transformed by and into ineffable magic.

The magic took another form. Suddenly I was surrounded by a cloud of butterflies, radiant in all colors and haloed in golden light, a rising, sighing enchantment. I remembered the little girl in the park when those children caught the butterfly. Now it was *I* who said, waving my hands at the beauty, "Now I let you go *and have your future* . . .," just as the girl had done. A magic spell, a spell of joy and goodness.

But the butterflies did not leave. They flew to me instead. Their scent was as perfumed as their wings were prismed. I could smell with my eyes and see with my nose, and my skin tingled and tickled as they covered me from head to foot with their fluttering wings, until I myself could fly. I went up and up, high over the garden, metamorphosized, no longer a human, no longer a woman, one with the magic, floating up beyond the soft clouds into endless space.

I woke up then. I was still floating. I did not fall and crash.

I still feel as if I am floating somewhere above my old self, Brian. And I hear the dream clearly, plainly, irrefutably. I am now telling myself that I am not going to arbitrarily lock myself away from our waiting garden. This has come from my deepest self, I cannot but recognize that truth. So we must at least meet and talk again.

I want the shade on the window to stay up in that white dream room. I don't want it to be pulled down by my concern for Arthur or my own fears.

Oddly, I am hearing music. But not harps and flutes—on the contrary. I am hearing Gary, my son, singing in a rasping, needling voice as he punches his guitar, "My eyes have seen the glory of the coming of the Clods." I resented it when he did it then. I despise it now, because I now have to face that he was not all wrong. In the end I did let life turn me into a Clod, didn't I?

It may be that I can never be anything else. It may simply be too late. But until I see you again I cannot be sure. That is all I can know for right now.

But accept this much for right now, my dear Brian—I am not saying No.

Trying hard,
Maggie

March 15

Dear Maggie:

Your letter was beautiful and opened a window of hope for me. I think it is too bad that none of us can remember being born, our first breath in this world, the wonder of being alive. People would live very differently if they had that memory to live by, and kept it undulled.

You are giving some of that back to me. It is the only way I can express the wonder of us, whatever happens.

I plan to come East earlier and stay later than the seminar, so we can talk without pressure. I wish all the clocks were not at such snail's pace.

I love you,
Brian

March 19

Brian dear:

We need plain speaking quite desperately. I told you I want to see you to talk and think and try for a decision together. I have to make it plain that I am still uncertain.

For the first time the possibility of divorcing Arthur and marrying you is a real fact in my life. I am not backing off that. I am facing into the truth that I am not happy with Arthur now. At the same time I must repeat that I am not yet entirely clear.

I can tell you this much. I keep having that dream. I think that augurs well for us.

Perhaps what I cannot get past is Arthur's devotion to me. The one thing in life that can never be feigned is loyalty, and he has given me that all of our married life.

So I am still not ready and must keep asking for patience.

Maggie

March 23

Maggie:

Then you must consider whether devotion is enough coin to buy a life with.

Brian

March 27

Brian:

I can understand your being out of sorts with me, but curtness does not become you. I have been adding up all the complications between us, Brian, and the columns simply won't foot!

I have come much further with you than I ever thought possible. I am torn and confused again, and I think it would be wisest not to make me say more at this time.

Maggie

April 1

Maggie:

Fool's Day, but we are in no joke. Of course your columns don't foot. You are not dealing with an accountant's ciphers. Except for our love, everything between us is without definition—and love lends itself to no arithmetic or calculus. It is intractably sloppy stuff. It spills over, it can't be sponged up, or squeezed into a measuring cup. Yet that is what you are trying to do. I have not intended to be curt, believe me, my dearest. Only trying to make you see what is so clear to me. My terror.

I mean I now have an absolute certainty in my heart that if you do not decide to marry me now, we will never have each other again.

That terrifies me.

Each day that has passed without you has been a mockery. We should not deny ourselves the happiness offered to us.

I don't want to go around that thorny circle again. You know it is the very truth.

Brian

April 5

Dear Brian:

You can stop scolding me.

I woke up this morning with a kind of . . . silent singing. Do you know the tradition of Silent Songs among certain peoples? Music comes into their minds, but it is never to be sung aloud. They accept the song with awe as a divine visitation from a spirit, to be cherished and held in lifelong privacy.

I see that I have made my decision, nothing less.

At this moment I feel my silent song is no longer mine alone, but to share with you. Surely that must be permitted. To share with love cannot be a violation. That is what you have been saying, and I have finally come to hear you, dear Brian.

I had no hint it would come this way, with all my doubts suddenly, completely, dissolved. Nothing special has happened here to account for it. There have been no problems, no quarrels with Arthur. On the contrary, he has never been more attentive, more pleasant, more considerate. And that is probably the reason! For, having the best of him, I must in honesty face the fierce question you hit me with. Is his devotion enough coin to buy the rest of my life?

I can avoid the answer no longer. Since you, I have known it in my heart for too long. Nothing can happen now to alter it.

I do want the rest of my life with you, Brian. Right now I find myself remembering with startling clarity the way I felt in Crete when I looked out over the spreading ruins at Knossos. I was overcome by a terrible, depressing message I drew from the ashes of the reaching, echoing centuries. So many dead generations of men and women, quite like me, once considered their lives consequential. In imagination I could hear voices and see people moving among the broken walls, could sense their laughter, their tears, their ambitions, their seasons of love—lying now in rubble and broken potsherds. I remember saying to Arthur that standing in such a place makes one realize how insignificant one's own mistakes are.

But I was wrong, dead wrong, Brian. I see that now. What the dead cities say to us is exactly the opposite! Not how insignificant our lives are, but how important, how vital and urgent and valuable. Not "You too will die," but *"Now it's YOUR turn to live!"*

How about that, Brian Curtiss? Margaret Fairfield has unblinded herself. Oh, how right you have been, my dear. We should not forfeit our turn!

Very soberly, I am a different woman than I have known. I can tell you, as I could never tell Arthur, that coming out of my bath this morning I saw how an artist might paint me. For the first time I *looked* at my body, stared at myself and enjoyed what I saw. For the first time in my life I did not hastily towel off and robe myself with only the most fleeting, puerile glance at my image in the mirror.

This morning I felt vain, and forward, and proud of it. Proud of myself as a good-looking woman! You have been prodding me to say that, and there it is. Oh, I wanted to see my nakedness as your eyes took me in that night. I was glad you had seen me. I received myself this morning with vanity and pleasure! I am delighted that I pleased you. And will please you again.

All at once I understood my butterfly dream in yet another light —not Monet's palette but *Renoir's*. Renoir was not making his women up, not being painterly. His brush stroked the tilts and planes of every woman's inner truth and beauty. His colors declare that whatever else a woman wants in life, she is and should always be a creature of romance and passion! I can say that now. I feel on my own skin the glow of Renoir's love affair with all women, and I see for myself every revealing tint and perfume of flesh across the whole lovely spectrum of desire.

How much of me there is still unknown to myself! For you to help me discover . . .

As I write, I am thinking of the John Donne poem I used as an excuse to say farewell. I take it back, every word. I have come upon a poem for saying the opposite now. It is by e.e. cummings, and I send it to you with what I am sure is John Donne's acquiescence and approval. Dearest Brian,

> *i carry your heart with me (i carry it in*
> *my heart) i am never without it (anywhere*
> *i go you go, my dear; and whatever is done*
> *by only me is your doing, my darling)*
>
>   *i fear*
> *no fate (for you are my fate, my sweet) i want*
> *no world (for beautiful you are my world, my true)*
> *and it's you are whatever a moon has always meant*
> *and whatever a sun will always sing is you*
>
> *here is the deepest secret nobody knows*
> *(here is the root of the root and the bud of the bud*
> *and the sky of the sky of a tree called life; which grows*
> *higher than soul can hope or mind can hide)*
> *and this is the wonder that's keeping the stars apart*
>
> *i carry your heart (i carry it in my heart)*

Brian, to be such a poet must be the best thing in the world. If I cannot be, and you know I'm not much in that line, then loving you and being your beloved is the next best thing . . .

It does turn out in the end to be that simple. All I require is courage! I have ten thousand apprehensions about starting a new life, but I have never been happier than I am in saying Yes to you.

Now I can say it with joy, now it need no longer be a silent singing. I do love you, Brian, more than I have ever dared to let myself know. I am flying with happiness, and I can't wait to be with you, my dearest.

Maggie

P.S. Add to our collection: An exultation of larks!

April 5

Dearest Brian:

I am back at the typewriter just after posting my last letter. When I returned upstairs from the mailbox, my phone was ringing. It turned out to be Albany, with a test of everything I had just settled in my mind! I need to tell you about this at once . . .

Albany wanted to set up an appointment on the very day of your panel. I cursed under my breath, gritted my teeth, and made the only judgment I considered right. I accepted their date. This is a major contract, and I have worked on it long and hard since I came back from the Coast. I decided I owed it to myself and to Charlie not to rock the boat. I told myself you would understand, you above all men, especially now that you have my answer about us . . .

But something in me gave way at that point. I was overcome by the conviction that if I missed your panel it would spell the end for us. We simply could not start our new life on that foot.

I became furious all over again. I asked myself why Albany (and Charlie) should be so enormously important to me. Why, to be "free," *must* I feel I have to put my work before my Brian? I was miserable. Your cleaning woman Tillie was right. I said "This too will pass" three times and it was a consolation, so I knew I was in trouble.

Well, Brian, I went back to the phone and called Albany to declare I needed to change the date. I waited for the sky to fall on my head. Instead, there was only a bit of fussing, and a new arrangement! I could have spared myself the aggravation of conjuring up their displeasure. How true of so many things we all do.

Including my concern for Arthur. It has been trailing around me like a mess of seaweed in which my feet keep tangling. Yet, despite everything Arthur has said about wanting our marriage, who really knows whether he, too, may not be relieved to be free? Even secretly happy! I would hope and pray that somewhere sometime he will be on another street corner free to accept a golden invitation to new happiness for himself. Yes, that is possible too, isn't it? None of us can ever know unless we risk it . . .

And now I have this Albany proof that I can make things happen my way instead of everyone else's! I once boasted of cutting my puppet strings, but I look back and realize I only rearranged them. What a wonderful, joyous feeling it is to take the scissors to them all, finally. The sharpest scissors in the world, my own deepest unapologizing truth, which you have helped me discover—the golden scissors of our love.

> All my love is yours,
> Maggie

April 8

Dearest one:

> I am here to say that Margaret Fairfield is *sensational!*
> I can't write my elation.
> I will be with you soon and we will share it then . . .

> With all my heart,
> Brian

Part Nine

April 9

Dear Brian:

Writing this letter is the hardest thing I have ever had to do in my life.

Margaret Webb died last night.

None of us was aware of the seriousness of her condition. It turns out she had deliberately lied about the lab reports after her operation. Actually, they showed a cancer.

Last night we learned she had insisted on two things from her doctor. First, that he tell *her* the absolute truth, and second, that he allow her to tell everyone else whatever she decided. So we were tragically unprepared for the sudden emergency.

The doctor believed there was a 50–50 chance for a full life after the surgery. We gather now that Margaret chose to believe in the brighter 50 percent, and so probably felt she was not really deceiving us. I suppose it was one reason she was eager to work with Charles Henley. She wanted to live as upbeat as possible all the way. She once told me she didn't like twilights. She wanted it to be bright day, and then quick night. There is some solace for us that it happened that way.

Please tell Mr. Henley that Mr. Webb will be in touch with him to settle their affairs.

Gary is taking his mother's death very hard. I scarcely recognize him myself and hope this doesn't send him off the narrow balance he has managed this past year.

Most important, Brian, I am writing because Margaret asked me to. I spent time alone with her at the hospital after she knew what was happening. She was calm and accepting, and she reminisced with open pleasure about your correspondence. She told me again she couldn't believe *she* had written to a man she did not know. It brought the twinkle back into her eyes. Margaret kept your letters and asked me to send them on to you. Of course you may be sure I have respected their privacy.

Margaret also asked me to send you something else she had put aside for you. It is a small red box, much worn and sort of scruffy, but Margaret apparently esteemed it greatly. She asked me to wrap it with special care. I did not inquire what it contained but I would guess it is fragile, so please handle it carefully when it arrives.

I am so brokenhearted to write this terrible news to you. I know you thought very highly of our friend, and that you will share our sense of tragic loss even though you knew Margaret only a little and at such a distance.

For her,
Lorna

Printed in the United States
1113800003B/308